W9-DFB-182

PENGUIN ESSENTIALS
The Pursuit of Love

Nancy Mitford (1904–73) was born in London, the eldest child of the second Baron Redesdale. Her childhood in a large, remote country house with her five sisters and one brother is recounted in the early chapters of *The Pursuit of Love* (1945), which, according to the author, is largely autobiographical. Apart from being taught to ride and speak French, Nancy Mitford always claimed she never received a proper education. She started writing before her marriage in 1932 in order 'to relieve the boredom of the intervals between the recreations established by the social conventions of her world' and had written four novels, including *Wigs on the Green* (1935), before the success of *The Pursuit of Love* in 1945. After the war she moved to Paris where she lived for the rest of her life. She followed *The Pursuit of Love* with *Love in a Cold Climate* (1949), *The Blessing* (1951) and *Don't Tell Alfred* (1960). She also wrote four works of biography: *Madame de Pompadour*, first published to great acclaim in 1954, *Voltaire in Love*, *The Sun King* and *Frederick the Great*. As well as being a novelist and a biographer she also translated Madame de Lafayette's classic novel *La Princesse de Clèves* into English, and edited *Noblesse Oblige*, a collection of essays concerned with the behaviour of the English aristocracy and the idea of 'U' and 'non-U'. Nancy Mitford was awarded the CBE in 1972.

Julianna Brion was born in New York City in 1989 to a family of artists, and illustrators. In 2011, She graduated from Maryland Institute College of Art in Baltimore, where she continues to work as a freelance illustrator and fine artist. Her work has been acknowledged by *American Illustration*, SCBWI, CMYK, 3x3, and The Society of Illustrators. You can find more at www.juliannabrion.com.

The Pursuit of Love

NANCY MITFORD

PENGUIN BOOKS

PENGUIN BOOKS

UK | USA | Canada | Ireland | Australia
India | New Zealand | South Africa

Penguin Books is part of the Penguin Random House group of companies
whose addresses can be found at global.penguinrandomhouse.com.

First published 1945
Published in Penguin Books 1949
This Penguin Essentials edition published 2018

006

Copyright © the Estate of Nancy Mitford, 1945

Printed and bound in Great Britain by Clays Ltd, Elcograf S.p.A.

The authorized representative in the EEA is Penguin Random House Ireland,
Morrison Chambers, 32 Nassau Street, Dublin D02 YH68

A CIP catalogue record for this book is available from the British Library

ISBN: 978-0-241-98407-9

www.greenpenguin.co.uk

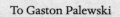To Gaston Palewski

I

There is a photograph in existence of Aunt Sadie and her six children sitting round the tea-table at Alconleigh. The table is situated, as it was, is now, and ever shall be, in the hall, in front of a huge open fire of logs. Over the chimney-piece plainly visible in the photograph hangs an entrenching tool, with which, in 1915, Uncle Matthew had whacked to death eight Germans one by one as they crawled out of a dug-out. It is still covered with blood and hairs, an object of fascination to us as children. In the photograph Aunt Sadie's face, always beautiful, appears strangely round, her hair strangely fluffy, and her clothes strangely dowdy, but it is unmistakably she who sits there with Robin, in oceans of lace, lolling on her knee. She seems uncertain what to do with his head, and the presence of Nanny waiting to take him away is felt though not seen. The other children, between Louisa's eleven and Matt's two years, sit round the table in party dresses or frilly bibs, holding cups or mugs according to age, all of them gazing at the camera with large eyes opened wide by the flash, and all looking as if butter would not melt in their round pursed-up mouths. There they are, held like flies, in the amber of that moment – click goes the camera and on goes life; the minutes, the days, the years, the decades, taking them further and further from that happiness and promise of youth, from the hopes Aunt Sadie must have had for them, and from the dreams they dreamed for themselves. I often think there is nothing quite so poignantly sad as old family groups.

When a child I spent my Christmas holidays at Alconleigh, it was a regular feature of my life, and, while some of them slipped by with nothing much to remember, others were distinguished by violent occurrences and had a definite character of their own.

There was the time, for example, when the servants' wing caught fire, the time when my pony lay on me in the brook and nearly drowned me (not very nearly, he was soon dragged off, but meanwhile bubbles were said to have been observed). There was drama when Linda, aged ten, attempted suicide in order to rejoin an old smelly Border Terrier which Uncle Matthew had had put down. She collected and ate a basketful of yew-berries, was discovered by Nanny and given mustard and water to make her sick. She was then 'spoken to' by Aunt Sadie, clipped over the ear by Uncle Matthew, put to bed for days and given a Labrador puppy, which soon took the place of the old Border in her affections. There was much worse drama when Linda, aged twelve, told the daughters of neighbours, who had come to tea, what she supposed to be the facts of life. Linda's presentation of the 'facts' had been so gruesome that the children left Alconleigh howling dismally, their nerves permanently impaired, their future chances of a sane and happy sex life much reduced. This resulted in a series of dreadful punishments, from a real beating, administered by Uncle Matthew, to luncheon upstairs for a week. There was the unforgettable holiday when Uncle Matthew and Aunt Sadie went to Canada. The Radlett children would rush for the newspapers every day hoping to see that their parents' ship had gone down with all aboard; they yearned to be total orphans – especially Linda, who saw herself as Katy in *What Katy Did*, the reins of the household gathered into small but capable hands. The ship met with no iceberg and weathered the Atlantic storms, but meanwhile we had a wonderful holiday, free from rules.

But the Christmas I remember most clearly of all was when I was fourteen and Aunt Emily became engaged. Aunt Emily was Aunt Sadie's sister, and she had brought me up from babyhood, my own mother, their youngest sister, having felt herself too beautiful and too gay to be burdened with a child at the age of nineteen. She left my father when I was a month old, and subsequently ran away so often, and with so many different people, that she became known to her family and friends as the Bolter; while my father's second, and presently his third, fourth, and fifth wives, very naturally had no great wish to look after me. Occasionally one of these impetuous parents would appear like a rocket, casting an unnatural glow upon my horizon. They had great glamour, and I longed to be caught up in their fiery trails and be carried away, though in my heart I knew how lucky I was to have Aunt Emily. By degrees, as I grew up, they lost all charm for me; the cold grey rocket cases mouldered where they happened to fall, my mother with a major in the South of France, my father, his estates sold up to pay his debts, with an old Rumanian countess in the Bahamas. Even before I was grown up much of the glamour with which they had been surrounded had faded, and finally there was nothing left, no foundation of childish memories to make them seem any different from other middle-aged people. Aunt Emily was never glamorous but she was always my mother, and I loved her.

At the time of which I write, however, I was at an age when the least imaginative child supposes itself to be a changeling, a Princess of Indian blood, Joan of Arc, or the future Empress of Russia. I hankered after my parents, put on an idiotic face which was intended to convey mingled suffering and pride when their names were mentioned, and thought of them as engulfed in deep, romantic, deadly sin.

Linda and I were very much preoccupied with sin, and our great hero was Oscar Wilde.

'But what did he *do*?'

'I asked Fa once and he roared at me – goodness, it was terrifying. He said: "If you mention that sewer's name again in this house I'll thrash you, do you hear, damn you?" So I asked Sadie and she looked awfully vague and said: "Oh, duck, I never really quite knew, but whatever it was was worse than murder, fearfully bad. And, darling, don't talk about him at meals, will you?"'

'We must find out.'

'Bob says he will, when he goes to Eton.'

'Oh, good! Do you think he was worse than Mummy and Daddy?'

'Surely he couldn't be. Oh, you are so lucky, to have wicked parents.'

This Christmas-time, aged fourteen, I stumbled into the hall at Alconleigh blinded by the light after a six-mile drive from Merlinford station. It was always the same every year, I always came down by the same train, arriving at tea-time, and always found Aunt Sadie and the children round the table underneath the entrenching tool, just as they were in the photograph. It was always the same table and the same tea-things; the china with large roses on it, the tea-kettle and the silver dish for scones simmering over little flames – the human beings of course were getting imperceptibly older, the babies were becoming children, the children were growing up, and there had been an addition in the shape of Victoria now aged two. She was waddling about with a chocolate biscuit clenched in her fist, her face was smothered in chocolate and was a horrible sight, but through the sticky mask shone unmistakably the blue of two steady Radlett eyes.

There was a tremendous scraping of chairs as I came in, and a pack of Radletts hurled themselves upon me with the intensity and almost the ferocity of a pack of hounds hurling itself upon a fox. All except Linda. She was the most pleased to see me, but determined not to show it. When the din had quieted down and I was seated before a scone and a cup of tea, she said:

'Where's Brenda?' Brenda was my white mouse.

'She got a sore back and died,' I said. Aunt Sadie looked anxiously at Linda.

'Had you been riding her?' said Louisa, facetiously. Matt, who had recently come under the care of a French nursery governess, said in a high-pitched imitation of her voice: '*C'était, comme d'habitude, les voies urinaires.*'

'Oh, dear,' said Aunt Sadie under her breath.

Enormous tears were pouring into Linda's plate. Nobody cried so much or so often as she; anything, but especially anything sad about animals, would set her off, and, once begun, it was a job to stop her. She was a delicate, as well as a highly nervous child, and even Aunt Sadie, who lived in a dream as far as the health of her children was concerned, was aware that too much crying kept her awake at night, put her off her food, and did her harm. The other children, and especially Louisa and Bob, who loved to tease, went as far as they dared with her, and were periodically punished for making her cry. *Black Beauty, Owd Bob, The Story of a Red Deer*, and all the Seton Thompson books were on the nursery index because of Linda, who, at one time or another, had been prostrated by them. They had to be hidden away, as, if they were left lying about, she could not be trusted not to indulge in an orgy of self torture.

Wicked Louisa had invented a poem which never failed to induce rivers of tears:

'A little, houseless match, it has no roof, no thatch,
It lies alone, it makes no moan, that little, houseless match.'

When Aunt Sadie was not around the children would chant this in a gloomy chorus. In certain moods one had only to glance at a match-box to dissolve poor Linda; when, however, she was feeling stronger, more fit to cope with life, this sort of teasing would force out of her very stomach an unwilling guffaw. Linda was not only my favourite cousin, but, then and for many years, my favourite human being. I adored all my cousins, and Linda distilled, mentally and physically, the very essence of the Radlett family. Her straight features, straight brown hair and large blue eyes were a theme upon which the faces of the others were a variation; all pretty, but none so absolutely distinctive as hers. There was something furious about her, even when she laughed, which she did a great deal, and always as if forced to against her will. Something reminiscent of pictures of Napoleon in youth, a sort of scowling intensity.

I could see that she was really minding much more about Brenda than I did. The truth was that my honeymoon days with the mouse were long since over; we had settled down to an uninspiring relationship, a form, as it were, of married blight, and, when she had developed a disgusting sore patch on her back, it had been all I could do to behave decently and treat her with common humanity. Apart from the shock it always is to find somebody stiff and cold in their cage in the morning, it had been a very great relief to me when Brenda's sufferings finally came to an end.

'Where is she buried?' Linda muttered furiously, looking at her plate.

'Beside the robin. She's got a dear little cross and her coffin was lined with pink satin.'

'Now, Linda darling,' said Aunt Sadie, 'if Fanny has finished her tea why don't you show her your toad?'

'He's upstairs asleep,' said Linda. But she stopped crying.

'Have some nice hot toast, then.'

'Can I have Gentleman's Relish on it?' she said, quick to make capital out of Aunt Sadie's mood, for Gentleman's Relish was kept strictly for Uncle Matthew, and supposed not to be good for children. The others made a great show of exchanging significant looks. These were intercepted, as they were meant to be, by Linda, who gave a tremendous bellowing boo-hoo and rushed upstairs.

'I wish you children wouldn't tease Linda,' said Aunt Sadie, irritated out of her usual gentleness, and followed her.

The staircase led out of the hall. When Aunt Sadie was beyond earshot, Louisa said: 'If wishes were horses beggars would ride. Child hunt to-morrow, Fanny.'

'Yes, Josh told me. He was in the car – been to see the vet.'

My Uncle Matthew had four magnificent bloodhounds, with which he used to hunt his children. Two of us would go off with a good start to lay the trail, and Uncle Matthew and the rest would follow the hounds on horseback. It was great fun. Once he came to my home and hunted Linda and me over Shenley Common. This caused the most tremendous stir locally, the Kentish week-enders on their way to church were appalled by the sight of four great hounds in full cry after two little girls. My uncle seemed to them like a wicked lord of fiction, and I became more than ever surrounded with an aura of madness, badness, and dangerousness for their children to know.

The child hunt on the first day of this Christmas visit was a great success. Louisa and I were chosen as hares. We ran across country, the beautiful bleak Cotswold uplands, starting soon after breakfast when the sun was still a red globe, hardly over the horizon, and the trees were etched in dark blue against a pale blue, mauve, and pinkish sky. The sun rose as we stumbled on, longing for our second wind; it shone, and there dawned a beautiful day, more like late autumn in its feeling than Christmas-time.

We managed to check the bloodhounds once by running through a flock of sheep, but Uncle Matthew soon got them on the scent again, and, after about two hours of hard running on our part, when we were only half a mile from home, the baying slavering creatures caught up with us, to be rewarded with lumps of meat and many caresses. Uncle Matthew was in a radiantly good temper, he got off his horse and walked home with us, chatting agreeably. What was most unusual, he was even quite affable to me.

'I hear Brenda has died,' he said. 'No great loss I should say. That mouse stank like merry hell. I expect you kept her cage too near the radiator, I always told you it was unhealthy, or did she die of old age?'

Uncle Matthew's charm, when he chose to turn it on, was considerable, but at that time I was always mortally afraid of him, and made the mistake of letting him see that I was.

'You ought to have a dormouse, Fanny, or a rat. They are much more interesting than white mice – though I must frankly say, of all the mice I ever knew, Brenda was the most utterly dismal.'

'She was dull,' I said, sycophantically.

'When I go to London after Christmas, I'll get you a dormouse. Saw one the other day at the Army & Navy.'

'Oh, Fa, it is unfair,' said Linda, who was walking her pony along beside us. 'You know how I've always longed for a dormouse.'

'It is unfair' was a perpetual cry of the Radletts when young. The great advantage of living in a large family is that early lesson of life's essential unfairness. With them I must say it nearly always operated in favour of Linda, who was the adored of Uncle Matthew.

To-day, however, my uncle was angry with her, and I saw in a flash that this affability to me, this genial chat about mice, was simply designed as a tease for her.

'You've got enough animals, miss,' he said, sharply. 'You can't control the ones you have got. And don't forget what I told you – that dog of yours goes straight to the kennel when we get back, and stays there.'

Linda's face crumpled, tears poured, she kicked her pony into a canter and made for home. It seemed that her dog Labby had been sick in Uncle Matthew's business-room after breakfast. Uncle Matthew was unable to bear dirtiness in dogs, he flew into a rage, and, in his rage, had made a rule that never again was Labby to set foot in the house. This was always happening, for one reason or another, to one animal or another, and, Uncle Matthew's bark being invariably much worse than his bite, the ban seldom lasted more than a day or two, after which would begin what he called the Thin End of the Wedge.

'Can I bring him in just while I fetch my gloves?'

'I'm so tired – I can't go to the stables – do let him stay just till after tea.'

'Oh, I see – the thin end of the wedge. All right, this time he can stay, but if he makes another mess – or I catch him on your bed – or he chews up the good furniture (according to whichever crime it was that had resulted in banishment), I'll have him destroyed, and don't say I didn't warn you.'

All the same, every time sentence of banishment was pronounced, the owner of the condemned would envisage her beloved moping his life away in the solitary confinements of a cold and gloomy kennel.

'Even if I take him out for three hours every day, and go and chat to him for another hour, that leaves twenty hours for him all alone with nothing to do. Oh, why can't dogs read?'

The Radlett children, it will be observed, took a highly anthropomorphic view of their pets.

To-day, however, Uncle Matthew was in a wonderfully good

temper, and, as we left the stables, he said to Linda, who was sitting crying with Labby in his kennel:

'Are you going to leave that poor brute of yours in there all day?'

Her tears forgotten as if they had never been, Linda rushed into the house with Labby at her heels. The Radletts were always either on a peak of happiness or drowning in black waters of despair; their emotions were on no ordinary plane, they loved or they loathed, they laughed or they cried, they lived in a world of superlatives. Their life with Uncle Matthew was a sort of perpetual Tom Tiddler's ground. They went as far as they dared, sometimes very far indeed, while sometimes, for no apparent reason, he would pounce almost before they had crossed the boundary. Had they been poor children they would probably have been removed from their roaring, raging, whacking papa and sent to an approved home, or, indeed, he himself would have been removed from them and sent to prison for refusing to educate them. Nature, however, provides her own remedies, and no doubt the Radletts had enough of Uncle Matthew in them to enable them to weather storms in which ordinary children like me would have lost their nerve completely.

2

It was an accepted fact at Alconleigh that Uncle Matthew loathed me. This violent, uncontrolled man, like his children, knew no middle course, he either loved or he hated, and generally, it must be said, he hated. His reason for hating me was that he hated my father; they were old Eton enemies. When it became obvious, and obvious it was from the hour of my conception, that my parents intended to doorstep me, Aunt Sadie had wanted to bring me up with Linda. We were the same age, and it had seemed a sensible plan. Uncle Matthew had categorically refused. He hated my father, he said, he hated me, but, above all, he hated children, it was bad enough to have two of his own. (He evidently had not envisaged so soon having seven, and indeed both he and Aunt Sadie lived in a perpetual state of surprise at having filled so many cradles, about the future of whose occupants they seemed to have no particular policy.) So dear Aunt Emily, whose heart had once been broken by some wicked dallying monster, and who intended on this account never to marry, took me on and made a life's work of me, and I am very thankful that she did. For she believed passionately in the education of women, she took immense pains to have me properly taught, even going to live at Shenley on purpose to be near a good day school. The Radlett daughters did practically no lessons. They were taught by Lucille, the French governess, to read and write, they were obliged, though utterly unmusical, to 'practise' in the freezing ballroom for one hour a day each, their eyes glued to the clock, they would thump out the 'Merry Peasant' and a few scales, they were made to go for a French walk with Lucille on all except hunting days, and that was the extent of their education. Uncle Matthew loathed clever females, but he considered that gentle-women ought, as well as being able to ride, to know French and play the piano. Although as a child I rather naturally envied them their freedom from thrall and bondage, from sums and science, I felt, nevertheless, a priggish satisfaction that I was not growing up unlettered, as they were.

Aunt Emily did not often come with me to Alconleigh. Perhaps she had an idea that it was more fun for me to be there on my own, and no doubt it was a change for her to get away and spend Christmas with the friends of her youth, and leave for a bit the responsibilities of her old age. Aunt Emily at this time was forty, and we children had long ago renounced on her behalf the world, the flesh, and the devil. This year, however, she had gone away from Shenley before the holidays began, saying that she would see me at Alconleigh in January.

On the afternoon of the child hunt Linda called a meeting of the Hons. The Hons was the Radlett secret society, anybody who was not a friend to the Hons was a Counter-Hon, and their battle-cry was 'Death to the horrible Counter-Hons.' I was a Hon, since my father, like theirs, was a lord.

There were also, however, many honorary Hons. It was not necessary to have been born a Hon in order to be one. As Linda once remarked: 'Kind hearts are more than coronets, and simple faith than Norman blood.' I'm not sure how much we really believed this, we were wicked snobs in those days, but we subscribed to the general idea. Head of the hon. Hons was Josh, the groom, who was greatly beloved by us all and worth buckets of Norman blood; chief of the horrible Counter-Hons was Craven, the game-keeper, against whom a perpetual war to the knife was waged. The Hons would creep into the woods, and hide Craven's steel traps, let out the chaffinches which, in wire cages without food or water, he used as bait for hawks, give decent burial to the victims of his gamekeeper's larder, and, before a meet of the hounds, unblock the earths which Craven had so carefully stopped.

The poor Hons were tormented by the cruelties of the coun-tryside, while, to me, holidays at Alconleigh were a perfect revelation of beastliness. Aunt Emily's little house was in a village; it was a Queen Anne box; red brick, white panelling, a magnolia tree and a delicious fresh smell. Between it and the country were a neat little garden, an ironwork fence, a village green and a village. The country one then came to was very different from Gloucestershire, it was emasculated, sheltered, over-cultivated, almost a suburban garden. At Alconleigh the cruel woods crept right up to the house; it was not unusual to be awoken by the screams of a rabbit running in horrified circles round a stoat, by the strange and awful cry of the dog-fox, or to see from one's bedroom window a live hen being carried away in the mouth of a vixen; while the roosting pheasant and the waking owl filled every night with wild primeval noise. In the winter, when snow covered the ground, we could trace the footprints of many creatures. These often ended in a pool of blood, a mass of fur or feathers, bearing witness to successful hunting by the carnivores.

On the other side of the house, within a stone's throw, was the Home Farm. Here the slaughtering of poultry and pigs, the castration of lambs and the branding of cattle took place as a matter of course, out in the open for whoever might be passing by to see. Even dear old Josh made nothing of firing, with red-hot irons, a favourite horse after the hunting season.

'You can only do two legs at a time,' he would say, hissing through his teeth as though one were a horse and he grooming one, 'otherwise they can't stand the pain.'

Linda and I were bad at standing pain ourselves, and found it intolerable that animals should have to lead such tormented lives and tortured deaths. (I still do mind, very much indeed, but in those days at Alconleigh it was an absolute obsession with us all.)

The humanitarian activities of the Hons were forbidden, on pain of punishment, by Uncle Matthew, who was always and entirely on the side of Craven, his favourite servant. Pheasants and partridges must be preserved, vermin must be put down rigorously, all except the fox, for whom a more exciting death was in store. Many and many a whacking did the poor Hons suffer, week after week their pocket-money was stopped, they were sent to bed early, given extra practising to do; nevertheless they bravely persisted with their discouraged and discouraging activities. Huge cases full of new steel traps would arrive periodically from the Army & Navy Stores, and lie stacked until required round Craven's hut in the middle of the wood (an old railway carriage was his headquarters, situated, most inappropriately, among the primroses and blackberry bushes of a charming little glade); hundreds of traps, making one feel the futility of burying, at great risk to life and property, a paltry three or four. Sometimes we would find a screaming animal held in one; it would take all our reserves of courage to go up to it and let it out, to see it run away with three legs and a dangling mangled horror. We knew that it then probably died of blood-poisoning in its lair; Uncle Matthew would rub in this fact, sparing no agonizing detail of the long drawn-out ordeal, but, though we knew it would be kinder, we could never bring ourselves to kill them; it was asking too much. Often, as it was, we had to go away and be sick after these episodes.

The Hons' meeting-place was a disused linen cupboard at the top of the house, small, dark, and intensely hot. As in so many country houses the central-heating apparatus at Alconleigh had been installed in the early days of the invention, at enormous expense, and was now thoroughly out of date. In spite of a boiler which would not have been too large for an Atlantic liner, in spite of the tons of coke which it consumed daily, the temperature of the living-rooms was hardly affected, and all the heat there was seemed to concentrate in the Hons' cupboard, which was always stifling. Here we would sit, huddled up on the slatted shelves, and talk for hours about life and death.

Last holidays our great obsession had been childbirth, on which entrancing subject we were informed remarkably late, having supposed for a long time that a mother's stomach swelled up for nine months and then burst open like a ripe pumpkin, shooting out the infant. When the real truth dawned upon us it seemed rather an anticlimax, until Linda produced, from some novel, and read out loud in ghoulish tones, the description of a woman in labour.

'Her breath comes in great gulps – sweat pours down her brow like water – screams as of a tortured animal rend the air – and can this face, twisted with agony, be that of my darling Rhona – can this torture-chamber really be our bedroom, this rack our marriage-bed? "Doctor, doctor," I cried, "do something" – I rushed out into the night' – and so on.

We were rather disturbed by this, realizing that too probably we in our turn would have to endure these fearful agonies. Aunt Sadie, who had only just finished having her seven children, when appealed to, was not very reassuring.

'Yes,' she said, vaguely. 'It is the worst pain in the world. But the funny thing is, you always forget in between what it's like. Each time, when it began, I felt like saying, "Oh, now I can remember, stop it, stop it." And, of course, by then it was nine months too late to stop it.'

At this point Linda began to cry, saying how dreadful it must be for cows, which brought the conversation to an end.

It was difficult to talk to Aunt Sadie about sex; something always seemed to prevent one; babies were the nearest we ever got to it. She and Aunt Emily, feeling at one moment that we ought to know more, and being, I suspect, too embarrassed to enlighten us themselves, gave us a modern textbook on the subject.

We got hold of some curious ideas.

'Jassy,' said Linda one day, scornfully, 'is obsessed, poor thing, with sex.'

'Obsessed with sex!' said Jassy, 'there's nobody so obsessed as you, Linda. Why if I so much as look at a picture you say I'm a pygmalionist.'

In the end we got far more information out of a book called *Ducks and Duck Breeding*.

'Ducks can only copulate,' said Linda, after studying this for a while, 'in running water. Good luck to them.'

This Christmas Eve we all packed into the Hons' meeting-place to hear what Linda had to say – Louisa, Jassy, Bob, Matt, and I.

'Talk about back-to-the-womb,' said Jassy.

'Poor Aunt Sadie,' I said. 'I shouldn't think she'd want you all back in hers.'

'You never know. Now rabbits eat their children – somebody ought to explain to them how it's only a complex.'

'How can one *explain* to *rabbits*? That's what is so worrying about animals, they simply don't understand when they're spoken to, poor angels. I'll tell you what about Sadie though, she'd like to be back in one herself, she's got a thing for boxes and that always shows. Who else – Fanny, what about you?'

'I don't think I would, but then I imagine the one I was in wasn't very comfortable at the time you know, and nobody else has ever been allowed to stay there.'

'Abortions?' said Linda with interest.

'Well, tremendous jumpings and hot baths anyway.'

'How *do* you know?'

'I once heard Aunt Emily and Aunt Sadie talking about it when I was very little, and afterwards I remembered. Aunt Sadie said: "How does she manage it?" and Aunt Emily said: "Skiing, or hunting, or just jumping off the kitchen table."'

'You are so lucky, having wicked parents.'

This was the perpetual refrain of the Radletts, and, indeed, my wicked parents constituted my chief interest in their eyes – I was really a very dull little girl in other respects.

'The news I have for the Hons to-day,' said Linda, clearing her throat like a grown-up person, 'while of considerable Hon interest generally, particularly concerns Fanny. I won't ask you to guess, because it's nearly tea-time and you never could, so I'll tell you straight out. Aunt Emily is engaged.'

There was a gasp from the Hons in chorus.

'Linda,' I said, furiously, 'you've made it up.' But I knew she couldn't have.

Linda brought a piece of paper out of her pocket. It was a half-sheet of writing-paper, evidently the end of a letter, covered with Aunt Emily's large babyish handwriting, and I looked over Linda's shoulder as she read it out:

'. . . not tell the children we're engaged, what d'you think darling, just at first? But then suppose Fanny takes a dislike to him, though I don't see how she could, but children are so funny, won't it be more of a shock? Oh, dear, I can't decide. Anyway, do what you think best, darling, we'll arrive on Thursday, and I'll telephone on Wednesday evening and see what's happened. All love from Emily.'

Sensation in the Hons' cupboard.

3

'But why?' I said, for the hundredth time.

Linda, Louisa, and I were packed into Louisa's bed, with Bob sitting on the end of it, chatting in whispers. These midnight talks were most strictly forbidden, but it was safer, at Alconleigh, to disobey rules during the early part of the night than at any other time in the twenty-four hours. Uncle Matthew fell asleep practically at the dinner-table. He would then doze in his business-room for an hour or so before dragging himself, in a somnambulist trance, to bed, where he slept the profound sleep of one who has been out of doors all day, until cockcrow the following morning, when he became very much awake. This was the time for his never-ending warfare with the housemaids over wood-ash. The rooms at Alconleigh were heated by wood fires, and Uncle Matthew maintained, rightly, that if these were to function properly, all the ash ought to be left in the fireplaces in a great hot smouldering heap. Every housemaid, however, for some reason (an early training with coal fires probably) was bent on removing this ash altogether. When shakings, imprecations, and being pounced out at by Uncle Matthew in his paisley dressing-gown at six a.m., had convinced them that this was not really feasible, they became absolutely determined to remove, by hook or by crook, just a little, a shovelful or so, every morning. I can only suppose they felt that like this they were asserting their personalities.

The result was guerrilla warfare at its most exciting. Housemaids are notoriously early risers, and can usually count upon three clear hours when a house belongs to them alone. But not at Alconleigh. Uncle Matthew was always, winter and summer alike, out of his bed by five a.m., and it was then his habit to wander about, looking like Great Agrippa in his dressing-gown, and drinking endless cups of tea out of a thermos flask, until about seven, when he would have his bath. Breakfast for my uncle, my aunt, family, and guests alike, was sharp at eight, and unpunctuality was not tolerated. Uncle Matthew was no respecter of other people's early morning sleep, and after five o'clock one could not count on any, for he raged round the house, clanking cups of tea, shouting at his dogs, roaring at the housemaids, cracking the stock whips which he had brought back from Canada on the lawn with a noise greater than gunfire, and all to the accompaniment of Galli Curci on his gramophone, an abnormally loud one, with an enormous horn, through which would be shrieked 'Una voce poco fà' – 'The Mad Song' from *Lucia* – 'Lo, here the gen-tel lar-ha-hark' – and so on, played at top speed, thus rendering them even higher and more screeching than they ought to be.

Nothing reminds me of my childhood days at Alconleigh so much as those songs. Uncle Matthew played them incessantly for years, until the spell was broken when he went all the way to Liverpool to hear Galli Curci in person. The disillusionment caused by her appearance was so great that the records remained ever after silent, and were replaced by the deepest bass voices that money could buy.

'Fearful the death of the diver must be,

Walking alone in the de-he-he-he-he-epths of the sea'
or 'Drake is going West, lads.'

These were, on the whole, welcomed by the family, as rather less piercing at early dawn.

'Why should she want to be married?'

'It's not as though she could be in love. She's forty.'

Like all the very young we took it for granted that making love is child's play.

'How old do you suppose he is?'

'Fifty or sixty I guess. Perhaps she thinks it would be nice to be a widow. Weeds, you know.'

'Perhaps she thinks Fanny ought to have a man's influence.'

'Man's influence!' said Louisa. 'I forsee trouble. Supposing he falls in love with Fanny, that'll be a pretty kettle of fish, like Somerset and Princess Elizabeth – he'll be playing rough games and pinching you in bed, see if he doesn't.'

'Surely not, at his age.'

'Old men love little girls.'

'And little boys,' said Bob.

'It looks as if Aunt Sadie isn't going to say anything about it before they come,' I said.

'There's nearly a week to go – she may be deciding. She'll talk it over with Fa. Might be worth listening next time she has a bath. You can, Bob.'

Christmas Day was spent, as usual at Alconleigh, between alternate bursts of sunshine and showers. I put, as children can, the disturbing news about Aunt Emily out of my mind, and concentrated upon enjoyment. At about six o'clock Linda and I unstuck our sleepy eyes and started on our stockings. Our real presents came later, at breakfast and on the tree, but the stockings were a wonderful hors d'œuvre and full of treasures. Presently Jassy came in and started selling us things out of hers. Jassy only cared about money because she was saving up to run away – she carried her post office book about with her everywhere, and always knew to a farthing what she had got. This was then translated by a miracle of determination as Jassy was very bad at sums, into so many days in a bed-sitting-room.

'How are you getting on, Jassy?'

'My fare to London and a month and two days and an hour and a half in a bed-sitter, with basin and breakfast.'

Where the other meals would come from was left to the imagination. Jassy studied advertisements of bed-sitters in *The Times* every morning. The cheapest she had found so far was in Clapham. So eager was she for the cash that would transform her dream into reality, that one could be certain of picking up a few bargains round about Christmas and her birthday. Jassy at this time was aged eight.

I must admit that my wicked parents turned up trumps at Christmas, and my presents from them were always the envy of the entire household. This year my mother, who was in Paris, sent a gilded bird-cage full of stuffed humming-birds which, when wound up, twittered and hopped about and drank at a fountain. She also sent a fur hat and a gold and topaz bracelet, whose glamour was enhanced by the fact that Aunt Sadie considered them unsuitable for a child, and said so. My father sent a pony and cart, a very smart and beautiful little outfit, which had arrived some days before, and been secreted by Josh in the stables.

'So typical of that damned fool Edward to send it here,' Uncle Matthew said, 'and give us all the trouble of getting it to Shenley. And I bet poor old Emily won't be too pleased. Who on earth is going to look after it?'

Linda cried with envy. 'It *is* unfair,' she kept saying, 'that you should have wicked parents and not me.'

We persuaded Josh to take us for a drive after luncheon. The pony was an angel and the whole thing easily managed by a child, even the harnessing. Linda wore my hat and drove the pony. We got back late for the Tree – the house was already full of tenants and their children; Uncle Matthew, who was struggling into his Father Christmas clothes, roared at us so violently that Linda had to go and cry upstairs, and was not there to collect her own present from him. Uncle Matthew had taken some trouble to get her longed-for dormouse and was greatly put out by this; he roared at everybody in turns, and ground his dentures. There was a legend in the family that he had already ground away four pairs in his rages.

The evening came to a climax of violence when Matt produced a box of fireworks which my mother had sent him from Paris. On the box they were called *pétards*. Somebody said to Matt: 'What do they do?' to which he replied: *'Bien, ça pète, quoi?'* This remark, overheard by Uncle Matthew, was rewarded with a first-class hiding, which was actually most unfair, as poor Matt was only repeating what Lucille had said to him earlier in the day. Matt, however, regarded hidings as a sort of natural phenomenon, unconnected with any actions of his own, and submitted to them philosophically enough. I have often wondered since how it was that Aunt Sadie could have chosen Lucille, who was the very acme of vulgarity, to look after her children. We all loved her, she was gay and spirited and read aloud to us without cease, but her language really was extraordinary, and provided dreadful pitfalls for the unwary.

'*Qu'est-ce que c'est ce custard, qu'on fout partout?*'

I shall never forget Matt quite innocently making this remark in Fuller's at Oxford, where Uncle Matthew had taken us for a treat. The consequences were awful.

It never seemed to occur to Uncle Matthew that Matt could not know these words by nature, and that it would really have been more fair to check them at their source.

4

I naturally awaited the arrival of Aunt Emily and her future intended with some agitation. She was, after all, my real mother, and, greatly as I might hanker after that glittering evil person who bore me, it was to Aunt Emily that I turned for the solid, sustaining, though on the face of it uninteresting relationship that is provided by motherhood at its best. Our little household at Shenley was calm and happy and afforded an absolute contrast to the agitations and tearing emotions of Alconleigh. It may have been dull, but it was a sheltering harbour, and I was always glad to get back to it. I think I was beginning dimly to realize how much it all centred upon me; the very time-table, with its early luncheon and high tea, was arranged to fit in with my lessons and bed-time. Only during those holidays when I went to Alconleigh did Aunt Emily have any life of her own, and even these breaks were infrequent, as she had an idea that Uncle Matthew and the whole stormy set-up there were bad for my nerves. I may not have been consciously aware of the extent to which Aunt Emily had regulated her existence round mine, but I saw, only too clearly, that the addition of a man to our establishment was going to change everything. Hardly knowing any men outside the family, I imagined them all to be modelled on the lines of Uncle Matthew, or of my own seldom seen, violently emotional papa, either of whom, plunging about in that neat little house, would have been sadly out of place. I was filled with apprehension, almost with horror, and, greatly assisted by the workings of Louisa's and Linda's vivid imaginations, had got myself into a real state of nerves. Louisa was now teasing me with the *Constant Nymph*. She read aloud the last chapters, and soon I was dying at a Brussels boarding-house, in the arms of Aunt Emily's husband.

On Wednesday Aunt Emily rang up Aunt Sadie, and they talked for ages. The telephone at Alconleigh was, in those days, situated in a glass cupboard half-way down the brilliantly lighted back passage; there was no extension, and eavesdropping was thus rendered impossible. (In later years it was moved to Uncle Matthew's business-room, with an extension, after which all privacy was at an end.) When Aunt Sadie returned to the drawing-room she said nothing except: 'Emily is coming to-morrow on the three-five. She sends you her love, Fanny.'

The next day we all went out hunting. The Radletts loved animals, they loved foxes, they risked dreadful beatings in order to unstop their earths, they read and cried and rejoiced over Reynard the Fox, in summer they got up at four to go and see the cubs playing in the pale-green light of the woods; nevertheless, more than anything in the world, they loved hunting. It was in their blood and bones and in my blood and bones, and nothing could eradicate it, though we knew it for a kind of original sin. For three hours that day I forgot everything except my body and my pony's body; the rushing, the scrambling, the splashing, struggling up the hills, sliding down them again, the tugging, the bucketing, the earth, and the sky. I forgot everything, I could hardly have told you my name. That must be the great hold that hunting has over people, especially stupid people; it enforces an absolute concentration, both mental and physical.

After three hours Josh took me home. I was never allowed to stay out long or I got tired and would be sick all night. Josh was out on Uncle Matthew's second horse; at about two o'clock they changed over, and he started home on the lathered, sweating first horse, taking me with him. I came out of my trance, and saw that the day, which had begun with brilliant sunshine, was now cold and dark, threatening rain.

'And where's her ladyship hunting this year?' said Josh, as we started on a ten-mile jog along Merlinford road, a sort of hog's back, more cruelly exposed than any road I have ever known, without a scrap of shelter or windscreen the whole of its fifteen miles. Uncle

Matthew would never allow motor-cars, either to take us to the meet or to fetch us home; he regarded this habit as despicably soft.

I knew that Josh meant my mother. He had been with my grandfather when she and her sisters were girls, and my mother was his heroine, he adored her.

'She's in Paris, Josh.'

'In Paris – what for?'

'I suppose she likes it.'

'Ho,' said Josh, furiously, and we rode for about half a mile in silence. The rain had begun, a thin cold rain, sweeping over the wide views on each side of the road; we trotted along, the weather in our faces. My back was not strong, and trotting on a side-saddle for any length of time was agony to me. I edged my pony on to the grass, and cantered for a bit, but I knew how much Josh disapproved of this, it was supposed to bring the horses back too hot; walking, on the other hand chilled them. It had to be jog, jog, back-breaking jog, all the way.

'It's my opinion,' said Josh at last, 'that her ladyship is wasted, downright wasted, every minute of her life that she's not on a 'oss.'

'She's a wonderful rider, isn't she?'

I had had all this before from Josh, many times, and could never have enough of it.

'There's no human being like her, that I've ever seen,' said Josh, hissing through his teeth. 'Hands like velvet, but strong like iron, and her seat – ! Now look at you, jostling about on that saddle, first here, then there – we shall have a sore back to-night, that's one thing certain we shall.'

'Oh, Josh – trotting. And I'm so tired.'

'Never saw her tired. I've seen 'er change 'osses after a ten-mile point, get on to a fresh young five-year-old what hadn't been out for a week – up like a bird – never know you had 'er foot in your hand, pick up the reins in a jiffy, catch up its head, and off over a post and rails and bucking over the ridge and furrow, sitting like a rock. Now his lordship (he meant Uncle Matthew) he can ride, I don't say the contrary, but look how he sends his 'osses home, so

darned tired they can't drink their gruel. He can ride all right, but
he doesn't study his 'oss. I never knew your mother bring them
home like this, she'd know when they'd had enough, and then
heads for home and no looking back. Mind you, his lordship's a
great big man, I don't say the contrary, rides every bit of sixteen
stone, but he has great big 'osses and half kills them, and then who
has to stop up with them all night? Me!'

The rain was pouring down by now. An icy trickle was feeling
its way past my left shoulder, and my right boot was slowly filling
with water, the pain in my back was like a knife. I felt that I couldn't
bear another moment of this misery, and yet I knew I must bear
another five miles, another forty minutes. Josh gave me scornful
looks as my back bent more and more double; I could see that he
was wondering how it was that I could be my mother's child.

'Miss Linda,' he said, 'takes after her ladyship something wonderful.'

At last, at last, we were off the Merlinford road, coming down
the valley into Alconleigh village, turning up the hill to Alconleigh
house, through the lodge gates, up the drive, and into the stable
yard. I got stiffly down, gave the pony to one of Josh's stable boys,
and stumped away, walking like an old man. I was nearly at the
front door before I remembered, with a sudden leap of my heart,
that Aunt Emily would have arrived by now, with HIM. It was quite
a minute before I could summon up enough courage to open the
front door.

Sure enough, standing with their backs to the hall fire, were
Aunt Sadie, Aunt Emily, and a small, fair, and apparently young
man. My immediate impression was that he did not seem at all
like a husband. He looked kind and gentle.

'Here is Fanny,' said my aunts in chorus.

'Darling,' said Aunt Sadie, 'can I introduce Captain Warbeck?'

I shook hands in the abrupt graceless way of little girls of fourteen, and thought that he did not seem at all like a captain either.

'Oh, darling, how wet you are. I suppose the others won't be
back for ages – where have you come from?'

'I left them drawing the spinney by the Old Rose.'

Then I remembered, being after all a female in the presence of a male, how dreadful I always looked when I got home from hunting, splashed from head to foot, my bowler all askew, my hair a bird's nest, my stocking a flapping flag, and, muttering something, I made for the back stairs, towards my bath and my rest. After hunting we were kept in bed for at least two hours. Soon Linda returned, even wetter than I had been, and got into bed with me. She, too, had seen the Captain, and agreed that he looked neither like a marrying nor like a military man.

'Can't see him killing Germans with an entrenching tool,' she said, scornfully.

Much as we feared, much as we disapproved of passionately as we sometimes hated Uncle Matthew, he still remained for us a sort of criterion of English manhood; there seemed something not quite right about any man who greatly differed from him.

'I bet Uncle Matthew gives him rat week,' I said, apprehensive for Aunt Emily's sake.

'Poor Aunt Emily, perhaps he'll make her keep him in the stables,' said Linda with a gust of giggles.

'Still, he looks rather nice to know, and, considering her age, I should think she's lucky to get anybody.'

'I can't wait to see him with Fa.'

However, our expectations of blood and thunder were disappointed, for it was evident at once that Uncle Matthew had taken an enormous fancy to Captain Warbeck. As he never altered his first opinion of people, and as his few favourites could commit nameless crimes without doing wrong in his eyes, Captain Warbeck was, henceforward, on a good wicket with Uncle Matthew.

'He's such a frightfully clever cove, literary you know, you wouldn't believe the things he does. He writes books and criticizes pictures, and whacks hell out of the piano, though the pieces he plays aren't up to much. Still, you can see what it would be like, if he learnt some of the tunes out of the *Country Girl*, for instance. Nothing would be too difficult for him, you can see that.'

At dinner Captain Warbeck sitting next to Aunt Sadie, and Aunt Emily next to Uncle Matthew, were separated from each other, not only by four of us children (Bob was allowed to dine down, as he was going to Eton next half), but also by pools of darkness. The dining-room table was lit by three electric bulbs hanging in a bunch from the ceiling, and screened by a curtain of dark-red jap silk with a gold fringe. One spot of brilliant light was thus cast into the middle of the table, while the diners themselves, and their plates, sat outside it in total gloom. We all, naturally, had our eyes fixed upon the shadowy figure of the fiancé, and found a great deal in his behaviour to interest us. He talked to Aunt Sadie at first about gardens, plants, and flowering shrubs, a topic which was unknown at Alconleigh. The gardener saw to the garden, and that was that. It was quite half a mile from the house, and nobody went near it, except as a little walk sometimes in the summer. It seemed strange that a man who lived in London should know the names, the habits, and the medicinal properties of so many plants. Aunt Sadie politely tried to keep up with him, but could not altogether conceal her ignorance, though she partly veiled it in a mist of absent-mindedness.

'And what is your soil here?' asked Captain Warbeck.

Aunt Sadie came down from the clouds with a happy smile, and said, triumphantly, for here was something she did know, 'Clay.'

'Ah, yes,' said the Captain.

He produced a little jewelled box, took from it an enormous pill, swallowed it, to our amazement, without one sip to help it down, and said, as though to himself, but quite distinctly, 'Then the water here will be madly binding.'

When Logan, the butler, offered him shepherd's pie (the food at Alconleigh was always good and plentiful, but of the homely schoolroom description) he said, again so that one did not quite know whether he meant to be overheard or not, 'No, thank you, no twice-cooked meat. I am a wretched invalid, I must be careful, or I pay.'

Aunt Sadie, who so much disliked hearing about health that people often took her for a Christian Scientist, which, indeed, she might have become had she not disliked hearing about religion even more, took absolutely no notice, but Bob asked with interest, what it was that twice-cooked meat did to one.

'Oh, it imposes a most fearful strain on the juices, you might as well eat leather,' replied Captain Warbeck, faintly, heaping onto his plate the whole of the salad. He said, again in that withdrawn voice: 'Raw lettuce, anti-scorbutic,' and, opening another box of even larger pills, he took two, murmuring, 'Protein.'

'How delicious your bread is,' he said to Aunt Sadie, as though to make up for his rudeness in refusing the twice-cooked meat. 'I'm sure it has the germ.'

'What?' said Aunt Sadie, turning from a whispered confabulation with Logan ('ask Mrs Crabbe if she could quickly make some more salad').

'I was saying that I feel sure your delicious bread is made of stone-ground flour, containing a high proportion of the germ. In my bedroom at home I have a picture of a grain of wheat (magnified, naturally) which shows the germ. As you know, in white bread the germ, with its wonderful health-giving properties, is eliminated – extracted, I should say – and put into chicken food. As a result the human race is becoming enfeebled, while hens grow larger and stronger with every generation.'

'So in the end,' said Linda, listening all agog, unlike Aunt Sadie, who had retired into a cloud of boredom, 'Hens will be Hons and Hons will be Hens. Oh, how I should love to live in a dear little Hon-house.'

'You wouldn't like your work,' said Bob. 'I once saw a hen laying an egg, and she had a most terrible expression on her face.'

'Only about like going to the lav,' said Linda.

'Now, Linda,' said Aunt Sadie, sharply, 'that's quite unnecessary. Get on with your supper and don't talk so much.'

Vague as she was, Aunt Sadie could not always be counted on to ignore everything that was happening around her.

'What were you telling me, Captain Warbeck, something about germs?'

'Oh, not germs – the germ –'

At this point I became aware that, in the shadows at the other end of the table, Uncle Matthew and Aunt Emily were having one of their usual set-tos, and that it concerned me. Whenever Aunt Emily came to Alconleigh these tussles with Uncle Matthew would occur, but, all the same, one could see that he was fond of her. He always liked people who stood up to him, and also he probably saw in her a reflection of Aunt Sadie, whom he adored. Aunt Emily was more positive than Aunt Sadie, she had more character and less beauty, and she was not worn out with childbirth, but they were very much sisters. My mother was utterly different in every respect, but then she, poor thing, was, as Linda would have said, obsessed with sex.

Uncle Matthew and Aunt Emily were now engaged upon an argument we had all heard many times before. It concerned the education of females.

Uncle Matthew: 'I hope poor Fanny's school (the word school pronounced in tones of withering scorn) is doing her all the good you think it is. Certainly she picks up some dreadful expressions there.'

Aunt Emily, calmly, but on the defensive: 'Very likely she does. She also picks up a good deal of education.'

Uncle Matthew: 'Education! I was always led to suppose that no educated person ever spoke of notepaper, and yet I hear poor Fanny asking Sadie for notepaper. What is this education? Fanny talks about mirrors and mantelpieces, handbags and perfume, she takes sugar in her coffee, has a tassel on her umbrella, and I have no doubt that, if she is ever fortunate enough to catch a husband, she will call his father and mother Father and Mother. Will the wonderful education she is getting make up to the unhappy brute for all these endless pinpricks? Fancy hearing one's wife talk about notepaper – the irritation!'

Aunt Emily: 'A lot of men would find it more irritating to have a wife who had never heard of George III. (All the same, Fanny darling, it is called writing-paper you know – don't let's hear any

29

more about the note, please.) That is where you and I come in, you see, Matthew, home influence is admitted to be a most important part of education.'

Uncle Matthew: 'There you are –'

Aunt Emily: 'A most important, but not by any means the most important.'

Uncle Matthew: 'You don't have to go to some awful middle-class establishment to know who George III was. Anyway, who was he, Fanny?'

Alas, I always failed to shine on these occasions. My wits scattered to the four winds by my terror of Uncle Matthew, I said, scarlet in my face:

'He was king. He went mad.'

'Most original, full of information,' said Uncle Matthew, sarcastically. 'Well worth losing every ounce of feminine charm to find that out, I must say. Legs like gateposts from playing hockey, and the worst seat on a horse of any woman I ever knew. Give a horse a sore back as soon as look at it. Linda, you're uneducated, thank God, what have you got to say about George III?'

'Well,' said Linda, her mouth full, 'he was the son of poor Fred and the father of Beau Brummel's fat friend, and he was one of those vacillators you know. "I am his Highness's dog at Kew, pray tell me, sir, whose dog are you?"' she added, inconsequently. 'Oh, how sweet!'

Uncle Matthew shot a look of cruel triumph at Aunt Emily. I saw that I had let down the side and began to cry, inspiring Uncle Matthew to fresh bouts of beastliness.

'It's a lucky thing that Fanny will have £15,000 a year of her own,' he said, 'not to speak of any settlements the Bolter may have picked up in the course of her career. She'll get a husband all right, even if she does talk about lunch, and *en*velope, and put the milk in first. I'm not afraid of that, I only say she'll drive the poor devil to drink when she has hooked him.'

Aunt Emily gave Uncle Matthew a furious frown. She had always tried to conceal from me the fact that I was an heiress, and, indeed,

I was one only until such time as my father, hale and hearty and in the prime of life, should marry somebody of an age to bear children. It so happened that, like the Hanoverian family, he cared for women only when they were over forty; after my mother had left him he had embarked upon a succession of middle-aged wives whom even the miracles of modern science were unable to render fruitful. It was also believed, wrongly, by the grown-ups that we children were ignorant of the fact that my mamma was called the Bolter.

'All this,' said Aunt Emily, 'is quite beside the point. Fanny may possibly, in the far future, have a little money of her own (though it is ludicrous to talk of £15,000). Whether she does, or does not, the man she marries may be able to support her – on the other hand, the modern world being what it is, she may have to earn her own living. In any case she will be a more mature, a happier, a more interested and interesting person if she –'

'If she knows that George III was a king and went mad.'

All the same, my aunt was right, and I knew it and she knew it. The Radlett children read enormously by fits and starts in the library at Alconleigh, a good representative nineteenth-century library, which had been made by their grandfather, a most cultivated man. But, while they picked up a great deal of heterogeneous informa-tion, and gilded it with their own originality, while they bridged gulfs of ignorance with their charm and high spirits, they never acquired any habit of concentration, they were incapable of solid hard work. One result, in later life, was that they could not stand boredom. Storms and difficulties left them unmoved, but day after day of ordinary existence produced an unbearable torture of ennui, because they completely lacked any form of mental discipline.

As we trailed out of the dining-room after dinner, we heard Captain Warbeck say:

'No port, no, thank you. Such a delicious drink, but I must refuse. It's the acid from port that makes one so delicate now.'

'Ah – you've been a great port drinker, have you?' said Uncle Matthew.

'Oh, not me, I've never touched it. My ancestors –'

Presently, when they joined us in the drawing-room, Aunt Sadie said: 'The children know the news now.'

'I suppose they think it's a great joke,' said Davey Warbeck, 'old people like us being married.'

'Oh, no, of course not,' we said, politely, blushing.

'He's an extraordinary fella,' said Uncle Matthew, 'knows everything. He says those Charles II sugar casters are only a Georgian imitation of Charles II, just fancy, not valuable at all. To-morrow we'll go round the house and I'll show you all our things and you can tell us what's what. Quite useful to have a fella like you in the family, I must say.'

'That will be very nice,' said Davey, faintly, 'and now I think, if you don't mind, I'll go to bed. Yes, please, early morning tea – so necessary to replace the evaporation of the night.'

He shook hands with us all, and hurried from the room, saying to himself: 'Wooing, so tiring.'

'Davey Warbeck is a Hon,' said Bob as we were all coming down to breakfast next day.

'Yes, he seems a terrific Hon,' said Linda, sleepily.

'No, I mean he's a real one. Look, there's a letter for him, The Hon. David Warbeck. I've looked him up, and it's true.'

Bob's favourite book at this time was Debrett, his nose was never out of it. As a result of his researches he was once heard informing Lucille that *les origines de la famille Radlett sont perdues dans les brumes de l'antiquité.*

'He's only a second son, and the eldest has got an heir, so I'm afraid Aunt Emily won't be a lady. And his father's only the second Baron, created 1860, and they only start in 1720, before that it's a female line.' Bob's voice was trailing off. 'Still –' he said.

We heard Davey Warbeck, as he was coming down the stairs, say to Uncle Matthew:

'Oh no, that couldn't be a Reynolds. Prince Hoare, at his very worst, if you're lucky.'

'Pig's thinkers, Davey?' Uncle Matthew lifted the lid of a hot dish.

'Oh, yes please, Matthew, if you mean brains. So digestible.'

'And after breakfast I'm going to show you our collection of minerals in the north passage. I bet you'll agree we've got something worth having there, it's supposed to be the finest collection in England – left me by an old uncle, who spent his life making it. Meanwhile, what'd you think of my eagle?'

'Ah, if that were Chinese now, it would be a treasure. But Jap I'm afraid, not worth the bronze it's cast in. Cooper's Oxford, please, Linda.'

After breakfast we all flocked to the north passage, where there were hundreds of stones in glass-fronted cupboards. Petrified this and fossilized that, blue-john and lapis were the most exciting, large flints which looked as if they had been picked up by the side of the road, the least. Valuable, unique, they were a family legend. 'The minerals in the north passage are good enough for a museum.' We children revered them. Davey looked at them carefully, taking some over to the window and peering into them. Finally, he heaved a great sigh and said:

'What a beautiful collection. I suppose you know they're all diseased?'

'Diseased?'

'Badly, and too far gone for treatment. In a year or two they'll all be dead – you might as well throw the whole lot away.'

Uncle Matthew was delighted.

'Damned fella,' he said, 'nothing's right for him, I never saw such a fella. Even the minerals have got foot-and-mouth, according to him.'

5

The year which followed Aunt Emily's marriage transformed Linda and me from children, young for our ages, into lounging adolescents waiting for love. One result of the marriage was that I now spent nearly all my holidays at Alconleigh. Davey, like all Uncle Matthew's favourites, simply could not see that he was in the least bit frightening, and scouted Aunt Emily's theory that to be too much with him was bad for my nerves.

'You're just a lot of little crybabies,' he said, scornfully, 'if you allow yourselves to be upset by that old cardboard ogre.'

Davey had given up his flat in London and lived with us at Shenley, where, during term-time, he made but little difference to our life, except in so far as a male presence in a female household is always salutary (the curtains, the covers, and Aunt Emily's clothes underwent an enormous change for the better), but, in the holidays, he liked to carry her off, to his own relations or on trips abroad, and I was parked at Alconleigh. Aunt Emily probably felt that, if she had to choose between her husband's wishes and my nervous system, the former should win the day. In spite of her being forty they were, I believe, very much in love; it must have been a perfect bore having me about at all, and it speaks volumes for their characters that never, for one moment, did they allow me to be aware of this. Davey, in fact was, and has been ever since, a perfect stepfather to me, affectionate, understanding, never in any way interfering. He accepted me at once as belonging to Aunt Emily, and never questioned the inevitability of my presence in his household.

By the Christmas holidays Louisa was officially 'out', and going to hunt balls, a source of bitter envy to us, though Linda said scornfully that she did not appear to have many suitors. We were not coming out for another two years – it seemed an eternity, and especially to Linda, who was paralysed by her longing for love, and had no lessons or work to do which could take her mind off it. In fact, she had no other interest now except hunting, even the animals seemed to have lost all charm for her. She and I did nothing on non-hunting days but sit about, too large for our tweed suits, whose hooks and eyes were always popping off at the waist, and play endless games of patience; or we lolled in the Hons' cupboard, and 'measured'. We had a tape-measure and competed as to the largeness of our eyes, the smallness of wrists, ankles, waist and neck, length of legs and fingers, and so on. Linda always won. When we had finished 'measuring' we talked of romance. These were most innocent talks, for to us, at that time, love and marriage were synonymous, we knew that they lasted for ever, to the grave and far, far beyond. Our preoccupation with sin was finished; Bob, back from Eton, had been able to tell us all about Oscar Wilde, and, now that his crime was no longer a mystery, it seemed dull, unromantic, and incomprehensible.

We were, of course, both in love, but with people we had never met; Linda with the Prince of Wales, and I with a fat, red-faced, middle-aged farmer, whom I sometimes saw riding through Shenley. These loves were strong, and painfully delicious; they occupied all our thoughts, but I think we half realized that they would be superseded in time by real people. They were to keep the house warm, so to speak, for its eventual occupant. What we never would admit was the possibility of lovers after marriage. We were looking for real love, and that could only come once in a lifetime; it hurried to consecration, and thereafter never wavered. Husbands, we knew, were not always faithful, this we must be prepared for, we must understand and forgive. 'I have been faithful to thee, Cynara, in my fashion' seemed to explain it beautifully. But women – that was different; only the lowest of the sex could love or give themselves more than once. I do not quite know how I reconciled these sentiments with the great hero-worship I still had for my mother, that adulterous doll. I suppose I put her in an entirely different category, in the face that launched a thousand ships class. A few historical characters must be allowed to have belonged to this, but Linda and I were perfectionists where love was concerned and did not ourselves aspire to that kind of fame.

This winter Uncle Matthew had a new tune on his gramophone, called 'Thora'. 'I live in a land of roses,' boomed a deep male voice, 'but dream of a land of snow. Speak, speak, SPEAK to me, Thora'. He played it morning, noon, and night; it suited our mood exactly, and Thora seemed the most poignantly beautiful of names.

Aunt Sadie was giving a ball for Louisa soon after Christmas, and to this we pinned great hopes. True, neither the Prince of Wales nor my farmer was invited, but, as Linda said, you never could tell in the country. Somebody might bring them. The Prince might break down in his motor-car, perhaps on his way to Badminton; what could be more natural than that he should while away the time by looking in on the revelry?

'Pray, who is that beautiful young lady?'

'My daughter Louisa, sir.'

'Ah, yes, very charming, but I really meant the one in white taffeta.'

'That is my youngest daughter Linda, Your Royal Highness.'

'Please present her to me.'

They would then whirl away in a waltz so accomplished that the other dancers would stand aside to admire. When they could dance no more they would sit for the rest of the evening absorbed in witty conversation.

The following day an A.D.C., asking for her hand –

'But she is so young!'

'His Royal Highness is prepared to wait a year. He reminds you that Her Majesty the Empress Elizabeth of Austria was married at sixteen. Meanwhile, he sends this jewel.'

A golden casket, a pink and white cushion, a diamond rose.

My daydreams were less exalted, equally improbable, and quite as real to me. I imagined my farmer carrying me away from Alconleigh, like young Lochinvar, on a pillion behind him to the nearest smith, who then declared us man and wife. Linda kindly said that we could have one of the royal farms, but I thought this would be a great bore, and that it would be much more fun to have one of our own.

Meanwhile, preparations for the ball went forward, occupying every single member of the household. Linda's and my dresses, white taffeta with floating panels and embroidered bead belts, were being made by Mrs Josh, whose cottage was besieged at all hours to see how they were getting on. Louisa's came from Reville, it was silver lamé in tiny frills, each frill edged with blue net. Dangling on the left shoulder, and strangely unrelated to the dress, was a large pink silk over-blown rose. Aunt Sadie, shaken out of her accustomed languor, was in a state of exaggerated preoccupation and worry over the whole thing; we had never seen her like this before. For the first time, too, that any of us could remember, she found herself in opposition to Uncle Matthew. It was over the following question: The nearest neighbour to Alconleigh was Lord Merlin; his estate marched with that of my uncle, and his house at Merlinford was about five miles away. Uncle Matthew loathed him, while, as for Lord Merlin, not for nothing was his telegraphic address Neighbourtease. There had, however, been no open breach between them, the fact that they never saw each other meant nothing, for Lord Merlin neither hunted, shot, nor fished, while Uncle Matthew had never in his life been known to eat a meal in anybody else's house. 'Perfectly good food at home,' he would say, and people had long ago stopped asking him. The two men, and indeed their two houses and estates afforded an absolute contrast. Alconleigh was a large, ugly, north-facing, Georgian house, built with only one intention, that of sheltering, when the weather was too bad to be out of doors, a succession of bucolic squires, their wives, their enormous families, their dogs, their horses, their father's relict, and their unmarried sisters. There was no attempt at decoration, at softening the lines, no apology for a façade, it was all as grim and as bare as a barracks, stuck upon the high hillside. Within, the keynote, the theme, was death. Not death of maidens, not death romantically accoutred with urns and weeping willows, cypresses and valedictory odes, but the death of warriors and of animals, stark, real. On the walls halberds and pikes and ancient muskets were arranged in crude patterns with the heads of beasts slaughtered in many lands, with the flags and uniforms of bygone Radletts. Glass-topped cases contained, not miniatures of ladies, but miniatures of the medals of their lords, badges, penholders made of tiger's teeth, the hoof of a favourite horse, telegrams announcing casualties in battle, and commissions written out on parchment scrolls, all lying together in a timeless jumble.

Merlinford nestled in a valley of south-westerly aspect, among orchards and old mellow farmhouses. It was a villa, built at about the same time as Alconleigh, but by a very different architect, and with a very different end in view. It was a house to live in, not to rush out from all day to kill enemies and animals. It was suitable for a bachelor, or a married couple with one, or at most two, beautiful, clever, delicate children. It had Angelica Kauffman ceilings, a Chippendale staircase, furniture by Sheraton and Hepplewhite; in the hall there hung two Watteaus; there was no entrenching tool to be seen, nor the head of any animal.

Lord Merlin added continually to its beauties. He was a great collector, and not only Merlinford, but also his houses in London and Rome flowed over with treasures. Indeed, a well-known antique dealer from St James's had found it worth his while to open a branch in the little town of Merlinford, to tempt his lordship with choice objects during his morning walk, and was soon followed there by a Bond Street jeweller. Lord Merlin loved jewels; his two black whippets wore diamond necklaces designed for whiter, but not slimmer or more graceful necks than theirs. This was a neighbour-tease of long standing; there was a feeling among the local gentry that it incited the good burghers of Merlinford to dishonesty. The neighbours were doubly teased, when year after year went by and the brilliants still sparkled on those furry necks intact.

His taste was by no means confined to antiques; he was an artist and a musician himself, and the patron of all the young. Modern music streamed perpetually from Merlinford, and he had built a small but exquisite playhouse in the garden, where his astonished neighbours were sometimes invited to attend such puzzlers as

Cocteau plays, the opera 'Mahagonny', or the latest Dada extravagances from Paris. As Lord Merlin was a famous practical joker, it was sometimes difficult to know where jokes ended and culture began. I think he was not always perfectly certain himself.

A marble folly on a nearby hill was topped with a gold angel which blew a trumpet every evening at the hour of Lord Merlin's birth (that this happened to be 9.20 p.m., just too late to remind one of the BBC news, was to be a great local grievance in years to come). The folly glittered by day with semi-precious stones, by night a powerful blue beam was trained upon it.

Such a man was bound to become a sort of legend to the bluff Cotswold squires among whom he lived. But, although they could not approve of an existence which left out of account the killing, though by no means the eating, of delicious game, and though they were puzzled beyond words by the aestheticism and the teases, they accepted him without question as one of themselves. Their families had always known his family, and his father, many years ago, had been a most popular M.F.H.; he was no upstart, no new rich, but simply a sport of all that was most normal in English country life. Indeed, the very folly itself, while considered absolutely hideous, was welcomed as a landmark by those lost on their way home from hunting.

The difference between Aunt Sadie and Uncle Matthew was not as to whether Lord Merlin should or should not be asked to the ball (that question did not arise, since all neighbours were automatically invited), but whether he should be asked to bring a house party. Aunt Sadie thought he should. Since her marriage the least wordly of women, she had known the world as a girl, and she knew that Lord Merlin's house party, if he consented to bring one, would have great decorative value. She also knew that, apart from this, the general note of her ball would be utter and unrelieved dowdiness, and she became aware of a longing to look once more upon young women with well brushed hair, London complexions, and Paris clothes. Uncle Matthew said: 'If we ask that brute Merlin to bring his friends, we shall get a lot of aesthetes, sewers from

Oxford, and I wouldn't put it past him to bring some foreigners. I hear he sometimes has Frogs and even Wops to stay with him. I will not have my house filled with Wops.'

In the end, however, as usual, Aunt Sadie had her way, and sat down to write:

'Dear Lord Merlin,
    We are having a little dance for Louisa, etc . . .'

while Uncle Matthew went gloomily off, having said his piece, and put on 'Thora'.

Lord Merlin accepted, and said he would bring a party of twelve people, whose names he would presently submit to Aunt Sadie. Very correct, perfectly normal behaviour. Aunt Sadie was quite agreeably surprised that his letter, when opened, did not contain some clockwork joke to hit her in the eye. The writing-paper did actually have a picture of his house on it, and this she concealed from Uncle Matthew. It was the kind of thing he despised.

A few days later there was another surprise. Lord Merlin wrote another letter, still jokeless, still polite, asking Uncle Matthew, Aunt Sadie and Louisa to dine with him for the Merlinford Cottage Hospital Ball. Uncle Matthew naturally could not be persuaded, but Aunt Sadie and Louisa went. They came back with their eyes popping out of their heads. The house, they said, had been boiling hot, so hot that one never felt cold for a single moment, not even getting out of one's coat in the hall. They had arrived very early, long before anyone else was down, as it was the custom at Alconleigh always to leave a quarter of an hour too soon when motoring, in case there should be a puncture. This gave them the opportunity to have a good look round. The house was full of spring flowers, and smelt wonderful. The hothouses at Alconleigh were full of spring flowers too, but somehow they never found their way into the house, and certainly would have died of cold if they had. The whippets did wear diamond necklaces, far grander ones than Aunt Sadie's, she said, and she was forced to admit that they looked very beautiful in them. Birds of paradise flew about the house, quite tame, and one of the young men told Louisa that, if she came in the daytime, she would see a flock of multi-coloured pigeons tumbling about like a cloud of confetti in the sky.

'Merlin dyes them every year, and they are dried in the linen cupboard.'

'But isn't that frightfully cruel?' said Louisa, horrified.

'Oh, no, they love it. It makes their husbands and wives look so pretty when they come out.'

'What about their poor eyes?'

'Oh, they soon learn to shut them.'

The house party, when they finally appeared (some of them shockingly late) from their bedrooms, smelt even more delicious than the flowers, and looked even more exotic than the birds of paradise. Everybody had been very nice, very kind to Louisa. She sat between two beautiful young men at dinner, and turned upon them the usual gambit:

'Where do you hunt?'

'We don't,' they said.

'Oh, then why do you wear pink coats?'

'Because we think they are so pretty.'

We all thought this dazzlingly funny, but agreed that Uncle Matthew must never hear of it, or he might easily, even now, forbid the Merlinford party his ball.

After dinner the girls had taken Louisa upstairs. She was rather startled at first to see printed notices in the guest rooms:

OWING TO AN UNIDENTIFIED CORPSE IN THE CISTERN VISITORS ARE REQUESTED NOT TO DRINK THE BATH WATER.

VISITORS ARE REQUESTED NOT TO LET OFF FIREARMS, BLOW BUGLES, SCREAM OR HOOT, BETWEEN THE HOURS OF MIDNIGHT AND SIX A.M.

and, on one bedroom door:

MANGLING DONE HERE

But it was soon explained to her that these were jokes.

The girls had offered to lend her powder and lipstick, but Louisa had not quite dared to accept, for fear Aunt Sadie would notice. She said it made the others look simply too lovely.

As the great day of the Alconleigh ball approached, it became obvious that Aunt Sadie had something on her mind. Everything appeared to be going smoothly, the champagne had arrived, the band, Clifford Essex's third string, had been ordered, and would spend the few hours of its rest in Mrs Craven's cottage. Mrs Crabbe, in conjunction with the Home Farm, Craven, and three women from the village who were coming in to help, was planning a supper to end all suppers. Uncle Matthew had been persuaded to get twenty oil-stoves, with which to emulate the caressing warmth of Merlinford, and the gardener was preparing to transfer to the house every pot-plant that he could lay his hands on. ('You'll be dyeing the White Leghorns next,' said Uncle Matthew, scornfully.)

But, in spite of the fact that the preparations seemed to be going forward without a single hitch, Aunt Sadie's brow was still furrowed with anxiety, because she had collected a large house-party of girls and their mammas, but not one single young man. The fact was that those of her own contemporaries who had daughters were glad to bring them, but sons were another matter. Dancing partners, sated with invitations at this time of the year, knew better than to go all the way down to Gloucestershire to a house as yet untried, where they were by no means certain of finding the warmth, the luxury and fine wines which they looked upon as their due, where there was no known female charmer to tempt them, where they had not been offered a mount, and where no mention had been made of a shoot, not even a day with the cocks.

Uncle Matthew had far too much respect for his horses and his pheasants to offer them up to be messed about by any callow unknown boy.

So here was a horrible situation. Ten females, four mothers and six girls, were advancing from various parts of England, to arrive at a household consisting of four more females (not that Linda and I counted, still, we wore skirts and not trousers, and were really too old to be kept all the time in the schoolroom) and only two males, one of whom was not yet in tails.

The telephone now became red-hot, telegrams flew in every direction. Aunt Sadie abandoned all pride, all pretence that things were as they should be, that people were asked for themselves alone, and launched a series of desperate appeals. Mr Wills, the vicar, consented to leave Mrs Wills at home, and dine, *en garçon*, at Alconleigh. It would be the first time they had been separated for forty years. Mrs Aster, the agent's wife, also made the same sacrifice, and Master Aster, the agent's son, aged not quite seventeen, was hurried off to Oxford to get himself a ready-made dress suit.

Davey Warbeck was ordered to leave Aunt Emily and come. He said he would, but unwillingly, and only after the full extent of the crisis had been divulged. Elderly cousins, and uncles who had been for many years forgotten as ghosts, were recalled from oblivion and urged to materialize. They nearly all refused, some of them quite rudely – they had, nearly all, at one time or another, been so deeply and bitterly insulted by Uncle Matthew that forgiveness was impossible.

At last Uncle Matthew saw that the situation would have to be taken in hand. He did not care two hoots about the ball, he felt no particular responsibility for the amusement of his guests, whom he seemed to regard as an onrushing horde of barbarians who could not be kept out, rather than as a group of delightful friends summoned for mutual entertainment and joyous revelry. But he did care for Aunt Sadie's peace of mind, he could not bear to see her looking so worried, and he decided to take steps. He went up to London and attended the last sitting of the House of Lords before the recess. His journey was entirely fruitful.

'Stromboli, Paddington, Fort William, and Curtley have accepted,' he told Aunt Sadie, with the air of a conjurer producing four wonderful fat rabbits out of one small wine-glass.

'But I had to promise them a shoot – Bob, go and tell Craven I want to see him in the morning.'

By these complicated devices the numbers at the dinner-table would now be even, and Aunt Sadie was infinitely relieved, though inclined to be giggly over Uncle Matthew's rabbits. Lord Stromboli, Lord Fort William, and the Duke of Paddington were old dancing partners of her own, Sir Archibald Curtley, Librarian of the House, was a well-known diner-out in the smart intellectual world, he was over seventy and very arthritic. After dinner, of course, the dance would be another matter. Mr Wills would then be joined by Mrs Wills, Captain Aster by Mrs Aster, Uncle Matthew and Bob could hardly be counted on as partners, while the House of Lords contingent were more likely to head for the bridge table than for the dancing floor.

'I fear it will be sink or swim for the girls,' said Aunt Sadie, dreamily.

In one way, however, it was all to the good. These old boys were Uncle Matthew's own choice, his own friends, and he would probably be polite to them; in any case they would know what he was like before they came. To have filled the house with strange young men would, she knew, have been taking a great risk. Uncle Matthew hated strangers, he hated the young, and he hated the idea of possible suitors for his daughters; Aunt Sadie saw rocks ahead, but this time they had been circumnavigated.

This then is a ball. This is life, what we have been waiting for all these years, here we are and here it is, a ball, actually going on now, actually in progress round us. How extraordinary it feels, such unreality, like a dream. But, alas, so utterly different from what one had imagined and expected; it must be admitted, not a good dream. The men so small and ugly, the women so frowsty, their clothes so messy and their faces so red, the oil-stoves so smelly, and not really very warm, but, above all, the men, either so old or so ugly. And when they ask one to dance (pushed to it, one cannot but suspect, by kind Davey, who is trying to see that we have a good time at our first party), it is not at all like floating away into a delicious cloud, pressed by a manly arm to a manly bosom, but stumble, stumble, kick, kick. They balance, like King Stork, on one leg, while, with the other, they come down, like King Log, on to one's toe. As for witty conversation, it is wonderful if any conversation, even of the most banal and jerky description, lasts through a whole dance and the sitting out. It is mostly: 'Oh, sorry – oh, my fault,' though Linda did get as far as taking one of her partners to see the diseased stones.

We had never learnt to dance, and, for some reason, we had supposed it to be a thing which everybody could do quite easily and naturally. I think Linda realized there and then what it took me years to learn, that the behaviour of civilized man really has nothing to do with nature, that all is artificiality and art more or less perfected.

The evening was saved from being an utter disillusionment by the Merlinford house party. They came immensely late, we had all forgotten about them in fact, but, when they had said how do you do to Aunt Sadie and taken the floor, they seemed at once to give the party a new atmosphere. They flourished and shone with jewels, lovely clothes, brilliant hair and dazzling complexions; when they danced they really did seem to float, except when it was the Charleston, and that, though angular, was so accomplished that it made us gasp with admiration. Their conversation was quite evidently both daring and witty, one could see it ran like a river, splashing, dashing, and glittering in the sun. Linda was entranced by them, and decided then and there that she would become one of these brilliant beings and live in their world, even if it took her a lifetime to accomplish. I did not aspire to this. I saw that they were admirable, but they were far removed from me and my orbit, belonging more to that of my parents; my back had been towards them from that day Aunt Emily had taken me home, and there was no return – nor did I wish for it. All the same, I found them fascinating as a spectacle, and, whether I sat out with Linda or stumped round the room with kind Davey, who, unable to persuade any more young men to take us on, gave us an occasional turn himself, my eyes were glued to them. Davey seemed to know them all quite well, and was evidently great friends with Lord Merlin. When he was not being kind to Linda and me, he attached himself to them, and joined in their accomplished chatter. He even offered to introduce us to them, but, alas, the floating panels of taffeta, which had seemed so original and pretty in Mrs Josh's cottage, looked queerly stiff beside their printed chiffons, so soft and supple; also, our experiences earlier in the evening had made us feel inferior, and we begged him not to.

That night in bed, I thought more than ever of the safe sheltering arms of my Shenley farmer. The next morning Linda told me that she had renounced the Prince of Wales.

'I have come to the conclusion,' she said, 'that Court circles would be rather dull. Lady Dorothy is a lady-in-waiting and look at her.'

6

The ball had a very unexpected sequel. Lord Fort William's mother invited Aunt Sadie and Louisa to stay at their place in Sussex for a hunt ball, and, shortly afterwards, his married sister asked them to a shoot and an Infirmary Ball. During this visit, Lord Fort William proposed to Louisa and was accepted. She came back to Alconleigh a fiancée, to find herself the centre of attention there for the first time since the birth of Linda had put her nose for ever out of joint. This was indeed an excitement, and tremendous chats took place in the Hons' cupboard, both with and without Louisa. She had a nice little diamond ring on her fourth finger, but was not as communicative as we could have wished on the subject of Lord (John now to us, but how could we remember that?) Fort William's lovemaking, retiring, with many blushes, behind the smoke-screen of such things as being too sacred to speak of. He soon appeared again in person, and we were able to observe him as an individual, instead of part, with Lord Stromboli and the Duke of Paddington, of a venerable trinity. Linda pronounced the summing-up. 'Poor old thing, I suppose she likes him, but, I must say, if he was one's dog one would have him put down.' Lord Fort William was thirty-nine, but he certainly looked much more. His hair seemed to be slipping off backwards, like an eiderdown in the night, Linda said, and he had a generally uncared-for middle-aged appearance. Louisa, however, loved him, and was happy for the first time in her life. She had always been more frightened of Uncle Matthew than any of the others, and with good reason; he thought she was a fool and was never at all nice to her, and she was in heaven at the prospect of getting away from Alconleigh for ever.

I think Linda, in spite of the poor old dog and the eiderdown, was really very jealous. She went off for long rides by herself, and spun more and more fantastic daydreams; her longing for love had become an obsession. Two whole years would have to be made away with somehow before she would come out in the world, but oh the days went dragging by. Linda would flop about in the drawing-room, playing (or beginning and then not finishing) endless games of patience, sometimes by herself, sometimes with Jassy, whom she had infected with her own restlessness.

'What's the time, darling?'

'Guess.'

'A quarter to six?'

'Better than that.'

'Six!'

'Not quite so good.'

'Five to?'

'Yes.'

'If this comes out I shall marry the man I love. If this comes out I shall marry at eighteen.'

If this comes out – shuffle – if this comes out – deal. A queen at the bottom of the pack, it can't come out, begin again.

Louisa was married in the spring. Her wedding dress, of tulle frills and sprays of orange blossom, was short to the knee and had a train, as was the hideous fashion then. Jassy got very worked up about it.

'So unsuitable.'

'Why, Jassy?'

'To be buried in, I mean. Women are always buried in their wedding dresses, aren't they? Think of your poor old dead legs sticking out.'

'Oh, Jassy, don't be such a ghoul. I'll wrap them up in my train.'

'Not very nice for the undertakers.'

Louisa refused to have bridesmaids. I think she felt that it would be agreeable, for once in her life, to be more looked at than Linda.

'You can't think how stupid you'll look from behind,' Linda said, 'without any. Still, have it your own way. I'm sure we don't want to be guyed up in blue chiffon, I'm only thinking what would be kinder for you.'

On Louisa's birthday John Fort William, an ardent antiquarian, gave her a replica of King Alfred's jewel. Linda, whose disagreeableness at this time knew no bounds, said that it simply looked like a chicken's mess. 'Same shape, same size, same colour. Not my idea of a jewel.'

'I think it's lovely,' said Aunt Sadie, but Linda's words had left their sting all the same.

Aunt Sadie had a canary then, which sang all day, rivalling even Galli Curci in the pureness and loudness of its trills. Whenever I hear a canary sing so immoderately it recalls that happy visit, the endless flow of wedding presents, unpacking them, arranging them in the ballroom with shrieks of admiration or of horror, the hustle, the bustle, and Uncle Matthew's good temper, which went on, as fine weather sometimes does, day after unbelievable day.

Louisa was to have two houses, one in London, Connaught Square, and one in Scotland. Her dress allowance would be three hundred a year, she would possess a diamond tiara, a pearl necklace, a motor-car of her own and a fur cape. In fact, granted that she could bear John Fort William, her lot was an enviable one. He was terribly dull.

The wedding day was fine and balmy, and, when we went in the morning to see how Mrs Wills and Mrs Josh were getting on with the decorations, we found the light little church bunchy with spring flowers. Later, its well-known outlines blurred with a most unaccustomed throng of human beings, it looked quite different. I thought that I personally should have liked better to be married in it when it was so empty and flowery and full of the Holy Ghost.

Neither Linda nor I had ever been to a wedding before, as Aunt Emily, most unfairly we thought at the time, had been married privately in the chapel at Davey's home in the North of England,

and we were hardly prepared for the sudden transformation on this day of dear old Louisa, of terribly dull John, into eternal types of Bride and Bridegroom, Heroine and Hero of romance.

From the moment when we left Louisa alone at Alconleigh with Uncle Matthew, to follow us in the Daimler in exactly eleven minutes, the atmosphere became positively dramatic. Louisa, enveloped from head to knee in tulle, sat gingerly on the edge of a chair, while Uncle Matthew, watch in hand, strode up and down the hall. We walked, as we always did, to the church, and arranged ourselves in the family pew at the back of it, from which vantage point we were able to observe with fascination, the unusual appearance of our neighbours, all tricked out in their best. The only person in the whole congregation who looked exactly as usual was Lord Merlin.

Suddenly there was a stir. John and his best man, Lord Stromboli, appearing like two jack-in-the-box from nowhere, stood beside the altar steps. In their morning coats, their hair heavily brilliantined, they looked quite glamorous, but we hardly had time to notice this fact before Mrs Wills struck up 'Here comes the Bride', with all the stops out, and Louisa, her veil over her face, was being dragged up the aisle at double quick time by Uncle Matthew. At this moment I think Linda would gladly have changed places with Louisa, even at the cost – the heavy cost – of being happy for ever after with John Fort William. In what seemed no time at all Louisa was being dragged down the aisle again by John, with her veil back, while Mrs Wills nearly broke the windows, so loud and triumphant was her 'Wedding March'.

Everything had gone like clockwork, and there was only one small incident. Davey slipped out of the family pew almost unobserved, in the middle of 'As pants the hart' (Louisa's favourite hymn) and went straight to London, making one of the wedding cars take him to Merlinford station. That evening he telephoned to say that he had twisted his tonsil, singing, and had thought it better to go immediately to Sir Andrew Macpherson, the nose, throat, and ear man, who was keeping him in bed for a week.

The most extraordinary accidents always seemed to overtake poor Davey.

When Louisa had gone away and the wedding guests had left Alconleigh, a sense of flatness descended upon the house, as always happens on these occasions. Linda then became plunged into such despairing gloom that even Aunt Sadie was alarmed. Linda told me afterwards that she thought a great deal about killing herself, and would most likely have done so had the material difficulties not been so great.

'You know what it is,' she said, 'trying to kill rabbits. Well, think of *oneself*!'

Two years seemed an absolute eternity, not worth ploughing through even with the prospect (which she never doubted, just as a religious person does not doubt the existence of heaven) of blissful love at the end of it. Of course, this was the time when Linda should have been made to work, as I was, all day and hard, with no time for silly dreaming except the few minutes before one went to sleep at night. I think Aunt Sadie dimly perceived this fact, she urged her to learn cooking, to occupy herself in the garden, to be prepared for confirmation. Linda furiously refused, nor would she do jobs in the village, nor help Aunt Sadie in the hundred and one chores which fall to the lot of a country squire's wife. She was, in fact, and Uncle Matthew told her so countless times every day, glaring at her with angry blue eyes, thoroughly bloody-minded.

Lord Merlin came to her rescue. He had taken a fancy to her at Louisa's wedding, and asked Aunt Sadie to bring her over to Merlinford some time. A few days later he rang up. Uncle Matthew answered the telephone, and shouted to Aunt Sadie, without taking his mouth away from the receiver:

'That hog Merlin wants to speak to you.'

Lord Merlin, who must have heard, was quite unmoved by this. He was an eccentric himself, and had a fellow feeling for the idiosyncrasies of others. Poor Aunt Sadie, however, was very much flustered, and, as a result, she accepted an invitation which she would otherwise most probably have refused, to take Linda over to Merlinford for luncheon.

Lord Merlin seemed to become immediately aware of Linda's state of mind, was really shocked to discover that she was doing no lessons at all, and did what he could to provide some interests for her. He showed her his pictures, explained them to her, talked at length about art and literature, and gave her books to read. He let fall the suggestion, which was taken up by Aunt Sadie, that she and Linda should attend a course of lectures in Oxford, and he also mentioned that the Shakespeare Festival was now in progress at Stratford-on-Avon.

Outings of this kind, which Aunt Sadie herself very much enjoyed, soon became a regular feature of life at Alconleigh. Uncle Matthew scoffed a bit, but never interfered with anything Aunt Sadie wanted to do; besides, it was not so much education that he dreaded for his daughters, as the vulgarizing effect that a boarding-school might have upon them. As for governesses, they had been tried, but none had ever been able to endure for more than a few days the terror of Uncle Matthew's grinding dentures, the piercing, furious blue flash of his eyes, the stock whips cracking under their bedroom windows at dawn. Their nerves, they said, and made for the station, often before they had had time to unpack enormous trunks, heavy as though full of stones, by which they were always accompanied.

Uncle Matthew went with Aunt Sadie and Linda on one occasion to a Shakespeare play, *Romeo and Juliet*. It was not a success. He cried copiously, and went into a furious rage because it ended badly. 'All the fault of that damned padre,' he kept saying on the way home, still wiping his eyes. 'That fella, what's 'is name, Romeo, might have known a blasted papist would mess up the whole thing. Silly old fool of a nurse too, I bet she was an R.C., dismal old bitch.'

So Linda's life, instead of being on one flat level plain of tedium, was now, to some extent, filled with outside interests. She perceived that the world she wanted to be in, the witty, sparkling world of Lord Merlin and his friends, was interested in things of the mind, and that she would be able to shine in it only if she became in some sort educated. The futile games of patience were abandoned, and she sat all day hunched up in a corner of the library, reading until her eyes gave out. She often rode over to Merlinford, and, unbeknownst to her parents, who never would have allowed her to go there, or indeed anywhere, alone, left Josh in the stable yard where he had congenial friends, and chatted for hours with Lord Merlin on all sorts of subjects. He knew that she had an intensely romantic character, he foresaw much trouble ahead, and he continually urged upon her the necessity for an intellectual background.

7

What could possibly have induced Linda to marry Anthony Kroesig? During the nine years of their life together people asked this question with irritating regularity, almost every time their names were mentioned. What was she after, surely she could never possibly have been in love with him, what was the idea, how could it have happened? He was admittedly very rich, but so were others and surely the fascinating Linda had only to choose? The answer was, of course, that, quite simply, she was in love with him. Linda was far too romantic to marry without love and indeed I, who was present at their first meeting and during most of their courtship, always understood why it had happened. Tony, in those days, and to unsophisticated country like us, seemed a glorious and glamorous creature. When we first saw him, at Linda's and my coming-out ball, he was in his last year at Oxford, a member of Bullingdon, a splendid young man with a Rolls-Royce, plenty of beautiful horses, exquisite clothes, and large luxurious rooms, where he entertained on a lavish scale. In person he was tall and fair, on the heavy side, but with a well-proportioned figure; he had already a faint touch of pomposity, a thing which Linda had never come across before, and which she found not unattractive. She took him, in short, at his own valuation.

What immediately gave him great prestige in her eyes was that he came to the ball with Lord Merlin. It was really most unlucky, especially as it happened that he had only been asked at the eleventh hour, as a stopgap.

Linda's ball was not nearly such a fiasco as Louisa's had been. Louisa, a married London lady now, produced a lot of young men for Aunt Sadie's house-party, dull, fair Scotch boys mostly, with nice manners; nothing to which Uncle Matthew could possibly take exception. They got on quite well with the various dull dark girls invited by Aunt Sadie, and the house-party seemed to 'go' very nicely, though Linda had her head in the air, saying they were all too impossibly dreary for words. Uncle Matthew had been implored by Aunt Sadie for weeks past to be kind to the young and not to shout at anybody, and he was quite subdued, almost pathetic in his wish to please, creeping about as though there were an invalid upstairs and straw in the street.

Davey and Aunt Emily were staying in the house to see me come out (Aunt Sadie had offered to bring me out with Linda and give us a London season together, an offer which was most gratefully accepted by Aunt Emily) and Davey constituted himself a sort of bodyguard to Uncle Matthew, hoping to stand as much as possible between him and the more unbearable forms of irritation.

'I'll be simply wonderful to everybody, but I won't have the sewers in my business-room, that's all,' Uncle Matthew had said, after one of Aunt Sadie's prolonged exhortations, and, indeed, spent most of the week-end (the ball was on a Friday and the house-party stayed on until Monday) locked into it, playing '1812' and the 'Haunted Ballroom' on the gramophone. He was rather off the human voice this year.

'What a pity,' said Linda, as we struggled into our ball dresses (proper London ones this time, with no floating panels), 'that we are dressing up like this, and looking so pretty, and all for those terrible productions of Louisa's. Waste, I call it.'

'You never know in the country,' I said, 'somebody may bring the Prince of Wales.'

Linda shot me a furious look under her eyelashes.

'Actually,' she said, 'I am pinning great hopes on Lord Merlin's party. I'm sure he'll bring some really interesting people.'

Lord Merlin's party arrived, as before, very late, and in very high spirits. Linda immediately noticed a large, blond young man in a beautiful pink coat. He was dancing with a girl who often stayed at Merlinford called Baby Fairweather, and she introduced him to Linda. He asked her to dance the next, and she abandoned one of Louisa's Scotch boys, to whom she had promised it, and strutted off with him in a quick one-step. Linda and I had both been having dancing lessons, and, if we did not exactly float round the room, our progress was by no means so embarrassing as it had been before.

Tony was in a happy mood, induced by Lord Merlin's excellent brandy, and Linda was pleased to find how well and easily she was getting on with this member of the Merlinford set. Everything she said seemed to make him laugh; presently they went to sit out, she chattered away, and Tony roared with laughter. This was the royal road to Linda's good books; she liked people who laughed easily more than anything; it naturally did not occur to her that Tony was a bit drunk. They sat out the next dance together. This was immediately noticed by Uncle Matthew, who began to walk up and down in front of them, giving them furious looks, until Davey, observing this danger signal, came up and hurried him away, saying that one of the oil-stoves in the hall was smoking.

'Who is that sewer with Linda?'

'Kroesig, Governor of the Bank of England, you know; his son.'

'Good God, I never expected to harbour a full-blooded Hun in this house – who on earth asked him?'

'Now, Matthew dear, don't get excited. The Kroesigs aren't Huns, they've been over here for generations, they are a very highly respected family of English bankers.'

'Once a Hun always a Hun,' said Uncle Matthew, 'and I'm not too set on bankers myself. Besides, the fella must be a gate-crasher.'

'No, he's not. He came with Merlin.'

'I knew that bloody Merlin would start bringing foreigners here sooner or later. I always said he would, but I didn't think even he would land one with a German.'

'Don't you think it's time somebody took some champagne to the band?' said Davey.

But Uncle Matthew stumped down to the boiler-room, where he had a long soothing talk with Timb, the odd man, about coke.

Tony, meanwhile, thought Linda ravishingly pretty, and great fun, which indeed she was. He told her so, and danced with her again and again, until Lord Merlin, quite as much put out as Uncle Matthew by what was happening, firmly and very early took his party home.

'See you at the meet to-morrow,' said Tony, winding a white scarf round his neck.

Linda was silent and preoccupied for the rest of the evening.

'You're not to go hunting, Linda,' said Aunt Sadie, the next day, when Linda came downstairs in her riding-habit, 'it's too rude, you must stay and look after your guests. You can't leave them like that.'

'Darling, darling Mummie,' said Linda, 'the meet's at Cock's Barn, and you know how one can't resist. And Flora hasn't been out for a week, she'll go mad. Be a love and take them to see the Roman villa or something, and I swear to come back early. And they've got Fanny and Louisa after all.'

It was this unlucky hunt that clinched matters as far as Linda was concerned. The first person she saw at the meet was Tony, on a splendid chestnut horse. Linda herself was always beautifully mounted, Uncle Matthew was proud of her horsemanship, and had given her two pretty, lively little horses. They found at once, and there was a short sharp run, during which Linda and Tony, both in a somewhat showing-off mood, rode side by side over the stone walls. Presently, on a village green, they checked. One or two hounds put up a hare, which lost its head, jumped into a duckpond, and began to swim about in a hopeless sort of way. Linda's eyes filled with tears.

'Oh, the poor hare!'

Tony got off his horse, and plunged into the pond. He rescued the hare, waded out again, his fine white breeches covered with green muck, and put it, wet and gasping, into Linda's lap. It was the one romantic gesture of his life.

At the end of the day Linda left the hounds to take a short cut home across country. Tony opened a gate for her, took off his hat, and said:

'You are a most beautiful rider, you know. Good night, when I'm back in Oxford I'll ring you up.'

When Linda got home she rushed me off to the Hons' cupboard and told me all this. She was in love.

Given Linda's frame of mind during the past two endless years, she was obviously destined to fall in love with the first young man who came along. It could hardly have been otherwise; she need not, however, have married him. This was made inevitable by the behaviour of Uncle Matthew. Most unfortunately Lord Merlin, the one person who might perhaps have been able to make Linda see that Tony was not all she thought him, went to Rome the week after the ball, and remained abroad for a year.

Tony went back to Oxford when he left Merlinford, and Linda sat about waiting, waiting, waiting for the telephone bell. Patience again. If this comes out he is thinking of me now this very minute – if this comes out he'll ring up to-morrow – if this comes out he'll be at the meet. But Tony hunted with the Bicester, and never appeared on our side of the country. Three weeks passed, and Linda began to feel in despair. Then one evening, after dinner, the telephone bell rang; by a lucky chance Uncle Matthew had gone down to the stables to see Josh about a horse that had colic, the business-room was empty, and Linda answered the telephone herself. It was Tony. Her heart was choking her, she could scarcely speak.

'Hullo, is that Linda? It's Tony Kroesig here. Will you come to lunch next Thursday?'

'Oh! But I should never be allowed to.'

'Oh, rot,' very impatiently, 'several other girls are coming down from London – bring your cousin if you like.'

'All right, that will be lovely.'

'See you then – about one – 7 King Edward Street, I expect you know the rooms. Altringham had them when he was up.'

Linda came away from the telephone trembling, and whispered for me to come quick to the Hons' cupboard. We were absolutely forbidden to see young men at any hour unchaperoned, and other girls did not count as chaperons. We knew quite well, though such a remote eventuality had never even been mooted at Alconleigh, that we would not be allowed to have luncheon with a young man in his lodgings with any chaperon at all, short of Aunt Sadie herself. The Alconleigh standards of chaperonage were medieval; they did not vary in the slightest degree from those applied to Uncle Matthew's sister, and to Aunt Sadie in youth. The principle was that one never saw any young man alone, under any circumstances, until one was engaged to him. The only people who could be counted on to enforce this rule were one's mother or one's aunts, therefore one must not be allowed beyond the reach of their ever-watchful eyes. The argument, often put forward by Linda, that young men were not very likely to propose to girls they hardly knew, was brushed aside as nonsense. Uncle Matthew had proposed, had he not? to Aunt Sadie, the very first time he ever saw her, by the cage of a two-headed nightingale at an Exhibition at the White City. 'They respect you all the more.' It never seemed to dawn upon the Alconleighs that respect is not an attitude of mind indulged in by modern young men, who look for other qualities in their wives than respectability. Aunt Emily, under the enlightened influence of Davey, was far more reasonable, but, of course, when staying with the Radletts, I had to obey the same rules.

In the Hons' cupboard we talked and talked. There was no question in our minds but that we must go, not to do so would be death for Linda, she would never get over it. But how to escape? There was only one way that we could devise, and it was full of risk. A very dull girl of exactly our age called Lavender Davis lived with her very dull parents about five miles away, and once in a blue moon, Linda, complaining vociferously, was sent over to luncheon with them, driving herself in Aunt Sadie's little car. We must pretend that we were going to do that, hoping that

Aunt Sadie would not see Mrs Davis, that pillar of the Women's Institute, for months and months, hoping also that Perkins, the chauffeur, would not remark on the fact that we had driven sixty miles and not ten.

As we were going upstairs to bed, Linda said to Aunt Sadie, in what she hoped was an off hand voice, but one which seemed to me vibrant with guilt:

'That was Lavender ringing up. She wants Fanny and me to lunch there on Thursday.'

'Oh, duck,' said Aunt Sadie, 'you can't have my car, I'm afraid.'

Linda became very white, and leant against the wall.

'Oh, please, Mummy, oh please do let me, I do so terribly want to go.'

'To the Davises,' said Aunt Sadie in astonishment, 'but, darling, last time you said you'd never go again as long as you lived – great haunches of cod you said, don't you remember? Anyhow, I'm sure they'll have you another day, you know.'

'Oh, Mummy, you don't understand. The whole point is, a man is coming who brought up a baby badger, and I do so want to meet him.'

It was known to be one of Linda's greatest ambitions, to bring up a baby badger.

'Yes, I see. Well, couldn't you ride over?'

'Staggers and ringworm,' said Linda, her large blue eyes slowly filling with tears.

'What did you say, darling?'

'In their stables – staggers and ringworm. You wouldn't want me to expose Flora to that.'

'Are you sure? Their horses always look so wonderful.'

'Ask Josh.'

'Well, I'll see. Perhaps I can borrow Fa's Morris, and if not, perhaps Perkins can take me in the Daimler. It's a meeting I must go to, though.'

'Oh, you are kind, you are kind. Oh, do try. I do so long for a badger.'

'If you go to London for the season you'll be far too busy to think of a badger. Good night then, ducks.'

'We must get hold of some powder.'

'And rouge.'

These commodities were utterly forbidden by Uncle Matthew, who liked to see female complexions in a state of nature, and often pronounced that paint was for whores and not for his daughters.

'I once read in a book that you can use geranium juice for rouge.'

'Geraniums aren't out at this time of year, silly.'

'We can blue our eyelids out of Jassy's paint-box.'

'And sleep in curlers.'

'I'll get the verbena soap out of Mummy's bathroom. If we let it melt in the bath, and soak for hours in it, we shall smell delicious.'

'I thought you loathed Lavender Davis.'

'Oh, shut up, Jassy.'

'Last time you went you said she was a horrible Counter-Hon, and you would like to bash in her silly face with the Hons' mallet.'

'I never said so. Don't invent lies.'

'Why have you got your London suit on for Lavender Davis?'

'Do go away, Matt.'

'Why are you starting already, you'll be hours too early.'

'We're going to see the badger before luncheon.'

'How red your face is, Linda. Oh, oh you do look so funny!'

'If you don't shut up and go away, Jassy, I swear I'll put your newt back in the pond.'

Persecution, however, continued until we were in the car and out of the garage yard.

'Why don't you bring Lavender back for a nice long cosy visit?' was Jassy's parting shot.

'Not very Honnish of them,' said Linda, 'do you think they can possibly have guessed?'

We left our car in the Clarendon yard, and, as we were very early, having allowed half an hour in case of two punctures, we made for Elliston & Cavell's ladies-room, and gazed at ourselves, with a tiny feeling of uncertainty, in the looking-glasses there. Our cheeks had round scarlet patches, our lips were the same colour, but only at the edges, inside it had already worn off, and our eyelids were blue, all out of Jassy's paint-box. Our noses were white, Nanny having produced some powder with which, years ago, she used to dust Robin's bottom. In short, we looked like a couple of Dutch dolls.

'We must keep our ends up,' said Linda, uncertainly.

'Oh, dear,' I said, 'the thing about me is, I always feel so much happier with my end down.'

We gazed and gazed, hoping thus, in some magical way, to make ourselves feel less peculiar. Presently we did a little work with damp handkerchiefs, and toned our faces down a bit. We then sallied forth into the street, looking at ourselves in every shop window that we passed. (I have often noticed that when women look at themselves in every reflection, and take furtive peeps into their hand looking-glasses, it is hardly ever, as is generally supposed, from vanity, but much more often from a feeling that all is not quite as it should be.)

Now that we had actually achieved our objective, we were beginning to feel horribly nervous, not only wicked, guilty and frightened, but also filled with social terrors. I think we would both gladly have got back into the car and made for home.

On the stroke of one o'clock we arrived in Tony's room. He was alone, but evidently a large party was expected, the table, a square one with a coarse white linen cloth, seemed to have a great many places. We refused sherry and cigarettes, and an awkward silence fell.

'Been hunting at all?' he asked Linda.

'Oh, yes, we were out yesterday.'

'Good day?'

'Yes, very. We found at once, and had a five-mile point and then
–' Linda suddenly remembered that Lord Merlin had once said to
her: 'Hunt as much as you like, but never talk about it, it's the most
boring subject in the world.'

'But that's marvellous, a five-mile point. I must come out with
the Heythrop again soon, they are doing awfully well this season,
I hear. We had a good day yesterday, too.'

He embarked on a detailed account of every minute of it, where
they found, where they ran to, how his first horse had gone lame,
how, luckily, he had then come upon his second horse, and so on.
I saw just what Lord Merlin meant. Linda, however, hung upon
his words with breathless interest.

At last noises were heard in the street, and he went to the
window.

'Good,' he said, 'here are the others.'

The others had come down from London in a huge Daimler,
and poured, chattering, into the room. Four pretty girls and a
young man. Presently some undergraduates appeared, and
completed the party. It was not really very enjoyable from our
point of view, they all knew each other too well. They gossiped
away, roared with laughter at private jokes, and showed off; still,
we felt that this was Life, and would have been quite happy just
looking on had it not been for that ghastly feeling of guilt, which
was now beginning to give us a pain rather like indigestion. Linda
turned quite pale every time the door opened, I think she really
felt that Uncle Matthew might appear at any moment, cracking a
whip. As soon as we decently could, which was not very soon,
because nobody moved from the table until after Tom had struck
four, we said good-bye, and fled for home.

The miserable Matt and Jassy were swinging on the garage gate.

'So how was Lavender? Did she roar at your eyelids? Better go
and wash before Fa sees you. You have been hours. Was it cod?
Did you see the the badger?'

Linda burst into tears.

'Leave me alone, you horrible Counter-Hons,' she cried, and rushed upstairs to her bedroom.

Love had increased threefold in one short day.

On Saturday the blow fell.

'Linda and Fanny, Fa wants you in the business-room. And sooner you than me by the look of him,' said Jassy, meeting us in the drive as we came in from hunting. Our hearts plunged into our boots. We looked at each other with apprehension.

'Better get it over,' said Linda, and we hurried to the business-room, where we saw at once that the worst had occurred.

Aunt Sadie, looking unhappy, and Uncle Matthew, grinding his teeth, confronted us with our crime. The room was full of blue lightning flashing from his eyes, and Jove's thunder was not more awful than what he now roared at us:

'Do you realize,' he said, 'that, if you were married women, your husbands could divorce you for doing this?'

Linda began to say no they couldn't. She knew the laws of divorce from having read the whole of the Russell case off newspapers with which the fires in the spare bedrooms were laid.

'Don't interrupt your father,' said Aunt Sadie, with a warning look.

Uncle Matthew, however, did not even notice. He was in the full flood and violence of his storm.

'Now we know you can't be trusted to behave yourselves, we shall have to take certain steps. Fanny can go straight home to-morrow, and I never want you here again, do you understand? Emily will have to control you in future, if she can, but you'll go the same way as your mother, sure as eggs is eggs. As for you, miss, there's no more question of a London season now – we shall have to watch you in future every minute of the day – not very agreeable, to have a child one can't trust – and there would be too many opportunities in London for slipping off. You can stew in your own juice here. And no more hunting this year. You're damned lucky not to be thrashed; most fathers would give you a good hiding, do you hear? Now you can both go to bed, and you're not to speak to each other before Fanny leaves. I'm sending her over in the car to-morrow.'

It was months before we knew how they found out. It seemed like magic, but the explanation was simple. Somebody had left a scarf in Tony Kroesig's rooms, and he had rung up to ask whether it belonged to either of us.

8

As always, Uncle Matthew's bark was worse than his bite, though, while it lasted, it was the most terrible row within living memory at Alconleigh. I was sent back to Aunt Emily the next day, Linda waving and crying out of her bedroom window: 'Oh, you *are* lucky, not to be me' (most unlike her, her usual cry being 'Isn't it lovely to be lovely *me*'); and she was stopped from hunting once or twice. Then relaxation began, the thin end of the wedge, and gradually things returned to normal, though it was reckoned in the family that Uncle Matthew had got through a pair of dentures in record time.

Plans for the London season went on being made, and went on including me. I heard afterwards that both Davey and John Fort William took it upon themselves to tell Aunt Sadie and Uncle Matthew (especially Uncle Matthew) that, according to modern ideas, what we had done was absolutely normal, though, of course, they were obliged to own that it was very wrong of us to have told so many and such shameless lies.

We both said we were very sorry, and promised faithfully that we would never act in such an underhand way again, but always ask Aunt Sadie if there was something we specially wanted to do.

'Only then, of course, it will always be no,' as Linda said, giving me a hopeless look.

Aunt Sadie took a furnished house for the summer near Belgrave Square. It was a house with so little character that I can remember absolutely nothing about it, except that my bed-room had a view over chimney-pots, and that on hot summer evenings I used to sit and watch the swallows, always in pairs, and wish sentimentally that I too could be a pair with somebody.

We really had great fun, although I don't think it was dancing that we enjoyed so much as the fact of being grown up and in London. At the dances the great bar of enjoyment was what Linda called the chaps. They were terribly dull, all on the lines of the ones Louisa had brought to Alconleigh; Linda, still in her dream of love for Tony, could not distinguish between them, and never even knew their names. I looked about hopefully for a possible life-partner, but, though I honestly tried to see the best in them, nothing remotely approximating to my requirements turned up.

Tony was at Oxford for his last term, and did not come to London until the end of the season.

We were chaperoned, as was to be expected, with Victorian severity. Aunt Sadie or Uncle Matthew literally never let us out of the sight of one or the other; as Aunt Sadie liked to rest in the afternoon, Uncle Matthew would solemnly take us off to the House of Lords, park us in the Peeresses' Gallery, and take his own forty winks on a back bench opposite. When he was awake in the House, which was not often, he was a perfect nuisance to the Whips, never voting with the same party twice running; nor were the workings of his mind too easy to follow. He voted, for instance, in favour of steel traps, of blood sports, and of steeplechasing, but against vivisection and the exporting of old horses to Belgium. No doubt he had his reasons, as Aunt Sadie would remark, with finality, when we commented on this inconsistency. I rather liked those drowsy afternoons in the dark Gothic chamber, fascinated by the mutterings and antics that went on the whole time, and besides, the occasional speech one was able to hear was generally rather interesting. Linda liked it too, she was far away, thinking her own thoughts. Uncle Matthew would wake up at tea-time, conduct us to the Peer's dining-room for tea and buttered buns, and then take us home to rest and dress for the dance.

Saturday to Monday was spent by the Radlett family at Alconleigh; they rolled down in their huge, rather sick-making Daimler; and by me at Shenley, where Aunt Emily and Davey were always longing to hear every detail of our week.

Clothes were probably our chief preoccupation at this time.

Once Linda had been to a few dress shows, and got her eye in, she had all hers made by Mrs Josh, and, somehow, they had a sort of originality and prettiness that I never achieved, although mine, which were bought at expensive shops, cost about five times as much. This showed, said Davey, who used to come and see us whenever he was in London, that either you get your clothes in Paris or it is a toss-up. Linda had one particularly ravishing ball-dress made of masses of pale grey tulle down to her feet. Most of the dresses were still short that summer, and Linda made a sensation whenever she appeared in her yards of tulle, very much disapproved of by Uncle Matthew, on the grounds that he had known three women burnt to death in tulle ball-dresses.

She was wearing this dress when Tony proposed to her in the Berkeley Square summer-house at six o'clock on a fine July morning. He had been down from Oxford about a fortnight, and it was soon obvious that he had eyes for nobody but her. He went to all the same dances, and, after stumping round with a few other girls, would take Linda to supper, and thereafter spend the evening glued to her side. Aunt Sadie seemed to notice nothing, but to the whole rest of the debutante world the outcome was a foregone conclusion, the only question being when and where Tony would propose.

The ball from which they had emerged (it was in a lovely old house on the east side of Berkeley Square, since demolished) was only just alive, the band sleepily thump-thumped its tunes through the nearly empty rooms; poor Aunt Sadie sat on a little gold chair trying to keep her eyes open and passionately longing for bed, with me beside her, dead tired and very cold, my partners all gone home. It was broad daylight. Linda had been away for hours, nobody seemed to have set eyes on her since supper-time, and Aunt Sadie, though dominated by her fearful sleepiness, was apprehensive, and rather angry. She was beginning to wonder whether Linda had not committed the unforgivable sin, and gone off to a night club.

Suddenly the band perked up and began to play 'John Peel' as a prelude to 'God Save the King'; Linda, in a grey cloud, was galloping up and down the room with Tony; one look at her face told all. We climbed into a taxi behind Aunt Sadie (she never would keep a chauffeur up at night), we splashed away past the great hoses that were washing the streets, we climbed the stairs to our rooms, without a word being spoken by any of us. A thin oblique sunlight was striking the chimney-pots as I opened my window. I was too tired to think, I fell into bed.

We were allowed to be late after dances, though Aunt Sadie was always up and seeing to the household arrangements by nine o'clock. As Linda came sleepily downstairs the next morning, Uncle Matthew shouted furiously at her from the hall:

'That bloody Hun Kroesig has just telephoned, he wanted to speak to you. I told him to get the hell out of it. I don't want you mixed up with any Germans, do you understand?'

'Well, I am mixed up,' said Linda, in an offhand, would-be casual voice, 'as it happens I'm engaged to him.'

At this point Aunt Sadie dashed out of her little morning-room on the ground floor, took Uncle Matthew by the arm, and led him away. Linda locked herself into her bedroom and cried for an hour, while Jassy, Matt, Robin, and I speculated upon further developments in the nursery.

There was a great deal of opposition to the engagement, not only from Uncle Matthew, who was beside himself with disappointment and disgust at Linda's choice, but also quite as much from Sir Leicester Kroesig. He did not want Tony to marry at all until he was well settled in his career in the City, and then he had hoped for an alliance with one of the other big banking families. He despised the landed gentry, whom he regarded as feckless, finished and done with in the modern world, he also knew that the vast, the enviable capital sums which such families undoubtedly still possessed, and of which they made so foolishly little use, were always entailed upon the eldest son, and that very small provision, if any, was made for the dowries of daughters. Sir Leicester and Uncle Matthew met, disliked each other on sight, and were at one in their determination to stop the marriage. Tony was sent off to

America, to work in a bank house in New York, and poor Linda, the season now being at an end, was taken home to eat her heart out at Alconleigh.

'Oh, Jassy, darling Jassy, lend me your running-away money to go to New York with.'

'No, Linda. I've saved and scraped for five years, ever since I was seven, I simply can't begin all over again now. Besides I shall want it for when I run away myself.'

'But, darling, I'll give it you back, Tony will, when we're married.'

'I know men,' said Jassy, darkly.

She was adamant.

'If only Lord Merlin were here,' Linda wailed. 'He would help me.' But Lord Merlin was still in Rome.

She had 15s 6d in the world, and was obliged to content herself with writing immense screeds to Tony every day. She carried about in her pocket a quantity of short, dull letters in an immature handwriting and with a New York postmark.

After a few months Tony came back, and told his father that he could not settle down to business or banking or think about his future career at all, until the date for his marriage had been fixed. This was quite the proper line to take with Sir Leicester. Anything that interfered with making money must be regulated at once. If Tony, who was a sensible fellow, and had never given his father one moment's anxiety in his life, assured him that he could be serious about banking only after marriage, then married he must be, the sooner the better. Sir Leicester explained at length what he considered the disadvantages of the union. Tony agreed in principle, but said that Linda was young, intelligent, energetic, that he had great influence with her, and did not doubt that she could be made into a tremendous asset. Sir Leicester finally gave his consent.

'It might have been worse,' he said, 'after all, she is a lady.'

Lady Kroesig opened negotiations with Aunt Sadie. As Linda had virtually worked herself into a decline, and was poisoning the lives of all around her by her intense disagreeableness, Aunt Sadie, secretly much relieved by the turn things had taken, persuaded Uncle Matthew that the marriage, though by no means ideal, was inevitable, and that, if he did not wish to alienate for ever his favourite child, he had better put a good face on it.

'I suppose it might have been worse,' Uncle Matthew said doubtfully, 'at least the fella's not a Roman Catholic.'

9

The engagement was duly announced in *The Times*. The Kroesigs now invited the Alconleighs to spend a Saturday to Monday at their house near Guildford. Lady Kroesig, in her letter to Aunt Sadie, called it a week-end, and said it would be nice to get to know each other better. Uncle Matthew flew into a furious temper. It was one of his idiosyncrasies that, not only did he never stay in other people's houses (except, very occasionally, with relations), but he regarded it as a positive insult that he should be invited to do so. He despised the expression 'week-end', and gave a sarcastic snort at the idea that it would be nice to know the Kroesigs better. When Aunt Sadie had calmed him down a bit, she put forward the suggestion that the Kroesig family, father, mother, daughter Marjorie, and Tony, should be asked instead if they would spend Saturday to Monday at Alconleigh. Poor Uncle Matthew, having swallowed the great evil of Linda's engagement, had, to do him justice, resolved to put the best face he could on it, and had no wish to make trouble for her with her future in-laws. He had at heart a great respect for family connexions, and once, when Bob and Jassy were slanging a cousin whom the whole family, including Uncle Matthew himself, very much disliked, he had turned upon them, knocked their heads together sharply, and said:

'In the first place he's a relation, and in the second place he's a clergyman, so shut up.'

It had become a classical saying with the Radletts.

So the Kroesigs were duly invited. They accepted, and the date was fixed. Aunt Sadie then got into a panic, and summoned Aunt Emily and Davey. (I was staying at Alconleigh anyhow, for a few weeks' hunting.) Louisa was feeding her second baby in Scotland, but hoped to come south for the wedding later on.

The arrival at Alconleigh of the four Kroesigs was not auspicious. As the car which had met them at the station was heard humming up the drive, every single light in the whole house fused – Davey had brought a new ultra-violet lamp with him, which had done the trick. The guests had to be led into the hall in pitch darkness, while Logan fumbled about in the pantry for a candle, and Uncle Matthew rushed off to the fuse box. Lady Kroesig and Aunt Sadie chatted politely about this and that, Linda and Tony giggled in the corner, and Sir Leicester hit his gouty foot on the edge of a refectory table, while the voice of an invisible Davey could be heard, apologizing in a high wail, from the top of the staircase. It was really very embarrassing.

At last the lights went up, and the Kroesigs were revealed. Sir Leicester was a tall fair man with grey hair, whose undeniable good looks were marred by a sort of silliness in his face; his wife and daughter were two dumpy little fluffy females. Tony evidently took after his father, and Marjorie after her mother. Aunt Sadie, thrown out of her stride by the sudden transformation of what had been mere voices in the dark into flesh and blood, and feeling herself unable to produce more topics of conversation, hurried them upstairs to rest, and dress for dinner. It was always considered at Alconleigh that the journey from London was an experience involving great exhaustion, and people were supposed to be in need of rest after it.

'What is this lamp?' Uncle Matthew asked Davey, who was still saying how sorry he was, still clad in the exiguous dressing-gown which he had put on for his sun-bath.

'Well, you know how one can never digest anything in the winter months.'

'I can, damn you,' said Uncle Matthew. This, addressed to Davey, could be interpreted as a term of endearment.

'You think you can, but you can't really. Now this lamp pours its rays into the system, your glands begin to work, and your food does you good again.'

'Well don't pour any more rays until we have had the voltage altered. When the house is full of bloody Huns one wants to be able to see what the hell they're up to.'

For dinner, Linda wore a white chintz dress with an enormous skirt, and a black lace scarf. She looked entirely ravishing, and it was obvious that Sir Leicester was much taken with her appearance – Lady Kroesig and Miss Marjorie, in bits of georgette and lace, seemed not to notice it. Marjorie was an intensely dreary girl, a few years older than Tony, who had failed so far to marry, and seemed to have no biological reason for existing.

'Have you read *Brothers*?' Lady Kroesig asked Uncle Matthew, conversationally, as they settled down to their soup.

'What's that?'

'The new Ursula Langdok – *Brothers* – it's about two brothers. You ought to read it.'

'My dear Lady Kroesig, I have only ever read one book in my life, and that is *White Fang*. It's so frightfully good I've never bothered to read another. But Davey here reads books – you've read *Brothers*, Davey, I bet.'

'Indeed, I have not,' said Davey, petulantly.

'I'll lend it to you,' said Lady Kroesig, 'I have it with me, and I finished it in the train.'

'You shouldn't,' said Davey, 'read in trains, ever. It's madly wearing to the optic nerve centres, it imposes a most fearful strain. May I see the menu, please? I must explain that I'm on a new diet, one meal white, one meal red. It's doing me so much good. Oh, dear, what a pity. Sadie – oh, she's not listening – Logan, could I ask for an egg, very lightly boiled, you know. This is my white meal, and we are having saddle of mutton I see.'

'Well, Davey, have your red meal now and your white meal for breakfast,' said Uncle Matthew. 'I've opened some Mouton Rothschild, and I know how much you like that – I opened it specially for you.'

'Oh, it is too bad,' said Davey, 'because I happen to know that there are kippers for breakfast, and I do so love them. What a ghastly decision. No! it must be an egg now, with a little hock. I could never

74

forgo the kippers, so delicious, so digestible, but, above all, so full of proteins.'

'Kippers,' said Bob, 'are brown.'

'Brown counts as red. Surely you can see that.'

But when a chocolate cream, in generous supply, but never quite enough when the boys were at home, came round, it was seen to count as white. The Radletts often had cause to observe that you could never entirely rely upon Davey to refuse food, however unwholesome, if it was really delicious.

Aunt Sadie was making heavy weather with Sir Leicester. He was full of boring herbaceous enthusiasms, and took it for granted that she was too.

'What a lot you London people always know about gardens,' she said. 'You must talk to Davey, he is a great gardener.'

'I am not really a London person,' said Sir Leicester, reproach-fully. 'I work in London, but my home is in Surrey.'

'I count that,' Aunt Sadie said, gently but firmly, 'as the same.'

The evening seemed endless. The Kroesigs obviously longed for bridge, and did not seem to care so much for racing demon when it was offered as a substitute. Sir Leicester said he had had a tiring week, and really should go to bed early.

'Don't know how you chaps can stand it,' said Uncle Matthew, sympathetically. 'I was saying to the bank manager at Merlinford only yesterday, it must be the hell of a life fussing about with other blokes' money all day, indoors.'

Linda went to ring up Lord Merlin, who had just returned from abroad. Tony followed her, they were gone a long time, and came back looking flushed and rather self-conscious.

The next morning, as we were hanging about in the hall waiting for the kippers, which had already announced themselves with a heavenly smell, two breakfast trays were seen going upstairs, for Sir Leicester and Lady Kroesig.

'No, really, that beats everything, dammit,' said Uncle Matthew, 'I never heard of a *man* having breakfast in bed before.' And he looked wistfully at his entrenching tool.

He was slightly mollified, however, when they came downstairs, just before eleven, all ready to go to church. Uncle Matthew was a great pillar of the church, read the lessons, chose the hymns, and took round the bag, and he liked his household to attend. Alas, the Kroesigs turned out to be blasted idolaters, as was proved when they turned sharply to the east during the creed. In short, they were of the company of those who could do no right, and sighs of relief echoed through the house when they decided to catch an evening train back to London.

'Tony is Bottom to Linda, isn't he?' I said, sadly.

Davey and I were walking through Hen's Grove the next day. Davey always knew what you meant, it was one of the nice things about him.

'Bottom,' he said sadly. He adored Linda.

'And nothing will wake her up?'

'Not before it's too late, I fear. Poor Linda, she has an intensely romantic character, which is fatal for a woman. Fortunately for them, and for all of us, most women are madly *terre à terre*, otherwise the world could hardly carry on.'

Lord Merlin was braver than the rest of us, and said right out what he thought. Linda went over to see him and asked him.

'Are you pleased about my engagement?' to which he replied:

'No, of course not. Why are you doing it?'

'I'm in love,' said Linda proudly.

'What makes you think so?'

'One doesn't think, one knows,' she said.

'Fiddlesticks.'

'Oh, you evidently don't understand about love, so what's the use of talking to you.'

Lord Merlin got very cross, and said that neither did immature little girls understand about love.

'Love,' he said, 'is for grown-up people, as you will discover one day. You will also discover that it has nothing to do with marriage.

I'm all in favour of you marrying soon, in a year or two, but for God's sake, and all of our sakes, don't go and marry a bore like Tony Kroesig.'

'If he's such a bore, why did you ask him to stay?'

'I didn't ask him. Baby brought him, because Cecil had 'flu and couldn't come. Besides, I can't guess you'll go and marry every stopgap I have in my house.'

'You ought to be more careful. Anyhow, I can't think why you say Tony's a bore, he knows everything.'

'Yes, that's exactly it, he does. And what about Sir Leicester? And have you seen Lady Kroesig?'

But the Kroesig family was illuminated for Linda by the great glow of perfection which shone around Tony, and she would hear nothing against them. She parted rather coldly from Lord Merlin, came home, and abused him roundly. As for him, he waited to see what Sir Leicester was giving her for a wedding present. It was a pigskin dressing-case with dark tortoiseshell fittings and her initials on them in gold. Lord Merlin sent her a morocco one double the size, fitted blonde tortoiseshell, and instead of initials, LINDA in diamonds.

He had embarked upon an elaborate series of Kroesig teases of which this was to be the first.

The arrangements for the wedding did not go smoothly. There was trouble without end over settlements. Uncle Matthew, whose estate provided a certain sum of money for younger children, to be allocated by him as he thought best, very naturally did not wish to settle anything on Linda, at the expense of the others, in view of the fact that she was marrying the son of a millionaire. Sir Leicester, however, refused to settle a penny unless Uncle Matthew did – he had no great wish to make a settlement in any case, saying that it was against the policy of his family to tie up capital sums. In the end, by sheer persistence, Uncle Matthew got a beggarly amount for Linda. The whole thing worried and upset him very much, and confirmed him, if need be, in his hatred of the Teutonic race.

Tony and his parents wanted a London wedding, Uncle Matthew

said he had never heard of anything so common and vulgar in his life. Women were married from their homes; he thought fashionable weddings the height of degradation, and refused to lead one of his daughters up the aisle of St Margaret's through a crowd of gaping strangers. The Kroesigs explained to Linda that, if she had a country wedding, she would only get half the amount of wedding presents, and also that the important, influential people, who would be of use, later, to Tony, would never come down to Gloucestershire in the depth of winter. All these arguments were lost on Linda. Since the days when she was planning to marry the Prince of Wales she had had a mental picture of what her wedding would be like, that is, as much like a wedding in a pantomime as possible, in a large church, with crowds both outside and in, with photographers, arum lilies, tulle, bridesmaids, and an enormous choir singing her favourite tune, 'The Lost Chord'. So she sided with the Kroesigs against poor Uncle Matthew, and, when fate tipped the scales in their favour by putting out of action the heating in Alconleigh church, Aunt Sadie took a London house, and the wedding was duly celebrated with every circumstance of publicized vulgarity at St Margaret's.

What with one thing and another, by the time Linda was married, her parents and her parents-in-law were no longer on speaking terms. Uncle Matthew cried without restraint all through the ceremony; Sir Leicester seemed to be beyond tears.

10

I think Linda's marriage was a failure almost from the beginning, but I really never knew much about it. Nobody did. She had married in the face of a good deal of opposition; the opposition proved to have been entirely well founded, and, Linda being what she was, maintained, for as long as possible, a perfect shop-front.

They were married in February, had a hunting honeymoon from a house they took at Melton, and settled down for good in Bryanston Square after Easter. Tony then started work in his father's old bank, and prepared to step into a safe Conservative seat in the House of Commons, an ambition which was very soon realized.

Closer acquaintance with their new in-laws did not make either the Radlett or the Kroesig families change their minds about each other. The Kroesigs thought Linda eccentric, affected, and extravagant. Worst of all, she was supposed not to be useful to Tony in his career. The Radletts considered that Tony was a first-class bore. He had a habit of choosing a subject, and then droning round and round it like an inaccurate bomb-aimer round his target, ever unable to hit; he knew vast quantities of utterly dreary facts, of which he did not hesitate to inform his companions, at great length and in great detail, whether they appeared to be interested or not. He was infinitely serious, he no longer laughed at Linda's jokes, and the high spirits which, when she first knew him, he had seemed to possess, must have been due to youth, drink, and good health. Now that he was grown up and married he put all three resolutely behind him, spending his days in the bank house and his evenings at Westminster, never having any fun or breathing fresh air: his true self emerged, and he was revealed as a pompous, money-grubbing ass, more like his father every day.

He did not succeed in making an asset out of Linda. Poor Linda was incapable of understanding the Kroesig point of view; try as she might (and in the beginning she tried very hard, having an infinite desire to please) it remained mysterious to her. The fact is that, for the first time in her life, she found herself face to face with the bourgeois attitude of mind, and the fate often foreseen for me by Uncle Matthew as a result of my middle-class education had actually befallen her. The outward and visible signs which he so deprecated were all there – the Kroesigs said notepaper, perfume, mirror, and mantelpiece, they even invited her to call them Father and Mother, which, in the first flush of love, she did, only to spend the rest of her married life trying to get out of it by addressing them to their faces as 'you', and communicating with them by postcard or telegram. Inwardly their spirit was utterly commercial, everything was seen by them in terms of money. It was their barrier, their defence, their hope for the future, their support for the present, it raised them above their fellowmen, and with it they warded off evil. The only mental qualities that they respected were those which produced money in substantial quantities, it was their one criterion of success, it was power and it was glory. To say that a man was poor was to label him a rotter, bad at his job, idle, feckless, immoral. If it was somebody whom they really rather liked, in spite of this cancer, they could add that he had been unlucky. They had taken care to insure against this deadly evil in many ways. That it should not overwhelm them through such cataclysms beyond their control as war or revolution they had placed huge sums of money in a dozen different countries; they owned ranches, and estancias, and South African farms, an hotel in Switzerland, a plantation in Malaya, and they possessed many fine diamonds, not sparkling round Linda's lovely neck to be sure, but lying in banks, stone by stone, easily portable.

Linda's upbringing had made all this incomprehensible to her; for money was a subject that was absolutely never mentioned at Alconleigh. Uncle Matthew had no doubt a large income, but it was derived from, tied up in, and a good percentage of it went back into, his land. His land was to him something sacred, and, sacred above that, was England. Should evil befall his country he would stay and share it, or die, never would the notion have entered his head that he might save himself, and leave old England in any sort of lurch. He, his family, and his estates were part of her and she was part of him, for ever and ever. Later on, when war appeared to be looming upon the horizon, Tony tried to persuade him to send some money to America.

'What for?' said Uncle Matthew.

'You might be glad to go there yourself, or send the children. It's always a good thing to have –'

'I may be old, but I can still shoot,' said Uncle Matthew, furiously, 'and I haven't got any children – for the purposes of fighting they are all grown up.'

'Victoria –'

'Victoria is thirteen. She would do her duty. I hope, if any bloody foreigners ever got here, that every man, woman, and child would go on fighting them until one side or the other was wiped out. Anyhow, I loathe abroad, nothing would induce me to live there, I'd rather live in the gamekeeper's hut in Hen's Grove, and, as for foreigners, they are all the same, and they all make me sick,' he said, pointedly, glowering at Tony, who took no notice, but went droning on about how clever he had been in transferring various funds to various places. He had always remained perfectly unaware of Uncle Matthew's dislike for him, and, indeed, such was my uncle's eccentricity of behaviour, that it was not very easy for somebody as thick-skinned as Tony to differentiate between Uncle Matthew's behaviour towards those he loved and those he did not.

On the first birthday she had after her marriage, Sir Leicester gave Linda a cheque for £1,000. Linda was delighted and spent it that very day on a necklace of large half pearls surrounded by rubies, which she had been admiring for some time in a Bond Street shop. The Kroesigs had a small family dinner party for her, Tony was to meet her there, having been kept late at his office. Linda arrived, wearing a very plain white satin dress cut very low, and her necklace, went straight up to Sir Leicester, and said: 'Oh, you were kind to give me such a wonderful present – look –'

Sir Leicester was stupefied.

'Did it cost all I sent you?' he said.

'Yes,' said Linda. 'I thought you would like me to buy one thing with it, and always remember it was you who gave it to me.'

'No, dear. That wasn't at all what I intended. £1,000 is what you might call a capital sum, that means something on which you expect a return. You should not spend it on a trinket which you wear three or four times a year, and which is most unlikely to appreciate in value. (And, by the way, if you buy jewels, let it always be diamonds – rubies and pearls are too easy to copy, they won't keep their price.) But, as I was saying, one hopes for a return. So you could either have asked Tony to invest it for you, or, which is what I really intended, you could have spent it on entertaining important people who would be of use to Tony in his career.'

These important people were a continual thorn in poor Linda's side. She was always supposed by the Kroesigs to be a great hindrance to Tony, both in politics and in the City, because, try as she might, she could not disguise how tedious they seemed to her. Like Aunt Sadie, she was apt to retire into a cloud of boredom on the smallest provocation, a vague look would come into her eyes, and her spirit would be absent itself. Important people did not like this; they were not accustomed to it; they liked to be listened and attended to by the young with concentrated deference when they were so kind as to bestow their company. What with Linda's yawns, and Tony informing them how many harbour-masters there were in the British Isles, important people were inclined to eschew the young Kroesigs. The old Kroesigs deeply deplored this state of affairs, for which they blamed Linda. They saw that she did not take the slightest interest in Tony's work. She tried to at first but it was beyond her; she simply could not understand how somebody who already had plenty of money could go and shut himself away from God's fresh air and blue skies, from the spring, the summer, the autumn, the winter, letting them merge into each other unaware that they were passing, simply in order to make more. She was far too young to be interested in politics, which were anyhow, in those days before Hitler came along to brighten them up, a very esoteric amusement.

'Your father was cross,' she said to Tony, as they walked home after dinner. Sir Leicester lived in Hyde Park Gardens, it was a beautiful night, and they walked.

'I don't wonder,' said Tony, shortly.

'But look, darling, how pretty it is. Don't you see how one couldn't resist it?'

'You are so affected. Do try and behave like an adult, won't you?'

The autumn after Linda's marriage Aunt Emily took a little house in St Leonard's Terrace, where she, Davey and I installed ourselves. She had been rather unwell, and Davey thought it would be a good thing to get her away from all her country duties and to make her rest, as no woman ever can at home. His novel, *The Abrasive Tube*, had just appeared, and was having a great success in intellectual circles. It was a psychological and physiological study of a South Polar explorer, snowed up in a hut where he knows he must eventually die, with enough rations to keep him going for a few months. In the end he dies. Davey was fascinated by Polar expeditions; he liked to observe, from a safe distance, how far the body can go when driven upon thoroughly indigestible foodstuffs deficient in vitamins.

'Pemmican,' he would say, gleefully, falling upon the delicious food for which Aunt Emily's cook was renowned, 'must have been so bad for them.'

Aunt Emily, shaken out of the routine of her life at Shenley, took up with old friends again, entertaining for us, and enjoyed herself so much that she talked of living half the year in London. As for me, I have never, before or since, been happier. The London season I had with Linda had been the greatest possible fun; it would be untrue and ungrateful to Aunt Sadie to deny that; I had even quite enjoyed the long dark hours we spent in the Peeresses' gallery; but there had been a curious unreality about it all, it was not related, one felt, to life. Now I had my feet firmly planted on the ground. I was allowed to do what I liked, see whom I chose, at any hour, peacefully, naturally, and without breaking rules, and it was wonderful to bring my friends home and have them greeted in a friendly, if somewhat detached manner, by Davey, instead of smuggling them up the back stairs for fear of a raging scene in the hall.

During this happy time I became happily engaged to Alfred Wincham, then a young don at, now Warden of, St Peter's College, Oxford. With this kindly scholarly man I have been perfectly happy ever since, finding in our home at Oxford that refuge from the storms and puzzles of life which I had always wanted. I say no more about him here; this is Linda's story, not mine.

We saw a great deal of Linda just then; she would come and chat for hours on end. She did not seem to be unhappy, though I felt sure she was already waking from her Titania-trance, but was obviously lonely, as her husband was at his work all day and at the House in the evening. Lord Merlin was abroad, and she had, as yet, no other very intimate friends; she missed the comings and goings, the cheerful bustle and hours of pointless chatter which had made up the family life at Alconleigh. I reminded her how much, when she was there, she had longed to escape, and she agreed, rather doubtfully, that it was wonderful to be on one's own. She was much pleased by my engagement, and liked Alfred.

'He has such a serious, clever look,' she said. 'What pretty little black babies you'll have, both of you so dark.'

He only quite liked her; he suspected that she was a tough nut, and rather, I must own, to my relief, she never exercised over him the spell in which she had entranced Davey and Lord Merlin.

One day, as we were busy with wedding invitations, she came in and announced:

'I am in pig, what d'you think of that?'

'A most hideous expression, Linda dear,' said Aunt Emily, 'but I suppose we must congratulate you.'

'I suppose so,' said Linda. She sank into a chair with an enormous sigh. 'I feel awfully ill, I must say.'

'But think how much good it will do you in the long run,' said Davey, enviously, 'such a wonderful clear-out.'

'I see just what you mean,' said Linda. 'Oh, we've got such a ghastly evening ahead of us. Some important Americans. It seems Tony wants to do a deal or something, and these Americans will only do the deal if they take a fancy to me. Now can you explain that? I know I shall be sick all over them, and my father-in-law will be so cross. Oh, the horror of important people – you are lucky not to know any.'

Linda's child, a girl, was born in May. She was ill for a long time before, and very ill indeed at her confinement. The doctors told her that she must never have another child, as it would almost certainly kill her if she did. This was a blow to the Kroesigs, as bankers, it seems, like kings, require many sons, but Linda did not appear to mind at all. She took no interest whatever in the baby she had got. I went to see her as soon as I was allowed to. She lay in a bower of blossom and pink roses, and looked like a corpse. I was expecting a baby myself, and naturally took a great interest in Linda's.

'What are you going to call her where is she, anyway?'

'In Sister's room – it shrieks. Moira, I believe.'

'Not Moira, darling, you can't. I never heard such an awful name.'

'Tony likes it, he had a sister called Moira who died, and what d'you think I found out (not from him, but from their old nanny)? She died because Marjorie whacked her on the head with a hammer when she was four months old. Do you call that interesting? And then they say we are an uncontrolled family – why even Fa has never actually murdered anybody, or do you count that beater?'

'All the same, I don't see how you can saddle the poor little thing with a name like Moira, it's too unkind.'

'Not really, if you think. It'll have to grow up a Moira if the Kroesigs are to like it (people always grow up to their names I've noticed) and they might as well like it because frankly, I don't.'

'Linda, how can you be so naughty, and, anyway, you can't possibly tell whether you like her or not, yet.'

'Oh, yes I can. I can always tell if I like people from the start, and I don't like Moira, that's all. She's a fearful Counter-Hon, wait till you see her.'

At this point the Sister came in, and Linda introduced us.

'Oh, you are the cousin I hear so much about,' she said. 'You'll want to see the baby.'

She went away and presently returned carrying a Moses basket full of wails.

'Poor thing,' said Linda indifferently. 'It's really kinder not to look.'

'Don't pay any attention to her,' said the Sister. 'She pretends to be a wicked woman, but it's all put on.'

I did look, and, deep down among the frills and lace, there was the usual horrid sight of a howling orange in a fine black wig.

'Isn't she sweet,' said the Sister. 'Look at her little hands.'

I shuddered slightly, and said:

'Well, I know it's dreadful of me, but I don't much like them as small as that; I'm sure she'll be divine in a year or two.'

The wails now entered on a crescendo, and the whole room was filled with hideous noise.

'Poor soul,' said Linda. 'I think it must have caught sight of itself in a glass. Do take it away, Sister.'

Davey now came into the room. He was meeting me there to drive me down to Shenley for the night. The Sister came back and shooed us both off, saying that Linda had had enough. Outside her room, which was in the largest and most expensive nursing home in London, I paused, looking for the lift.

'This way,' said Davey, and then, with a slightly self-conscious giggle: '*Nourri dans le sérail, j'en connais les détours.* Oh, how are you, Sister Thesiger? How very nice to see you.'

'Captain Warbeck – I must tell Matron you are here.'

And it was nearly an hour before I could drag Davey out of this home from home. I hope I am not giving the impression that Davey's whole life was centred round his health. He was fully occupied with his work, writing, and editing a literary review, but his health was his hobby, and, as such, more in evidence during his

86

spare time, the time when I saw most of him. How he enjoyed it! He seemed to regard his body with the affectionate preoccupation of a farmer towards a pig – not a good doer, the small one of the litter, which must somehow be made to be a credit to the farm. He weighed it, sunned it, aired it, exercised it, and gave it special diets, new kinds of patent food and medicine, but all in vain. It never put on so much as a single ounce of weight, it never became a credit to the farm, but, somehow, it lived, enjoying good things, enjoying its life, though falling victim to the ills that flesh is heir to, and other, imaginary ills as well, through which it was nursed with unfailing care, with concentrated attention, by the good farmer and his wife.

Aunt Emily said at once, when I told her about Linda and poor Moira:

'She's too young. I don't believe very young mothers ever get wrapped up in their babies. It's when women are older that they so adore their children, and maybe it's better for the children to have young unadoring mothers and to lead more detached lives.'

'But Linda seems to loathe her.'

'That's so like Linda,' said Davey. 'She has to do things by extremes.'

'But she seemed so gloomy. You must say that's not very like her.'

'She's been terribly ill,' said Aunt Emily. 'Sadie was in despair. Twice they thought she would die.'

'Don't talk of it,' said Davey. 'I can't imagine the world without Linda.'

II

Living in Oxford, engrossed with my husband and young family, I
saw less of Linda during the next few years than at any time of my
life. This, however, did not affect the intimacy of our relationship,
which remained absolute, and, when we did meet, it was still as
though we were seeing each other every day. I stayed with her in
London from time to time, and she with me in Oxford, and we
corresponded regularly. I may as well say here that the one thing
she never discussed with me was the deterioration of her marriage;
in any case it would not have been necessary, the whole thing being
as plain as relations between married people can ever be. Tony was,
quite obviously, not good enough as a lover to make up, even at
first, for his shortcomings in other respects, the boredom of his
company and the mediocrity of his character. Linda was out of love
with him by the time the child was born, and, thereafter, could not
care a rap for the one or the other. The young man she had fallen
in love with, handsome, gay, intellectual, and domineering, melted
away upon closer acquaintance, and proved to have been a chimera,
never to have existed outside her imagination. Linda did not commit
the usual fault of blaming Tony for what was entirely her own
mistake, she merely turned from him in absolute indifference. This
was made easier by the fact that she saw so little of him.

Lord Merlin now launched a tremendous Kroesig-tease. The
Kroesigs were always complaining that Linda never went out,
would not entertain, unless absolutely forced to, and did not care
for society. They told their friends that she was a country girl,
entirely sporting, that if you went into her drawing-room she
would be found training a retriever with dead rabbits hidden
behind the sofa cushions. They pretended that she was an amiable,

half-witted, beautiful rustic, incapable of helping poor Tony, who was obliged to battle his way through life alone. There was a grain of truth in all this, the fact being that the Kroesig circle of acquaintances was too ineffably boring; poor Linda, having been unable to make any headway at all in it, had given up the struggle, and retired to the more congenial company of retrievers and dormice.

Lord Merlin, in London for the first time since Linda's marriage, at once introduced her into his world, the world towards which she had always looked, that of smart bohemianism; and here she found her feet, was entirely happy, and had an immediate and great success. She became very gay and went everywhere. There is no more popular unit in London society than a young, beautiful, but perfectly respectable woman who can be asked to dinner without her husband, and Linda was soon well on the way to having her head turned. Photographers and gossip writers dogged her footsteps, and indeed one could not escape the impression, until half an hour of her company put one right again, that she was becoming a bit of a bore. Her house was full of people from morning till night, chatting. Linda, who loved to chat, found many congenial spirits in the carefree, pleasure-seeking London of those days, when unemployment was rife as much among the upper as the lower classes. Young men, pensioned off by their relations, who would sometimes suggest in a perfunctory manner that it might be a good thing if they found some work, but without seriously helping them to do so (and, anyhow, what work was there for such as they?) clustered round Linda like bees round honey, buzz, buzz, buzz, chat, chat, chat. In her bedroom, on her bed, sitting on the stairs outside while she had a bath, in the kitchen while she ordered the food, shopping, walking round the park, cinema, theatre, opera, ballet, dinner, supper, night clubs, parties, dances, all day, all night – endless, endless, chat.

'But what do you suppose they talk about?' Aunt Sadie, disapproving, used to wonder. What, indeed?

Tony went early to his bank, hurrying out of the house with an air of infinite importance, an attaché case in one hand and a sheaf of newspapers under his arm. His departure heralded the swarm of chatterers, almost as if they had been waiting round the street corner to see him leave, and thereafter the house was filled with them. They were very nice, very good-looking, and great fun – their manners were perfect. I never was able, during my short visits, to distinguish them much one from another, but I saw their attraction, the unfailing attraction of vitality and high spirits. By no stretch of the imagination, however, could they have been called 'important', and the Kroesigs were beside themselves at this turn of affairs.

Tony did not seem to mind; he had long given up Linda as hopeless from the point of view of his career, and was rather pleased and flattered by the publicity which now launched her as a beauty. 'The beautiful wife of a clever young M.P.' Besides, he found that they were invited to large parties and balls, to which it suited him very well to go, coming late after the House, and where there were often to be found not only Linda's unimportant friends, with whom she would amuse herself, but also colleagues of his own, and by no means unimportant ones, whom he could button-hole and bore at the bar. It would have been useless, however, to explain this to the old Kroesigs, who had a deeply rooted mistrust of smart society, of dancing, and of any kind of fun, all of which led, in their opinion, to extravagance, without compensating material advantages. Fortunately for Linda, Tony at this time was not on good terms with his father, owing to a conflict of policies in the bank; they did not go to Hyde Park Gardens as much as when they were first married, and visits to Planes, the Kroesig house in Surrey, were, for the time being, off. When they did meet, however, the old Kroesigs made it clear to Linda that she was not proving a satisfactory daughter-in-law. Even Tony's divergence of views was put down to her, and Lady Kroesig told her friends, with a sad shake of the head, that Linda did not bring out the best in him.

Linda now proceeded to fritter away years of her youth, with nothing whatever to show for them. If she had had an intellectual upbringing the place of all this pointless chatter, jokes, and parties might have been taken by a serious interest in the arts, or by reading; if she had been happy in her marriage that side of her nature which craved for company could have found its fulfilment by the nursery fender; things being as they were, however, all was frippery and silliness.

Alfred and I once had an argument with Davey about her, during which we said all this. Davey accused us of being prigs, though at heart he must have known that we were right.

'But Linda gives one so much pleasure,' he kept saying, 'she is like a bunch of flowers. You don't want people like that to bury themselves in serious reading; what would be the good?'

However, even he was forced to admit that her behaviour to poor little Moira was not what it should be. (The child was fat, fair, placid, dull, and backward, and Linda still did not like her; the Kroesigs, on the other hand, adored her, and she spent more and more time, with her nanny, at Planes. They loved having her there, but that did not stop them from ceaseless criticism of Linda's behaviour. They now told everybody that she was a silly society butterfly, hard-hearted neglecter of her child.)

Alfred said, almost angrily:

'It's so odd that she doesn't even have love affairs. I don't see what she gets out of her life, it must be dreadfully empty.'

Alfred likes people to be filed neatly away under some heading that he can understand; careerist, social climber, virtuous wife and mother, or adulteress.

Linda's social life was completely aimless; she simply collected around her an assortment of cosy people who had the leisure to chat all day; whether they were millionaires or paupers, princes or refugee Rumanians, was a matter of complete indifference to her. In spite of the fact that, except for me and her sisters, nearly all her friends were men, she had such a reputation for virtue that she was currently suspected of being in love with her husband.

'Linda believes in love,' said Davey, 'she is passionately romantic. At the moment I am sure she is, subconsciously, waiting for an irresistible temptation. Casual affairs would not interest her in the least. One must hope that when it comes it will not prove to be another Bottom.'

'I suppose she is really rather like my mother,' I said, 'and all of hers have been Bottoms.'

'Poor Bolter!' said Davey, 'but she's happy now, isn't she, with her white hunter?'

Tony soon became, as was to be expected, a perfect mountain of pomposity, more like his father every day. He was full of large, clear-sighted ideas for bettering the conditions of the capitalist classes, and made no bones of his hatred and distrust of the workers.

'I hate the lower classes,' he said one day, when Linda and I were having tea with him on the terrace of the House of Commons. 'Ravening beasts, trying to get my money. Let them try, that's all.'

'Oh, shut up, Tony,' said Linda, bringing a dormouse out of her pocket, and feeding it with crumbs. 'I love them, anyway I was brought up with them. The trouble with you is you don't know the lower classes and you don't belong to the upper classes, you're just a rich foreigner who happens to live here. Nobody ought to be in Parliament who hasn't lived in the country, anyhow part of their life – why, my old Fa knows more what he's talking about, when he does talk in the House, than you do.'

'I have lived in the country,' said Tony. 'Put that dormouse away, people are looking.'

He never got cross, he was far too pompous.

'Surrey,' said Linda, with infinite contempt.

'Anyhow, last time your Fa made a speech, about the Peeresses in their own right, his only argument for keeping them out of the House was that, if once they got in, they might use the Peers' lavatory.'

'Isn't he a love?' said Linda. 'It's what they all thought, you know, but he was the only one who dared to say it.'

'That's the worst of the House of Lords,' said Tony. 'These backwoodsmen come along just when they think they will, and bring the whole place into disrepute with a few dotty remarks, which get an enormous amount of publicity and give people the impression that we are governed by a lot of lunatics. These old peers ought to realize that it's their duty to their class to stay at home and keep quiet. The amount of excellent, solid, necessary work done in the House of Lords is quite unknown to the man in the street.'

Sir Leicester was expecting soon to become a peer, so this was a subject close to Tony's heart. His general attitude to what he called the man in the street was that he ought constantly to be covered by machine-guns; this having become impossible, owing to the weakness, in the past, of the great Whig families, he must be doped into submission with the fiction that huge reforms, to be engineered by the Conservative party, were always just round the next corner. Like this he could be kept quiet indefinitely, as long as there was no war. War brings people together and opens their eyes, it must be avoided at all costs, and especially war with Germany, where the Kroesigs had financial interests and many relations. (They were originally a Junker family, and snobbed their Prussian connexions as much as the latter looked down on them for being in trade.)

Both Sir Leicester and his son were great admirers of Herr Hitler: Sir Leicester had been to see him during a visit to Germany, and had been taken for a drive in a Mercedes-Benz by Dr Schacht.

Linda took no interest in politics, but she was instinctively and unreasonably English. She knew that one Englishman was worth a hundred foreigners, whereas Tony thought that one capitalist was worth a hundred workers. Their outlook upon this, as upon most subjects, differed fundamentally.

12

By a curious irony of fate it was at her father-in-law's house in Surrey that Linda met Christian Talbot. The little Moira, aged six, now lived permanently at Planes; it seemed a good arrangement as it saved Linda, who disliked housekeeping, the trouble of running two establishments, while Moira was given the benefit of country air and food. Linda and Tony were supposed to spend a couple of nights there every week, and Tony generally did so. Linda, in fact, went down for Sunday about once a month.

Planes was a horrible house. It was an overgrown cottage, that is to say, the rooms were large, with all the disadvantages of a cottage, low ceilings, small windows with diamond panes, uneven floorboards, and a great deal of naked knotted wood. It was furnished neither in good nor in bad taste, but simply with no attempt at taste at all, and was not even very comfortable. The garden which lay around it would be a lady water-colourist's heaven, herbaceous borders, rockeries, and water-gardens were carried to a perfection of vulgarity, and flaunted a riot of huge and hideous flowers, each individual bloom appearing twice as large, three times as brilliant as it ought to have been and if possible of a different colour from that which nature intended. It would be hard to say whether it was more frightful, more like glorious Technicolor, in spring, in summer, or in autumn. Only in the depth of winter, covered by the kindly snow, did it melt into the landscape and become tolerable.

One April Saturday morning, in 1937, Linda, with whom I had been staying in London, took me down there for the night, as she sometimes did. I think she liked to have a buffer between herself and the Kroesigs, perhaps especially between herself and Moira. The old Kroesigs were by way of being very fond of me, and Sir

94

Leicester sometimes took me for walks and hinted how much he wished that it had been me, so serious, so well educated, such a good wife and mother, whom Tony had married.

We motored down past acres of blossom.

'The great difference,' said Linda, 'between Surrey and proper, real country, is that in Surrey, when you see blossom, you know there will be no fruit. Think of the Vale of Evesham, and then look at all this pointless pink stuff – it gives you quite a different feeling. The garden at Planes will be a riot of sterility, just you wait.'

It was. You could hardly see any beautiful, pale, bright, yellow-green of spring, every tree appeared to be entirely covered with a waving mass of pink or mauve tissue-paper. The daffodils were so thick on the ground that they too obscured the green, they were new varieties of a terrifying size, either dead white or dark yellow, thick and fleshy; they did not look at all like the fragile friends of one's childhood. The whole effect was of a scene for musical comedy, and it exactly suited Sir Leicester, who, in the country, gave a surprisingly adequate performance of the old English squire. Picturesque. Delightful.

He was pottering in the garden as we drove up, in an old pair of corduroy trousers, so much designed as an old pair that it seemed improbable that they had ever been new, an old tweed coat on the same lines, secateurs in his hand, a depressed Corgi at his heels, and a mellow smile on his face.

'Here you are,' he said, heartily. (One could almost see, as in the strip advertisements, a bubble coming out of his head – thinks – 'You are a most unsatisfactory daughter-in-law, but nobody can say it's our fault, we always have a welcome and a kind smile for you.') 'Car going well, I hope? Tony and Moira have gone out riding, I thought you might have passed them. Isn't the garden looking grand just now, I can hardly bear to go to London and leave all this beauty with no one to see it. Come for a stroll before lunch – Foster will see to your gear – just ring the front-door bell, Fanny, he may not have heard the car.'

He led us off into Madame Butterfly-land.

'I must warn you,' he said, 'that we have got rather a rough diamond coming to lunch. I don't know if you've ever met old Talbot who lives in the village, the old professor? Well, his son, Christian. He's by way of being rather a Communist, a clever chap gone all wrong, and a journalist on some daily rag. Tony can't bear him, never could as a child, and he's very cross with me for asking him to-day, but I always think it's as well to see something of these Left-wing fellows. If people like us are nice to them they can be tamed wonderfully.'

He said this in the tone of one who might have saved the life of a Communist in the war, and, by this act, turned him, through gratitude, into a true blue Tory. But in the first world war Sir Leicester had considered that, with his superior brain, he would have been wasted as cannon fodder, and had fixed himself in an office in Cairo. He neither saved nor took any lives, nor did he risk his own, but built up many valuable business contacts, became a major and got an O.B.E., thus making the best of all worlds.

So Christian came to luncheon, and behaved with the utmost intransigence. He was an extraordinarily handsome young man, tall and fair, in a completely different way from that of Tony, thin and very English-looking. His clothes were outrageous – he wore a really old pair of grey flannel trousers, full of little round moth-holes in the most embarrassing places, no coat, and a flannel shirt, one of the sleeves of which had a tattered tear from wrist to elbow.

'Has your father been writing anything lately?' Lady Kroesig asked, as they sat down to luncheon.

'I suppose so,' said Christian, 'as it's his profession. I can't say I've asked him, but one assumes he has, just as one assumes that Tony has been banking something lately.'

He then planted his elbow, bare through the rent, onto the table between himself and Lady Kroesig and swivelling right round to Linda, who was on his other side, he told her, at length and in immense detail, of a production of *Hamlet* he had seen lately in Moscow. The cultured Kroesigs listened attentively, throwing off occasional comments calculated to show that they knew *Hamlet* well – 'I don't think that quite fits in with my idea of Ophelia', or 'But Polonius was a very old man', to all of which Christian turned an utterly deaf ear, gobbling his food with one hand, his elbow on the table, his eyes on Linda.

After luncheon he said to Linda:

'Come back and have tea with my father, you'd like him,' and they went off together, leaving the Kroesigs to behave for the rest of the afternoon like a lot of hens who have seen a fox.

Sir Leicester took me to his water-garden, which was full of enormous pink forget-me-nots, and dark-brown irises, and said:

'It is really too bad of Linda, little Moira has been so much looking forward to showing her the ponies. That child idolizes her mother.'

She didn't, actually, in the least. She was fond of Tony and quite indifferent to Linda, calm and stolid and not given to idolatry, but it was part of the Kroesigs' creed that children should idolize their mothers.

'Do you know Pixie Townsend?' he asked me, suddenly.

'No,' I said, which was true, nor did I then know anything about her. 'Who is she?'

'She's a very delightful person.' He changed the subject.

Linda returned just in time to dress for dinner, looking extremely beautiful. She made me come and chat while she had her bath – Tony was reading to Moira upstairs in the night nursery. Linda was perfectly enchanted with her outing. Christian's father, she said, lived in the smallest house imaginable, an absolute contrast to what Christian called the Kroesighof, because, although absolutely tiny, it had nothing whatever of a cottage about it – it was in the grand manner, and full of books. Every available wall space was covered with books, they lay stacked on tables and chairs and in heaps on the floor. Mr Talbot was the exact opposite of Sir Leicester, there was nothing picturesque about him, or anything to indicate that he was a learned man, he was brisk and matter-of-fact, and had made some very funny jokes about Davey, whom he knew well.

'He's perfect heaven,' Linda kept saying, her eyes shining. What she really meant, as I could see too clearly, was that Christian was perfect heaven. She was dazzled by him. It seemed that he had talked without cease, and his talk consisted of variations upon a single theme – the betterment of the world through political change. Linda, since her marriage, had heard no end of political shop talked by Tony and his friends, but this related politics entirely to personalities and jobs. As the persons all seemed to her infinitely old and dull, and as it was quite immaterial to her whether they got jobs or not, Linda had classed politics as a boring subject, and used to go off into a dream when they were discussed. But Christian's politics did not bore her. As they walked back from his father's house that evening he had taken her for a tour of the world. He showed her Fascism in Italy, Nazism in Germany, civil war in Spain, inadequate Socialism in France, tyranny in Africa, starvation in Asia, reaction in America, and Right-wing blight in England. Only the U.S.S.R., Norway, and Mexico came in for a modicum of praise.

Linda was a plum ripe for shaking. The tree was now shaken, and down she came. Intelligent and energetic, but with no outlet for her energies, unhappy in her marriage, uninterested in her child, and inwardly oppressed with a sense of futility, she was in the mood either to take up some cause, or to embark upon a love affair. That a cause should now be presented by an attractive young man made both it and him irresistible.

13

The poor Alconleighs were now presented with crises in the lives of three of their children almost simultaneously. Linda ran away from Tony, Jassy ran away from home, and Matt ran away from Eton. The Alconleighs were obliged to face the fact, as parents must sooner or later, that their children had broken loose from control and had taken charge of their own lives. Distracted, disapproving, worried to death, there was nothing they could do; they had become mere spectators of a spectacle which did not please them in the least. This was the year when the parents of our contemporaries would console themselves, if things did not go quite as they hoped for their own children, by saying: 'Never mind, just think of the poor Alconleighs!'

Linda threw discretion, and what worldly wisdom she may have picked up during her years in London society, to the winds; she became an out-and-out Communist, bored and embarrassed everybody to death by preaching her new-found doctrine, not only at the dinner-table, but also from a soap-box in Hyde Park, and other equally squalid rostra, and finally, to the infinite relief of the Kroesig family, she went off to live with Christian. Tony started proceedings for divorce. This was a great blow to my aunt and uncle. It is true that they had never liked Tony, but they were infinitely old-fashioned in their ideas; marriage, to their way of thinking, was marriage, and adultery was wrong. Aunt Sadie was, in particular, profoundly shocked by the light-hearted way in which Linda had abandoned the little Moira. I think it all reminded her too much of my mother, and that she envisaged Linda's future from now on as a series of uncontrollable bolts.

Linda came to see me in Oxford. She was on her way back to London after having broken the news at Alconleigh. I thought it was really very brave of her to do it in person, and indeed, the first thing she asked for (most unlike her) was a drink. She was quite unnerved.

'Goodness,' she said. 'I'd forgotten how terrifying Fa can be – even now, when he's got no power over one. It was just like after we lunched with Tony; in the business-room just the same, and he simply roared, and poor Mummy looked miserable, but she was pretty furious too, and you know how sarcastic she can be. Oh, well, that's over. Darling, it's heaven to see you again.'

I hadn't seen her since the Sunday at Planes when she met Christian, so I wanted to hear all about her life.

'Well,' she said, 'I'm living with Christian in his flat, but it's very small, I must say, but perhaps that is just as well, because I'm doing the housework, and I don't seem to be very good at it, but luckily he is.'

'He'll need to be,' I said.

Linda was notorious in the family for her unhandiness, she could never even tie her own stock, and on hunting days either Uncle Matthew or Josh always had to do it for her. I so well remember her standing in front of a looking-glass in the hall, with Uncle Matthew tying it from behind, both the very picture of concentration, Linda saying: 'Oh, now I see. Next time I know I shall be able to manage.' As she had never in her life done so much as make her own bed, I could not imagine that Christian's flat could be very tidy or comfortable if it was being run by her.

'You are horrid. But oh how dreadful it is, cooking, I mean. That oven – Christian puts things in and says: "Now you take it out in about half an hour." I don't dare tell him how terrified I am, and at the end of half an hour I summon up all my courage and open the oven, and there is that awful hot blast hitting one in the face. I don't wonder people sometimes put their heads in and leave them in out of sheer misery. Oh, dear, and I wish you could have seen the Hoover running away with me, it suddenly took the bit between its teeth and made for the lift shaft. How I shrieked – Christian only just rescued me in time. I think housework is far more tiring and frightening than hunting is, no comparison, and yet after hunting we had eggs for tea and were made to rest for hours, but after housework people expect one to go on just as if nothing special had happened.' She sighed.

'Christian is very strong,' she said, 'and very brave. He doesn't like it when I shriek.'

She seemed tired I thought and rather worried, and I looked in vain for signs of great happiness or great love.

'So what about Tony – how has he taken it?'

'Oh, he's awfully pleased, actually, because he can now marry his mistress without having a scandal, or being divorced, or upsetting the Conservative Association.'

It was so like Linda never to have hinted, even to me, that Tony had a mistress.

'Who is she?' I asked.

'Called Pixie Townsend. You know the sort, young face, with white hair dyed blue. She adores Moira, lives near Planes, and takes her out riding every day. She's a terrific Counter-Hon, but I'm only too thankful now that she exists, because I needn't feel in the least bit guilty – they'll all get on so much better without me.'

'Married?'

'Oh, yes, and divorced her husband years ago. She's frightfully good at all poor Tony's things, golf and business and Conservatism, just like I wasn't, and Sir Leicester think's she's perfect. Goodness, they'll be happy.'

'Now, I want to hear more about Christian, please.'

'Well, he's heaven. He's a frightfully serious man, you know, a Communist, and so am I now, and we are surrounded by comrades all day, and they are terrific Hons, and there's an anarchist. The comrades don't like anarchists, isn't it queer? I always thought they were the same thing, but Christian likes this one because he threw a bomb at the King of Spain; you must say it's romantic. He's called Ramón, and he sits about all day and broods over the miners at Oviedo because his brother is one.'

'Yes, but, darling, tell about Christian.'

'Oh, he's perfect heaven – you must come and stay – or perhaps that wouldn't be very comfortable – come and see us. You can't think what an extraordinary man he is, so detached from other human beings that he hardly notices whether they are there or not. He only cares for ideas.'

'I hope he cares for you.'

'Well, I think he does, but he is very strange and absent-minded. I must tell you, the evening before I ran away with him (I only moved down to Pimlico in a taxi, but running away sounds romantic) he dined with his brother, so naturally I thought they'd talk about me and discuss the whole thing, so I couldn't resist ringing him up at about midnight and saying: "Hullo, darling, did you have a nice evening, and what did you talk about?" and he said: "I can't remember – oh, guerrilla warfare, I think."'

'Is his brother a Communist too?'

'Oh, no, he's in the Foreign Office. Fearfully grand, looks like a deep-sea monster – you know.'

'Oh, that Talbot – yes, I see. I hadn't connected them. So now what are your plans?'

'Well, he says he's going to marry me when I'm divorced. I think it's rather silly, I rather agree with Mummy that once is enough, for marriage, but she says I'm the kind of person one marries if one's living with them, and the thing is it would be bliss not to be called Kroesig any more. Anyway, we'll see.'

'Then what's your life? I suppose you don't go to parties and things now, do you?'

'Darling, such killing parties, you can't think – he won't let us go to ordinary ones at all. Grandi had a dinner-dance last week, and he rang me up himself and asked me to bring Christian, which I thought was awfully nice of him actually – he always has been nice to me – but Christian got into quite a temper and said if I couldn't see any reason against going I'd better go, but nothing would induce him to. So in the end, of course, neither of us went, and I heard afterwards it was the greatest fun. And we mayn't go to the Ribs or to . . .' and she mentioned several families known as much for their hospitality as for their Right-wing convictions.

'The worst of being a Communist is that the parties you may go to are – well – awfully funny and touching, but not very gay, and they're always in such gloomy places. Next week, for instance, we've got three, some Czechs at the Sacco and Vanzetti Memorial Hall at Golders Green, Ethiopians at the Paddington Baths, and the Scotsboro' boys at some boring old rooms or other. You know.'

'The Scotsboro' boys,' I said. 'Are they really still going? They must be getting on.'

'Yes, and they've gone downhill socially,' said Linda, with a giggle. 'I remember a perfectly divine party Brian gave for them – it was the first party Merlin ever took me to so I remember it well, oh, dear, it was fun. But next Thursday won't be the least like that. (Darling, I am being disloyal, but it is such heaven to have a chat after all these months. The comrades are sweet, but they never chat, they make speeches all the time.) But I'm always saying to Christian how much I wish his buddies would either brighten up their parties a bit or else stop giving them, because I don't see the point of sad parties, do you? And Left-wing people are always sad because they mind dreadfully about their causes, and the causes are always going so badly. You see, I bet the Scotsboro' boys will be electrocuted in the end, if they don't die of old age first, that is. One does feel so much on their side, but it's no good, people like Sir Leicester always come out on top, so what can one do? However, the comrades don't seem to realize that, and, luckily for them, they don't know Sir Leicester, so they feel they must go on giving these sad parties.'

'What do you wear at them?' I asked, with some interest, thinking that Linda, in her expensive-looking clothes, must seem very much out of place at these baths and halls.

'You know, that was a great tease at first, it worried me dreadfully, but I've discovered that, so long as one wears wool or cotton, everything is all right. Silk and satin would be the blunder. But I only ever do wear wool and cotton, so I'm on a good wicket. No jewels, of course, but then I left them behind at Bryanston Square, it's the way I was brought up but I must say it gave me a pang. Christian doesn't know about jewellery – I told him, because I thought he'd be rather pleased I'd given them all up for him, but he only said: "Well, there's always the Burma Jewel Company." Oh, dear, he is such a funny man, you must meet him again soon. I must go, darling, it has so cheered me up to see you.'

I don't quite know why, but I felt somehow that Linda had been once more deceived in her emotions, that this explorer in the sandy waste had seen only another mirage. The lake was there, the trees were there, the thirsty camels had gone down to have their evening drink; alas, a few steps forward would reveal nothing but dust and desert as before.

A few minutes only after Linda had left me to go back to London, Christian and the comrades, I had another caller. This time it was Lord Merlin. I liked Lord Merlin very much, I admired him, I was predisposed in his favour, but I was by no means on such intimate terms with him as Linda was. To tell the real truth he frightened me. I felt that, in my company, boredom was for him only just round the corner, and that, anyhow, I was merely regarded as pertaining to Linda, not existing on my own except as a dull little don's wife. I was nothing but the confidante in white linen.

'This is a bad business,' he said, abruptly, and without preamble, though I had not seen him for several years. 'I'm just back from Rome, and what do I find – Linda and Christian Talbot. It's an extraordinary thing that I can't ever leave England without Linda getting herself mixed up with some thoroughly undesirable character. This is a disaster – how far has it gone? Can nothing be done?'

I told him that he had just missed Linda, and said something about her marriage with Tony having been unhappy. Lord Merlin waved this remark aside – it was a disconcerting gesture and made me feel a fool.

'Naturally she never would have stayed with Tony – nobody expected that. The point is that she's out of the frying-pan into an empty grate. How long has it been going on?'

I said I thought it was partly the Communism that had attracted her.

'Linda has always felt the need of a cause.'

'Cause,' he said, scornfully. 'My dear Fanny, I think you are mixing up cause with effect. No, Christian is an attractive fellow, and I quite see that he would provide a perfect reaction from Tony, but it is a disaster. If she is in love with him he will make her miserable, and, if not, it means she has embarked upon a career like your mother's, and that, for Linda, would be very bad indeed. I don't see a ray of comfort anywhere. No money either, of course, and she needs money, she ought to have it.'

He went to the window, and looked across the street at Christ Church gilded by the westerly sun.

'I've known Christian,' he said, 'from a child – his father is a great friend of mine. Christian is a man who goes through the world attached to nobody – people are nothing in his life. The women who have been in love with him have suffered bitterly because he has not even noticed that they are there. I expect he is hardly aware that Linda has moved in on him – his head is in the clouds and he is always chasing after some new idea.'

'This is rather what Linda has just been saying.'

'Oh, she's noticed it already? Well, she is not stupid, and, of course, at first it adds to the attraction – when he comes out of the clouds he is irresistible, I quite see that. But how can they ever settle down? Christian has never had a home, or felt the need for one; he wouldn't know what to do with it – it would hamper him. He'll never sit and chat to Linda, or concentrate upon her in any way, and she is a woman who requires, above all things, a great deal of concentration. Really it is too provoking that I should have been away when this happened, I'm sure I could have stopped it. Now, of course, nobody can.'

He turned from the window and looked at me so angrily that I felt it had all been my fault – actually I think he was unaware of my presence.

'What are they living on?' he said.

'Very little. Linda has a small allowance from Uncle Matthew, I believe, and I suppose Christian makes something from his journalism. I hear the Kroesigs go about saying that there is one good thing, she is sure to starve.'

'Oh, they do, do they?' said Lord Merlin, taking out his notebook, 'can I have Linda's address, please, I am on my way to London now.'

Alfred came in, as usual unaware of exterior events and buried in some pamphlet he was writing.

'You don't happen to know,' he said to Lord Merlin, 'what the daily consumption of milk is in the Vatican City?'

'No, of course not,' said Lord Merlin, angrily, 'Ask Tony Kroesig, he'll be sure to. Well, good-bye, Fanny, I'll have to see what I can do.'

What he did was to present Linda with the freehold of a tiny house far down Cheyne Walk. It was the prettiest little doll's house that ever was seen, on that great bend of the river where Whistler had lived. The rooms were full of reflections of water and full of south and west sunlight; it had a vine and a Trafalgar balcony. Linda adored it. The Bryanston Square house, with an easterly outlook, had been originally, dark, cold, and pompous. When Linda had had it done up by some decorating friend, it had become white, cold, and tomblike. The only thing of beauty that she had possessed was a picture, a fat tomato-coloured bathing-woman, which had been given her by Lord Merlin to annoy the Kroesigs. It had annoyed them, very much. This picture looked wonderful in the Cheyne Walk house, you could hardly tell where the real water-reflections ended and the Renoir one began. The pleasure which Linda derived from her new surroundings, the relief which she felt at having once and for all got rid of the Kroesigs, were, I think, laid by her at Christian's door, and seemed to come from him. Thus the discovery that real love and happiness had once more eluded her was delayed for quite a long time.

14

The Alconleighs were shocked and horrified over the whole Linda affair, but they had their other children to think of, and were, just now, making plans for the coming out of Jassy, who was as pretty as a peach. She, they hoped, would make up to them for their disappointment with Linda. It was most unfair, but very typical of them, that Louisa, who had married entirely in accordance with their wishes and had been a faithful wife and most prolific mother, having now some five children, hardly seemed to count any more. They were really rather bored by her.

Jassy went with Aunt Sadie to a few London dances at the end of the season, just after Linda had left Tony. She was thought to be rather delicate, and Aunt Sadie had an idea that it would be better for her to come out properly in the less strenuous autumn season, and, accordingly, in October, took a little house in London into which she prepared to move with a few servants, leaving Uncle Matthew in the country, to kill various birds and animals. Jassy complained very much that the young men she had met so far were dull and hideous, but Aunt Sadie took no notice. She said that all girls thought this at first, until they fell in love.

A few days before they were to have moved to London Jassy ran away. She was to have spent a fortnight with Louisa in Scotland, had put Louisa off without telling Aunt Sadie, had cashed her savings, and, before anybody even knew that she was missing, had arrived in America. Poor Aunt Sadie received, out of the blue, a cable saying: 'On way to Hollywood. Don't worry. Jassy.'

At first the Alconleighs were completely mystified. Jassy had never shown the smallest interest in stage or cinema, they felt certain she had no wish to become a film star, and yet, why Hollywood? Then it occurred to them that Matt might know something, he and Jassy being the two inseparables of the family, and Aunt Sadie got into the Daimler and rolled over to Eton. Matt was able to explain everything. He told Aunt Sadie that Jassy was in love with a film star called Gary Coon (or Gary Goon, he could not remember which), and that she had written to Hollywood to ask him if he were married, telling Matt that if he proved not to be she was going straight out there to marry him herself. Matt said all this, in his wobbling half grown-up, half little-boy voice, as if it were the most ordinary situation imaginable.

'So I suppose,' he ended up, 'that she got a letter saying he's not married and just went off. Lucky she had her running away money. What about some tea, Mum?'

Aunt Sadie, deeply preoccupied as she was, knew the rules of behaviour and what was expected of her, and stayed with Matt while he consumed sausages, lobsters, eggs, bacon, fried sole, banana mess, and a chocolate sundae.

As always in times of crisis, the Alconleighs now sent for Davey, and, as always, Davey displayed a perfect competence to deal with the situation. He found out in no time that Cary Goon was a second-rate film actor whom Jassy must have seen when she was in London for the last parties of the summer. He had been in a film then showing called *One Splendid Hour*. Davey got hold of the film, and Lord Merlin put it on his private cinema for the benefit of the family. It was about pirates, and Cary Goon was not even the hero, he was just a pirate and seemed to have nothing in particular to recommend him; no good looks, talent, or visible charm, though he did display a certain agility shinning up and down ropes. He also killed a man with a weapon not unlike the entrenching tool, and this, we felt, may have awakened some hereditary emotion in Jassy's bosom. The film itself was one of those of which it is very difficult for the ordinary English person, as opposed to the film fan, to make head or tail, and every time Cary Goon appeared the scene had to be played over again for Uncle Matthew, who had come determined that no detail should escape him. He absolutely identified the actor with his part, and kept saying:

'What does the fella want to do that for? Bloody fool, he might know there would be an ambush there. I can't hear a word the fella says – put that bit on again, Merlin.'

At the end he said he didn't think much of the cove, he appeared to have no discipline and had been most impertinent to his commanding officer. 'Needs a haircut! and I shouldn't wonder if he drinks.'

Uncle Matthew said how-do-you-do and good-bye quite civilly to Lord Merlin. He really seemed to be mellowing with age and misfortune.

After great consultations it was decided that some member of the family, not Aunt Sadie or Uncle Matthew, would have to go to Hollywood and bring Jassy home. But who? Linda, of course, would have been the obvious person, had she not been under a cloud and, furthermore, engrossed with her own life. But it would be no use to send one bolter to fetch back another bolter, so somebody else must be found. In the end, after some persuasion ('madly inconvenient just now that I have started this course of *piqûres*') Davey consented to go with Louisa – the good, the sensible Louisa.

By the time this had been decided, Jassy had arrived in Hollywood, had broadcast her matrimonial intentions to all and sundry, and the whole thing appeared in the newspapers, which devoted pages of space to it, and (it was a silly season with nothing else to occupy their readers) turned it into a sort of serial story. Alconleigh now entered upon a state of siege. Journalists braved Uncle Matthew's stock-whips, his bloodhounds, his terrifying blue flashes, and hung around the village, penetrating even into the house itself in their search for local colour. Their stories were a daily delight. Uncle Matthew was made into something between Heathcliff, Dracula, and the Earl of Dorincourt, Alconleigh a sort of Nightmare Abbey or House of Usher, and Aunt Sadie a character not unlike David Copperfield's mother. Such courage, ingenuity, and toughness were displayed by these correspondents that it came as no surprise to any of us when, later on, they did so well in the war. 'War report by So-and-So –'

Uncle Matthew would then say:

'Isn't that the damned sewer I found hiding under my bed?'

He greatly enjoyed the whole affair. Here were opponents worthy of him, not jumpy housemaids, and lachrymose governesses with wounded feelings, but tough young men who did not care what methods they used so long as they could get inside his house and produce a story.

He also seemed greatly to enjoy reading about himself in the newspapers and we all began to suspect that Uncle Matthew had a hidden passion for publicity. Aunt Sadie, on the other hand, found the whole thing very distasteful indeed.

It was thought most vital to keep it from the press that Davey and Louisa were leaving on a voyage of rescue, as the sudden surprise of seeing them might prove an important element in influencing Jassy to return. Unfortunately, Davey could not embark on so long and so trying a journey without a medicine chest, specially designed. While this was being made they missed one boat, and, by the time it was ready, the sleuths were on their track – this unlucky medicine chest having played the same part that Marie Antoinette's *nécessaire* did in the escape to Varennes.

Several journalists accompanied them on the crossing, but did not reap much of a reward, as Louisa was prostrated with sea-sickness and Davey spent his whole time closeted with the ship's doctor, who asserted that his trouble was a cramped intestine, which could easily be cured by manipulation, rays, diet, exercises, and injections, all of which, or resting after which, occupied every moment of his day.

On their arrival in New York, however, they were nearly torn to pieces, and we were able, in common with the whole of the two great English-speaking nations, to follow their every move. They even appeared on the newsreel, looking worried and hiding their faces behind books.

It proved to have been a useless trip. Two days after their arrival in Hollywood Jassy became Mrs Cary Goon. Louisa telegraphed this news home, adding, 'Cary is a terrific Hon.'

There was one comfort, the marriage killed the story.

'He's a perfect dear,' said Davey, on his return. 'A little man like a nut. I'm sure Jassy will be madly happy with him.'

Aunt Sadie, however, was neither reassured nor consoled. It seemed hard luck to have reared a pretty love of a daughter in order for her to marry a little man like a nut, and live with him thousands of miles away. The house in London was cancelled, and the Alconleighs lapsed into such a state of gloom that the next blow, when it fell, was received with fatalism.

Matt, aged sixteen, ran away from Eton, also in a blaze of newspaper publicity, to the Spanish war. Aunt Sadie minded this very much, but I don't think Uncle Matthew did. The desire to fight seemed to him entirely natural, though, of course, he deplored the fact that Matt was fighting for foreigners. He did not take a particular line against the Spanish reds, they were brave boys and had had the good sense to bump off a lot of idolatrous monks, nuns, and priests, a proceeding of which he approved, but it was surely a pity to fight in a second-class war when there would so soon be a first-class one available. It was decided that no steps should be taken to retrieve Matt.

Christmas that year was a very sad one at Alconleigh. The children seemed to be melting away like the ten little nigger boys. Bob and Louisa, neither of whom had given their parents one moment of disquiet in their lives, John Fort William, as dull as a man could be, Louisa's children, so good, so pretty, but lacking in any sort of originality, could not make up for the absence of Linda, Matt, and Jassy, while Robin and Victoria, full as they were of jokes and fun, were swamped by the general atmosphere, and kept themselves to themselves as much as possible in the Hons' cupboard.

Linda was married in the Caxton Hall as soon as her divorce was through. The wedding was as different from her first as the Left-wing parties were different from the other kind. It was not exactly sad, but dismal, uncheerful, and with no feeling of happiness. Few of Linda's friends, and none of her relations except Davey and me were there; Lord Merlin sent two Aubusson rugs and some orchids but did not turn up himself. The pre-Christian chatters had faded out of Linda's life, discouraged, loudly bewailing the great loss she was in theirs.

Christian arrived late, and hurried in, followed by several comrades.

'I must say he is wonderful-looking,' Davey hissed in my ear, 'but oh, bother it all!'

There was no wedding breakfast, and, after a few moments of aimless and rather embarrassed hanging about in the street outside the hall, Linda and Christian went off home. Feeling provincial, up in London for the day and determined to see a little life, I made Davey give me luncheon at the Ritz. This had a still further depressing effect on my spirits. My clothes, so nice and suitable for the George, so much admired by the other dons' wives ('My dear, where did you get that lovely tweed?'), were, I now realized, almost bizarre in their dowdiness; it was the floating panels of taffeta all over again. I thought of those dear little black children, three of them now, in their nursery at home, and of dear Alfred in his study, but just for the moment this thought was no consolation. I passionately longed to have a tiny fur hat, or a tiny ostrich hat, like the two ladies at the next table. I longed for a neat black dress, diamond clips and a dark mink coat, shoes like surgical boots, long crinkly black suède gloves, and smooth polished hair. When I tried to explain all this to Davey, he remarked, absentmindedly:

'Oh, but it doesn't matter a bit for you, Fanny, and, after all, how can you have time for *les petits soins de la personne* with so many other, more important things to think of.'

I suppose he thought this would cheer me up.

Soon after her marriage the Alconleighs took Linda back into the fold. They did not count second weddings of divorced people, and Victoria had been severely reprimanded for saying that Linda was engaged to Christian.

'You can't be engaged when you're married.'

It was not the fact of the ceremony which had mollified them, in their eyes Linda would be living from now on in a state of adultery, but they felt the need of her too strongly to keep up a quarrel. The thin end of the wedge (luncheon with Aunt Sadie at Gunters) was inserted, and soon everything was all right again between them. Linda went quite often to Alconleigh, though she never took Christian there, feeling that it would benefit nobody were she to do so.

Linda and Christian lived in their house in Cheyne Walk, and, if Linda was not as happy as she had hoped to be, she exhibited, as usual, a wonderful shop-front. Christian was certainly very fond of her, and, in his way, he tried to be kind to her, but, as Lord Merlin had prophesied, he was much too detached to make any ordinary woman happy. He seemed, for weeks on end, hardly to be aware of her presence; at other times he would wander off and not reappear for days, too much engrossed in whatever he was doing to let her know where he was or when she might expect to see him again. He would eat and sleep where he happened to find himself – on a bench at St Pancras' station, or just sitting on the doorstep of some empty house. Cheyne Walk was always full of comrades, not chatting to Linda, but making speeches to each other, restlessly rushing about, telephoning, typewriting, drinking, quite often sleeping in their clothes, but without their boots, on Linda's drawing-room sofa.

Money troubles accrued. Christian, though he never appeared to spend any money, had a disconcerting way of scattering it. He had few, but expensive amusements, one of his favourites being to ring up the Nazi leaders in Berlin, and other European politicians, and have long teasing talks with them, costing pounds a minute. 'They can never resist a call from London,' he would say, nor, unfortunately, could they. At last, greatly to Linda's relief, the telephone was cut off, as the bill could not be paid.

I must say that Alfred and I both liked Christian very much. We are intellectual pinks ourselves, enthusiastic agreers with the *New Statesman*, so that his views, while rather more advanced than ours, had the same foundation of civilized humanity, and he seemed to us a great improvement on Tony. All the same, he was a hopeless husband for Linda. Her craving was for love, personal and particular, centred upon herself; wider love, for the poor, the sad, and the unattractive, had no appeal for her, though she honestly tried to believe that it had. The more I saw of Linda at this time, the more certain I felt that another bolt could not be very far ahead.

Twice a week Linda worked in a Red bookshop. It was run by a huge, perfectly silent comrade, called Boris. Boris liked to get drunk from Thursday afternoon, which was closing day in that district, to Monday morning, so Linda said she would take it over on Friday and Saturday. An extraordinary transformation would then occur. The books and tracts which mouldered there month after month, getting damper and dustier until at last they had to be thrown away, were hurried into the background, and their place taken by Linda's own few but well-loved favourites. Thus for *Whither British Airways?* was substituted *Round the World in Forty Days, Karl Marx, the Formative Years* was replaced by *The Making of a Marchioness,* and *The Giant of the Kremlin* by *Diary of a Nobody,* while *A Challenge to Coal-Owners* made way for *King Solomon's Mines.*

Hardly would Linda have arrived in the morning on her days there, and taken down the shutters, than the slummy little street would fill with motor-cars, headed by Lord Merlin's electric brougham. Lord Merlin did great propaganda for the shop, saying that Linda was the only person who had ever succeeded in finding him *Froggie's Little Brother* and *Le Père Goriot.* The chatters came back in force, delighted to find Linda so easily accessible again, and without Christian, but sometimes there were embarrassing moments when they came face to face with comrades. Then they would buy a book and beat a hasty retreat, all except Lord Merlin, who had never felt disconcerted in his life. He took a perfectly firm line with the comrades.

'How are you to-day?' he would say with great emphasis, and then glower furiously at them until they left the shop.

All this had an excellent effect upon the financial side of the business. Instead of showing, week by week, an enormous loss, to be refunded from one could guess where, it now became the only Red bookshop in England to make a profit. Boris was greatly praised by his employers, the shop received a medal, which was stuck upon the sign, and the comrades all said that Linda was a good girl and a credit to the Party.

The rest of her time was spent in keeping house for Christian and the comrades, an occupation which entailed trying to induce a series of maids to stay with them, and making sincere, but sadly futile, efforts to take their place when they had left, which they usually did at the end of the first week. The comrades were not very nice or very thoughtful to maids.

'You know, being a Conservative is much more restful,' Linda said to me once in a moment of confidence, when she was being unusually frank about her life, 'though one must remember that it is bad, not good. But it does take place within certain hours, and then finish, whereas Communism seems to eat up all one's life and energy. And the comrades are such Hons, but sometimes they make me awfully cross, just as Tony used to make one furious when he talked about the workers. I often feel rather the same when they talk about us – you see, just like Tony, they've got it all wrong. I'm all for them stringing up Sir Leicester, but if they started on Aunt Emily and Davey, or even on Fa, I don't think I could stand by and watch. I suppose one is neither fish, nor good red herring, that's the worst of it.'

'But there is a difference,' I said, 'between Sir Leicester and Uncle Matthew.'

'Well, that's what I'm always trying to explain. Sir Leicester grubs up his money in London, goodness knows how, but Fa gets it from his land, and he puts a great deal back into the land, not only money, but work. Look at all the things he does for no pay – all those boring meetings. County Council, J.P., and so on. And he's a good landlord, he takes trouble. You see, the comrades don't know the country – they didn't know you could get a lovely cottage with a huge garden for 25 6d a week until I told them, and then they hardly believed it. Christian knows, but he says the system is wrong, and I expect it is.'

'What exactly does Christian do?' I said.

'Oh, everything you can think of. Just at the moment he's writing a book on famine – goodness! it's sad – and there's a dear little Chinese comrade who comes and tells him what famine is like, you never saw such a fat man in your life.'

I laughed.

Linda said, hurriedly and guiltily:

'Well, I may seem to laugh at the comrades, but at least one does know they are doing good not harm, and not living on other people's slavery like Sir Leicester, and really you know I do simply love them, though I sometimes wish they were a little more fond of chatting, and not quite so sad and earnest and down on everybody.'

15

Early in 1939, the population of Catalonia streamed over the Pyrenees into the Roussillon, a poor and little-known province of France, which now, in a few days, found itself inhabited by more Spaniards than Frenchmen. Just as the lemmings suddenly pour themselves in a mass suicide off the coast of Norway, knowing neither whence they come nor whither bound, so great is the compulsion that hurls them into the Atlantic, thus half a million men, women, and children suddenly took flight into the bitter mountain weather, without pausing for thought. It was the greatest movement of population, in the time it took, that had ever hitherto been seen. Over the mountains they found no promised land; the French government, vacillating in its policy, neither turned them back with machine-guns at the frontier, nor welcomed them as brothers-in-arms against Fascism. It drove them like a herd of beasts down to the cruel salty marshes of that coast, enclosed them, like a herd of beasts, behind barbed-wire fences, and forgot all about them.

Christian, who had always, I think, had a half-guilty feeling about not having fought in Spain, immediately rushed off to Perpignan to see what was happening, and what, if anything, could be done. He wrote an endless series of reports, memoranda, articles, and private letters about the conditions he had found in the camps, and then settled down to work in an office financed by various English humanitarians with the object of improving the camps, putting refugee families in touch again, and getting as many as possible out of France. This office was run by a young man who had lived many years in Spain called Robert Parker. As soon as it became clear that there would not be, as at first was expected, an outbreak of typhus, Christian sent for Linda to join him in Perpignan.

It so happened that Linda had never before been abroad in her life. Tony had found all his pleasures, hunting, shooting, and golf, in England, and had grudged the extra days out of his holiday which would have been spent in travelling; while it would never have occurred to the Alconleighs to visit the Continent for any other purpose than that of fighting. Uncle Matthew's four years in France and Italy between 1914 and 1918 had given him no great opinion of foreigners.

'Frogs,' he would say, 'are slightly better than Huns or Wops, but abroad is unutterably bloody and foreigners are fiends.'

The bloodiness of abroad, the fiendishness of foreigners had, in fact, become such a tenet of the Radlett family creed that Linda set forth on her journey with no little trepidation. I went to see her off at Victoria, she was looking intensely English in her long blond mink coat, the *Tatler* under her arm, and Lord Merlin's morocco dressing-case, with a canvas cover, in her hand.

'I hope you have sent your jewels to the bank,' I said.

'Oh, darling, don't tease, you know how I haven't got any now. But my money,' she said with a self conscious giggle, 'is sewn into my stays. Fa rang up and begged me to, and I must say it did seem quite an idea. Oh, why aren't you coming? I do feel so terrified – think of sleeping in the train, all alone.'

'Perhaps you won't be alone,' I said. 'Foreigners are greatly given, I believe, to rape.'

'Yes, that would be nice, so long as they didn't find my stays. Oh, we are off – good-bye, darling, do think of me,' she said, and, clenching her suède-covered fist, she shook it out of the window in a Communist salute.

I must explain that I know everything that now happened to Linda, although I did not see her for another year, because afterwards, as will be shown, we spent a long quiet time together, during which she told it all to me, over and over again. It was her way of re-living happiness.

Of course the journey was an enchantment to her. The porters in their blue overalls, the loud, high conversations, of which, although she thought she knew French quite well, she did not understand a single word, the steamy, garlic-smelling heat of the French train, the delicious food, to which she was summoned by a little hurried bell, it was all from another world, like a dream.

She looked out of the window and saw chateaux, lime avenues, ponds, and villages exactly like those in the *Bibliothèque Rose* – she thought she must, at any moment, see Sophie in her white dress and unnaturally small black pumps cutting up goldfish, gorging herself on new bread and cream, or scratching the face of good, uncomplaining Paul. Her very stilted, very English French, got her across Paris and into the train for Perpignan without a hitch. Paris. She looked out of the window at the lighted dusky streets, and thought that never could any town have been so hauntingly beautiful.

A strange stray thought came into her head that, one day, she would come back here and be very happy, but she knew that it was not likely, Christian would never want to live in Paris. Happiness and Christian were still linked together in her mind at this time.

At Perpignan she found him in a whirl of business. Funds had been raised, a ship had been chartered, and plans were on foot for sending six thousand Spaniards out of the camps to Mexico. This entailed an enormous amount of staff work, as families (no Spaniard would think of moving without his entire family) had to be reunited from camps all over the place, assembled in a camp in Perpignan, and taken by train to the port of Cette, whence they finally embarked. The work was greatly complicated by the fact that Spanish husbands and wives do not share a surname. Christian explained all this to Linda almost before she was out of the train; he gave her an absent-minded peck on the forehead and rushed her to his office, hardly giving her time to deposit her luggage at an hotel on the way and scouting the idea that she might like a bath. He did not ask how she was or whether she had had a good journey – Christian always assumed that people were all right unless they told him to the contrary, when, except in the case of destitute, coloured, oppressed, leprous, or otherwise unattractive strangers, he would take absolutely no notice. He was really only interested in mass wretchedness, and never much cared for individual cases, however genuine their misery, while the idea that it is possible to have three square meals a day and a roof and yet be unhappy or unwell, seemed to him intolerable nonsense.

The office was a large shed with a yard round it. This yard was permanently full of refugees with mountains of luggage and quantities of children, dogs, donkeys, goats, and other appurtenances, who had just struggled over the mountains in their flight from Fascism, and were hoping that the English would be able to prevent them being put into camps. In certain cases they could be lent money, or given railway tickets enabling them to join relations in France and French Morocco, but the vast majority waited hours for an interview, only to be told that there was no hope for them. They would then, with great and heart-breaking politeness, apologize for having been a nuisance and withdraw. Spaniards have a highly developed sense of human dignity.

Linda was now introduced to Robert Parker and to Randolph Pine, a young writer who, having led a more or less playboy existence in the South of France, had gone to fight in Spain, and was now working in Perpignan from a certain feeling of responsibility towards those who had once been fellow soldiers. They seemed pleased that Linda had arrived, and were most friendly and welcoming, saying that it was nice to see a new face.

'You must give me some work to do,' said Linda.

'Yes, now what can we think of for you?' said Robert. 'There's masses of work, never fear, it's just a question of finding the right kind. Can you speak Spanish?'

'No.'

'Oh, well, you'll soon pick it up.'

'I'm quite sure I shan't,' said Linda doubtfully.

'What do you know about welfare work?'

'Oh, dear, how hopeless I seem to be. Nothing, I'm afraid.'

'Lavender will find her a job,' said Christian, who had settled down at his table and was flapping over a card index.

'Lavender?'

'A girl called Lavender Davis.'

'No! I know her quite well, she used to live near us in the country. In fact she was one of my bridesmaids.'

'That's it,' said Robert, 'she said she knew you, I'd forgotten. She's wonderful, she really works with the Quakers in the camps, but she helps us a great deal too. There's absolutely nothing she doesn't know about calories and babies' nappies, and expectant mummies, and so on, and she's the hardest worker I've ever come across.'

'I'll tell you,' said Randolph Pine, 'what you can do. There's a job simply waiting for you, and that is to arrange the accommodation on this ship that's going off next week.'

'Oh, yes, of course,' said Robert, 'the very thing. She can have this table and start at once.'

'Now look,' said Randolph. 'I'll show you. (What delicious scent you have, Après l'Ondée? I thought so.) Now here is a map of the ship – see – best cabins, not such good cabins, lousy cabins, and battened down under the hatches. And here is a list of the families who are going. All you have to do is to allocate each family its cabin – when you have decided which they are to have, you put the number of the cabin against the family – here – you see? And the number of the family on the cabin here, like that. Quite easy, but it takes time, and must be done so that when they arrive on the boat they will know exactly where to go with their things.'

'But how do I decide who gets the good ones and who is battened? Awfully tricky, isn't it?'

'Not really. The point is it's a strictly democratic ship run on republican principles, class doesn't enter into it. I should give decent cabins to families where there are small children or babies. Apart from that do it any way you like. Take a pin if you like. The only thing that matters is that it should be done, otherwise there'll be a wild scramble for the best places when they get on board.'

Linda looked at the list of families. It took the form of a card index, the head of each family having a card on which was written the number and names of his dependants.

'It doesn't give their ages,' said Linda. 'How am I to know if there are young babies?'

'That's a point,' said Robert. 'How is she to?'

'Quite easy,' said Christian. 'With Spaniards you can always tell. Before the war they were called either after saints or after episodes in the life of the Virgin – Anunciación, Asunción, Purificación, Concepción, Consuelo, etc. Since the Civil War they are called Carlos after Charlie Marx, Frederigo after Freddie Engels, or Estalina (very popular until the Russians let them down with a wallop), or else nice slogans like Solidaridad-Obrera, Libertad, and so on. Then you know the children are under three. Couldn't be simpler, really.'

Lavender Davis now appeared. She was indeed the same Lavender, dowdy, healthy, and plain, wearing an English country tweed and brogues. Her short brown hair curled over her head, and she had no make-up. She greeted Linda with enthusiasm, indeed, it had always been a fiction in the Davis family that Lavender and Linda were each other's greatest friends. Linda was delighted to see her, as one always is delighted to see a familiar face, abroad.

'Come on,' said Randolph, 'now we're all here let's go and have a drink at the Palmarium.'

For the next weeks, until her private life began to occupy Linda's attention, she lived in an atmosphere of alternate fascination and horror. She grew to love Perpignan, a strange little old town, so different from anything she had ever known, with its river and broad quays, its network of narrow streets, its huge wild-looking plane trees, and all around it the bleak vine-growing country of the Roussillon bursting into summery green under her very eyes. Spring came late and slowly, but when it came it was hand-in-hand with summer, and almost at once everything was baking and warm, and in the villages the people danced every night on concrete dancing floors under the plane trees. At week-ends the English, unable to eradicate such a national habit, shut up the office and made for Collioure on the coast, where they bathed and sunbathed and went for Pyrenean picnics.

But all this had nothing to do with the reason for their presence in these charming surroundings – the camps. Linda went to the camps nearly every day, and they filled her soul with despair. As she could not help much in the office owing to her lack of Spanish, nor with the children, since she knew nothing about calories, she was employed as a driver, and was always on the road in a Ford van full of supplies, or of refugees, or just taking messages to and from the camps. Often she had to sit and wait for hours on end while a certain man was found and his case dealt with; she would quickly be surrounded by a perfect concourse of men talking to her in their heavy guttural French. By this time the camps were quite decently organized; there were rows of orderly though depressing huts, and the men were getting regular meals, which, if not very appetizing, did at least keep body and soul together. But the sight of these thousands of human beings, young and healthy, herded behind wire away from their womenfolk, with nothing on earth to do day after dismal day, was a recurring torture to Linda. She began to think that Uncle Matthew had been right – that abroad, where such things could happen, was indeed un-utterably bloody, and that foreigners, who could inflict them upon each other, must be fiends.

One day as she sat in her van, the centre, as usual, of a crowd of Spaniards, a voice said:

'Linda, what on earth are you doing here?'

And it was Matt.

He looked ten years older than when she had last seen him, grown up, in fact, and extremely handsome, his Radlett eyes infinitely blue in a dark-brown face.

'I've seen you several times,' he said, 'and I thought you had been sent to fetch me away so I made off, but then I found out you are married to that Christian fellow. Was he the one you ran away from Tony with?'

'Yes,' said Linda. 'I'd no idea, Matt. I thought you'd have been sure to go back to England.'

'Well, no,' said Matt. 'I'm an officer, you see – must stay with the boys.'

'Does Mummy know you're all right?'

'Yes, I told her – at least if Christian posted a letter I gave him.'

'I don't suppose so – he's never been known to post a letter in his life. He is funny, he might have told me.'

'He didn't know – I sent it under cover to a friend of mine to forward. Didn't want any of the English to find out I was here, or they would start trying to get me home. I know.'

'Christian wouldn't,' said Linda. 'He's all for people doing what they want to in life. You're very thin, Matt, is there anything you'd like?'

'Yes,' said Matt, 'some cigarettes and a couple of thrillers.'

After this Linda saw him most days. She told Christian, who merely grunted and said: 'He'll have to be got out before the world war begins. I'll see to that,' and she wrote and told her parents. The result was a parcel of clothes from Aunt Sadie, which Matt refused to accept, and a packing-case full of vitamin pills from Davey, which Linda did not even dare to show him. He was cheerful and full of jokes and high spirits, but then there is a difference, as Christian said, between staying in a place because you are obliged to, and staying there because you think it right. But in any case, with the Radlett family, cheerfulness was never far below the surface.

The only other cheerful prospect was the ship. It was only going to rescue from hell a few thousand of the refugees, a mere fraction of the total amount, but, at any rate, they would be rescued, and taken to a better world, with happy and useful future prospects.

When she was not driving the van Linda worked hard over the cabin arrangements, and finally got the whole thing fixed and finished in time for the embarkation.

All the English except Linda went to Cette for the great day, taking with them two M.P.s and a duchess, who had helped the enterprise in London and had come out to see the fruit of their work. Linda went over by bus to Argelès to see Matt.

'How odd the Spanish upper classes must be,' she said, 'they don't raise a finger to help their own people, but leave it all to strangers like us.'

'You don't know Fascists,' Matt said, gloomily.

'I was thinking yesterday when I was taking the Duchess round Barcarès – yes, but why an English duchess, aren't there any Spanish ones, and, come to that, why is it nothing but English working in Perpignan? I knew several Spaniards in London, why don't they come and help a bit? They'd be awfully useful. I suppose they speak Spanish.'

'Fa was quite right about foreigners being fiends,' said Matt, 'upper-class ones are, at least. All these boys are terrific Hons, I must say.'

'Well, I can't see the English leaving each other in the lurch like this, even if they did belong to different parties. I think it's shameful.'

Christian and Robert came back from Cette in a cheerful mood. The arrangements had gone like clockwork, and a baby which had been born during the first half-hour on the ship was named Embarcación. It was the kind of joke Christian very much enjoyed. Robert said to Linda:

'Did you work on any special plan when you were arranging the cabins, or how did you do it?'

'Why? Wasn't it all right?'

'Perfect. Everybody had a place, and made for it. But I just wondered what you went by when you allocated the good cabins, that's all.'

'Well, I simply,' said Linda, 'gave the best cabins to the people who had *Labrador* on their card, because I used to have one when I was little and he was such a terrific . . . so sweet, you know.'

'Ah,' said Robert, gravely, 'all is now explained. *Labrador* in Spanish happens to mean labourer. So you see under your scheme (excellent by the way, most democratic) the farm hands all found themselves in luxury while the intellectuals were battened. That'll teach them not to be so clever. You did very well, Linda, we were all most grateful.'

'He was such a sweet Labrador,' said Linda dreamily. 'I wish you could have seen him. I do miss not having pets.'

'Can't think why you don't make an offer for the *sangsue*,' said Robert.

One of the features of Perpignan was a leech in a bottle in the window of a chemist's shop, with a typewritten notice saying: SI LA SANGSUE MONTE DANS LA BOUTEILLE IL FERA BEAU TEMPS. SI LA SANGSUE DESCEND – L'ORAGE.'

'It might be nice,' said Linda, 'but I can't somehow imagine her getting fond of one – too busy fussing about the weather all day, up and down, up and down – no time for human relationships.'

16

Linda never could remember afterwards whether she had really minded when she discovered that Christian was in love with Lavender Davis, and, if so, how much. She could not at all remember her emotions at that time. Certainly wounded pride must have played a part, though perhaps less so with Linda than it would have many women, as she did not suffer from much inferiority feeling. She must have seen that the past two years, her running away from Tony, all now went for nothing – but was she stricken at the heart, was she still in love with Christian, did she suffer the ordinary pangs of jealousy? I think not.

All the same, it was not a flattering choice. Lavender had seemed for years and years, stretching back into childhood, to epitomize everything that the Radletts considered most unromantic: a keen girl guide, hockey player, tree climber, head girl at her school, rider astride. She had never lived in a dream of love; the sentiment was, quite obviously, far removed from her thoughts, although Louisa and Linda, unable to imagine that anybody could exist without some tiny spark of it, used to invent romances for Lavender – the games mistress at her school or Dr Simpson of Merlinford (of whom Louisa had made up one of her nonsense rhymes – 'He's doctor and king's proctor too, and she's in love with him but he's in love with you'). Since those days she had trained as a nurse and as a welfare worker, had taken a course of law and political economy, and, indeed, might have done it all, Linda saw only too well, with the express intention of fitting herself to be a mate for Christian. The result was that in their present surroundings, with her calm assured confidence in her own ability, she easily outshone poor Linda. There was no competition, it was a walkover.

Linda did not discover their love in any vulgar way – surprising a kiss, or finding them in bed together. It was all far more subtle, more dangerous than that, being quite simply borne in upon her week after week that they found perfect happiness in each other, and that Christian depended entirely on Lavender for comfort and encouragement in his work. As this work now absorbed him heart and soul, as he thought of nothing else and never relaxed for a moment, dependence upon Lavender involved the absolute exclusion of Linda. She felt uncertain what to do. She could not have it out with Christian; there was nothing tangible to have out, and, in any case, such a proceeding would have been absolutely foreign to Linda's character. She dreaded scenes and rows more than anything else in the world, and she had no illusions about what Christian thought of her. She felt that he really rather despised her for having left Tony and her child so easily, and that, in his opinion, she took a silly, light-hearted, and superficial view of life. He liked serious, educated women, especially those who had made a study of welfare, especially Lavender. She had no desire to hear all this said. On the other hand she began to think that it would be as well for her to get away from Perpignan herself before Christian and Lavender went off together, as it seemed to her most probable that they would, wandering off hand in hand to search for and relieve other forms of human misery. Already she felt embarrassed when she was with Robert and Randolph, who were obviously very sorry for her and were always making little manoeuvres to prevent her noticing that Christian was spending every minute of the day with Lavender.

One afternoon, looking idly out of the window of her hotel bedroom, she saw them walking up the Quai Sadi Carnot together, completely absorbed, utterly contented in each other's company, radiating happiness. Linda was seized by an impulse and acted on it. She packed her things, wrote a hasty letter to Christian saying that she was leaving him for good, as she realized that their marriage had been a failure. She asked him to look after Matt. She then burnt her boats by adding a post-script (a fatal feminine practice), 'I think you had much better marry Lavender'. She bundled herself and her luggage into a taxi and took the night train for Paris.

The journey this time was horrible. She was, after all, very fond of Christian, and as soon as the train had left the station, she began to ask herself whether she had not in fact behaved stupidly and badly. He probably had a passing fancy for Lavender, based on common interests, which would fade away as soon as he got back to London. Possibly it was not even that, but simply that he was obliged, for his work, to be with Lavender all the time. His absent-minded treatment of Linda was, after all, nothing new, it had begun almost as soon as he had got her under his roof. She began to feel that she had done wrong to write that letter.

She had her return ticket, but very little money indeed, just enough, she reckoned, for dinner on the train and some food for the next day. Linda always had to translate French money into pounds, shillings, and pence before she knew where she was with it. She seemed to have about 18s 6d with her, so there could be no question of a sleeper. She had never sat up all night in a train, and the experience appalled her; it was like some dreadful feverish illness, when the painful hours drag by, each one longer than a week. Her thoughts brought her no comfort. She had torn up her life of the past two years, all that she had tried to put into her relationship with Christian, and thrown it away like so much waste-paper. If this was to be the outcome why had she ever left Tony, her real husband for better for worse, and her child? That was where her duty had lain, and well she knew it. She thought of my mother and shuddered. Could it be that she, Linda, was from now on doomed to a life that she utterly despised, that of a bolter?

And in London what would she find? A little empty, dusty house. Perhaps, she thought, Christian would pursue her, come and insist that she belonged to him. But in her heart she knew that he would not, and that she did not, and that this was the end. Christian believed too sincerely that people must be allowed to do as they wish in life, without interference. He was fond of Linda, she knew, but disappointed in her, she also knew; he would not himself have made the first move to separate, but would not much regret the fact that she had done so. Soon he would have some new scheme in his head, some new plan for suffering mortals, any mortals, anywhere, so long as there were enough of them and their misery was great. Then he would forget Linda, and possibly also Lavender, as if they had never been. Christian was not in passionate quest of love, he had other interests, other aims, and it mattered very little to him what woman happened to be in his life at a given moment. But in his nature, she knew, there was a certain ruthlessness. She felt that he would not forgive what she had done, or try to persuade her to go back on it, nor, indeed, was there any reason why he should do so.

It could not be said, thought Linda, as the train pursued its way through the blackness, that her life so far had been a marked success. She had found neither great love nor great happiness, and she had not inspired them in others. Parting with her would have been no death blow to either of her husbands; on the contrary, they would both have turned with relief to a much preferred mistress, who was more suited to them in every way. Whatever quality it is that can hold indefinitely the love and affection of a man she plainly did not possess, and now she was doomed to the lonely, hunted life of a beautiful but unattached woman. Where now was love that would last to the grave and far beyond? What had she done with her youth? Tears for her lost hopes and ideals, tears of self-pity in fact, began to pour down her cheeks. The three fat Frenchmen who shared the carriage with her were in a snoring sleep, she wept alone.

Sad and tired as Linda was, she could not but perceive the beauty of Paris that summer morning as she drove across it to the Gare du Nord. Paris in the early morning has a cheerful, bustling aspect, a promise of delicious things to come, a positive smell of coffee and croissants, quite peculiar to itself.

The people welcome a new day as if they were certain of liking it, the shopkeepers pull up their blinds serene in the expectation of good trade, the workers go happily to their work, the people who have sat up all night in night clubs go happily to their rest, the orchestra of motor-car horns, of clanking trams, of whistling policemen tunes up for the daily symphony, and everywhere is joy. This joy, this life, this beauty did not underline poor Linda's fatigue and sadness, she felt it but was not of it. She turned her thoughts to old familiar London, she longed above all for her own bed, feeling as does a wounded beast when it crawls home to its lair. She only wanted to sleep undisturbed in her own bedroom.

But when she presented her return ticket at the Gare du Nord she was told, furiously, loudly, and unsympathetically, that it had expired.

'Voyons, madame – le 29 Mai. C'est aujourd'hui le 30, n'est-ce pas? Donc – !' Tremendous shruggings.

Linda was paralysed with horror. Her 18s 6d was by now down to 6s 3d, hardly enough for a meal. She knew nobody in Paris, she had absolutely no idea what she ought to do, she was too tired and too hungry to think clearly. She stood like a statue of despair. Her porter, tired of waiting beside a statue of despair, deposited the luggage at its feet and went grumbling off. Linda sank onto her suitcase and began to cry; nothing so dreadful had ever happened to her before. She cried bitterly, she could not stop. People passed to and fro as if weeping ladies were the most ordinary phenomenon at the Gare du Nord. 'Fiends! fiends!' she sobbed. Why had she not listened to her father, why had she ever come to this bloody abroad? Who would help her? In London there was a society, she knew, which looked after ladies stranded at railway stations; here, more likely, there would be one for shipping them off to South America. At any moment now somebody, some genial-looking old woman might come up and give her an injection, after which she would disappear for ever.

She became aware that somebody was standing beside her, not an old lady, but a short, stocky, very dark Frenchman in a black Homburg hat. He was laughing. Linda took no notice, but went on crying. The more she cried the more he laughed. Her tears were tears of rage now, no longer of self-pity.

At last she said, in a voice which was meant to be angrily impressive, but which squeaked and shook through her handkerchief:

'Allez-vous en.'

For answer he took her hand and pulled her to her feet.

'Bonjour, bonjour,' he said.

'Voulez-vous vous en aller?' said Linda, rather more doubtfully, here at least was a human being who showed signs of taking some interest in her. Then she thought of South America.

'Il faut expliquer que je ne suis pas,' she said, 'une esclave blanche. Je suis la fille d'un très important lord anglais.'

The Frenchman gave a great bellow of laughter.

'One does not,' he said in the early perfect English of somebody who has spoken it from a child, 'have to be Sherlock Holmes to guess that.'

Linda was rather annoyed. An Englishwoman abroad may be proud of her nationality and her virtue without wishing them to jump so conclusively to the eye.

'French ladies,' he went on, 'covered with les marques extérieurs de la richesse never never sit crying on their suitcases at the Gare du Nord in the very early morning, while esclaves blanches always have protectors, and it is only too clear that you are unprotected just now.'

This sounded all right, and Linda was mollified.

'Now,' he said, 'I invite you to luncheon with me, but first you must have a bath and rest and a cold compress on your face.'

He picked up her luggage and walked to a taxi.

'Get in, please.'

Linda got in. She was far from certain that this was not the road to Buenos Aires, but something made her do as he said. Her powers of resistance were at an end, and she really saw no alternative.

'Hotel Montalembert,' he told the taxi man. 'Rue du Bac. Je m'excuse, madame, for not taking you to the Ritz, but I have a feeling for the Hotel Montalembert just now, that it will suit your mood this morning.'

Linda sat upright in her corner of the taxi, looking, she hoped, very prim. As she could not think of anything pertinent to say she remained silent. Her companion hummed a little tune, and seemed vastly amused. When they arrived at the hotel, he took a room for her, told the liftman to show her to it, told the *concierge* to send her up a *café complet*, kissed her hand, and said:

'*A tout à l'heure* – I will fetch you a little before one o'clock and we will go out to luncheon.'

Linda had her bath and breakfast and got into bed. When the telephone bell rang she was so sound asleep that it was a struggle to wake up.

'*Un monsieur qui demande, madame.*'

'*Je descends tout de suite,*' said Linda, but it took her quite half an hour to get ready.

17

'Ah! You keep me waiting,' he said, kissing her hand, or at least making a gesture of raising her hand towards his lips and then dropping it rather suddenly. 'That is a very good sign.'

'Sign of what?' said Linda. He had a two-seater outside the hotel and she got into it. She was feeling more like herself again.

'Oh, of this and that,' he said, letting in the clutch, 'a good augury for our affair, that it will be happy and last long.'

Linda became intensely stiff, English, and embarrassed, and said, self-consciously:

'We are not having an affair.'

'My name is Fabrice – may one ask yours?'

'Linda.'

'Linda. *Comme c'est joli.* With me, it usually lasts five years.'

He drove to a restaurant where they were shown, with some deference, to a table in a red plush corner. He ordered the luncheon and the wine in rapid French, the sort of French that Linda frankly could not follow, then, putting his hands on his knees, he turned to her and said:

'*Allons, racontez, madame.*'

'*Racontez* what?'

'Well, but of course, the story. Who was it that left you to cry on that suitcase?'

'He didn't. I left him. It was my second husband and I have left him for ever because he has fallen in love with another woman – a welfare worker, not that you'd know what that is, because I'm sure they don't exist in France. It just makes it worse, that's all.'

'What a very curious reason for leaving one's second husband. Surely with your experience of husbands you must have noticed that falling in love with other women is one of the things they do?

However, it's an ill wind, and I don't complain. But why the suit-case? Why didn't you put yourself in the train and go back to Monsieur the important lord, your father?'

'That's what I was doing until they told me that my return ticket had expired. I only had 6s 3d, and I don't know anybody in Paris, and I was awfully tired, so I cried.'

'The second husband – why not borrow some money from him? Or had you left a note on his pillow – women never can resist these little essays in literature, and they do make it rather embarrassing to go back, I know.'

'Well, anyhow he's in Perpignan, so I couldn't have.'

'Ah, you come from Perpignan. And what were you doing there, in the name of heaven?'

'In the name of heaven we were trying to stop you frogs from teasing the poor Epagnards,' said Linda with some spirit.

'E-spa-gnols! So we are teasing them, are we?'

'Not so badly now – terribly at the beginning.'

'What were we supposed to do with them? We never invited them to come, you know.'

'You drove them into camps in that cruel wind, and gave them no shelter for weeks. Hundreds died.'

'It is quite a job to provide shelter, at a moment's notice, for half a million people. We did what we could – we fed them – the fact is that most of them are still alive.'

'Still herded in camps.'

'My dear Linda, you could hardly expect us to turn them loose on the countryside with no money – what would be the result? Do use your common sense.'

'You should mobilize them to fight in the war against Fascism that's coming any day now.'

'Talk about what you know and you won't get so angry. We haven't enough equipment for our own soldiers in the war against Germany that's coming – not any day, but after the harvest, prob-ably in August. Now go on telling me about your husbands. It's so very much more interesting.'

'Only two. My first was a Conservative, and my second is a Communist.'

'Just as I guessed, your first is rich, your second is poor. I could see you once had a rich husband, the dressing-case and the fur coat, though it is a hideous colour, and no doubt, as far as one could see, with it bundled over your arm, a hideous shape. Still, *vison* usually betokens a rich husband somewhere. Then this dreadful linen suit you are wearing has ready-made written all over it.'

'You are rude, it's a very pretty suit.'

'And last year's. Jackets are getting longer you will find. I'll get you some clothes – if you were well dressed you would be quite good-looking, though it's true your eyes are small. Blue, a good colour, but small.'

'In England,' said Linda, 'I am considered a beauty.'

'Well, you have points.'

So this silly conversation went on and on, but it was only froth on the surface. Linda was feeling, what she had never so far felt for any man, an overwhelming physical attraction. It made her quite giddy, it terrified her. She could see that Fabrice was perfectly certain of the outcome, so was she perfectly certain, and that was what frightened her. How could she, Linda, with the horror and contempt she had always felt for casual affairs, allow herself to be picked up by any stray foreigner, and, having seen him only for an hour, long and long and long to be in bed with him? He was not even good-looking, he was exactly like dozens of other dark men in Homburgs that can be seen in the streets of any French town. But there was something about the way he looked at her which seemed to be depriving her of all balance. She was profoundly shocked, and, at the same time, intensely excited.

After luncheon they strolled out of the restaurant into brilliant sunshine.

'Come and see my flat,' said Fabrice.

'I would rather see Paris,' said Linda.

'Do you know Paris well?'

'I've never been here before in my life.'

Fabrice was really startled.

'Never been here before?' He could not believe it. 'What a pleasure for me, to show it all to you. There is so much to show, it will take weeks.'

'Unfortunately,' said Linda, 'I leave for England to-morrow.'

'Yes, of course. Then we must see it all this afternoon.'

They drove slowly round a few streets and squares, and then went for a stroll in the Bois. Linda could not believe that she had only just arrived there, that this was still the very day which she had seen unfolding itself, so full of promise, through her mist of morning tears.

'How fortunate you are to live in such a town,' she said to Fabrice. 'It would be impossible to be very unhappy here.'

'Not impossible,' he said. 'One's emotions are intensified in Paris – one can be more happy and also more unhappy here than in any other place. But it is always a positive source of joy to live here, and there is nobody so miserable as a Parisian in exile from his town. The rest of the world seems unbearably cold and bleak to us, hardly worth living in.' He spoke with great feeling.

After tea, which they had out of doors in the Bois, he drove slowly back into Paris. He stopped the car outside an old house in the Rue Bonaparte, and said, again:

'Come and see my flat.'

'No, no,' said Linda. 'The time has now come for me to point out that I am *une femme sérieuse*.'

Fabrice gave his great bellow of laughter.

'Oh,' he said, shaking helplessly, 'how funny you are. What a phrase, *femme sérieuse*, where did you find it? And if so serious, how do you explain the second husband?'

'Yes, I admit that I did wrong, very wrong indeed, and made a great mistake. But that is no reason for losing control, for sliding down the hill altogether, for being picked up by strange gentlemen at the Gare du Nord and then immediately going with them to see their flat. And please, if you will be so kind as to lend me some money, I want to catch the London train to-morrow morning.'

'Of course, by all means,' said Fabrice.

He thrust a roll of banknotes into her hand, and drove her to the Hotel Montalembert. He seemed quite unmoved by her speech, and announced he would come back at eight o'clock to take her out to dinner.

Linda's bedroom was full of roses, it reminded her of when Moira was born.

'Really,' she thought with a giggle, 'this is a very penny-novelettish seduction, how can I be taken in by it?'

But she was filled with a strange, wild, unfamiliar happiness, and knew that this was love. Twice in her life she had mistaken something else for it; it was like seeing somebody in the street who you think is a friend, you whistle and wave and run after him, and it is not only not the friend, but not even very like him. A few minutes later the real friend appears in view, and then you can't imagine how you ever mistook that other person for him. Linda was now looking upon the authentic face of love, and she knew it, but it frightened her. That it should come so casually, so much by a series of accidents, was frightening. She tried to remember how she had felt when she had first loved her two husbands. There must have been strong and impelling emotion; in both cases she had disrupted her own life, upset her parents and friends remorselessly, in order to marry them, but she could not recall it. Only she knew that never before, not even in dreams, and she was a great dreamer of love, had she felt anything remotely like this. She told herself, over and over again, that to-morrow she must go back to London, but she had no intention of going back, and she knew it.

Fabrice took her out to dinner and then to a night club, where they did not dance, but chatted endlessly. She told him about Uncle Matthew, Aunt Sadie and Louisa and Jassy and Matt, and he could not hear enough, and egged her on to excesses of exaggeration about her family and all their various idiosyncrasies.

'*Et* Jassy – *et* Matt – *alors, racontez.*'

And she recounted, for hours.

In the taxi on their way home she refused again to go back with him or to let him come into the hotel with her. He did not insist, he did not try to hold her hand, or touch her at all. He merely said:

'*C'est une résistance magnifique, je vous félicite de tout mon cœur, madame.*'

Outside the hotel she gave him her hand to say good night. He took it in both of his and really kissed it.

'*A demain,*' he said, and got into the taxi.

'*Allô – allô.*'

'Hullo.'

'Good morning. Are you having breakfast?'

'Yes.'

'I thought I heard a coffee-cup clattering. Is it good?'

'It's so delicious that I have to keep stopping, for fear of finishing it too quickly. Are you having yours?'

'Had it. I must tell you that I like very long conversations in the morning, and I shall expect you to *raconter des histoires.*'

'Like Schéhérazade?'

'Yes, just like. And you're not to get that note in your voice of "now I'm going to ring off"', as English people always do.'

'What English people do you know?'

'I know some. I was at school in England, and at Oxford.'

'No! When?'

'1920.'

'When I was nine. Fancy, perhaps I saw you in the street – we used to do all our shopping in Oxford.'

'Elliston & Cavell?'

'Oh, yes, and Webbers.'

There was a silence.

'Go on,' he said.

'Go on, what?'

'I mean don't ring off. Go on telling.'

'I shan't ring off. As a matter of fact I adore chatting. It's my favourite thing, and I expect you will want to ring off ages before I do.'

They had a long and very silly conversation, and, at the end of it, Fabrice said:

'Now get up, and in an hour I will fetch you and we will go to Versailles.'

At Versailles, which was an enchantment to Linda, she was reminded of a story she had once read about two English ladies who had seen the ghost of Marie Antoinette sitting in her garden at the Little Trianon. Fabrice found this intensely boring, and said so.

'Histoires,' he said, 'are only of interest when they are true, or when you have made them up specially to amuse me. Histoires de revenants, made up by some dim old English virgins, are neither true nor interesting. Donc plus d'histoires de revenants, madame, s'il vous plaît.'

'All right,' said Linda, crossly. 'I'm doing my best to please – you tell me a story.'

'Yes, I will – and this story is true. My grandmother was very beautiful and had many lovers all her life, even when she was quite old. A short time before she died she was in Venice with my mother, her daughter, and one day, floating up some canal in their gondola, they saw a little palazzo of pink marble, very exquisite. They stopped the gondola to look at it, and my mother said: "I don't believe anybody lives there, what about trying to see the inside?"

'So they rang the bell, and an old servant came and said that nobody had lived there for many, many years, and he would show it to them if they liked. So they went in and upstairs to the salone, which had three windows looking over the canal and was decorated with fifteenth-century plaster work, white on a pale blue background. It was a perfect room. My grandmother seemed strangely moved, and stood for a long time in silence. At last she said to my mother:

'"If, in the third drawer of that bureau there is a filigree box containing a small gold key on a black velvet ribbon, this house belongs to me."

'And my mother looked, and there was, and it did. One of my grandmother's lovers had given it to her years and years before, when she was quite young, and she had forgotten all about it.'

'Goodness,' said Linda, 'what fascinating lives you foreigners do lead.'

'And it belongs to me now.'

He put up his hand to Linda's forehead and stroked back a strand of hair which was loose:

'And I would take you there to-morrow if –'

'If what?'

'One must wait here now, you see, for the war.'

'Oh, I keep forgetting the war,' said Linda.

'Yes, let's forget it. *Comme vous êtes mal coiffée, ma chère.*'

'If you don't like my clothes and don't like my hair and think my eyes are so small, I don't know what you see in me.'

'*Quand même j'avoue qu'il y a quelquechose,*' said Fabrice.

Again they dined together.

Linda said: 'Haven't you any other engagements?'

'Yes, of course. I have cancelled them.'

'Who are your friends?'

'*Les gens du monde.* And yours?'

'When I was married to Tony, that is, my first husband, I used to go out in the *monde*, it was my life. In those days I loved it. But then Christian didn't approve of it, he stopped me going to parties and frightened away my friends, whom he considered frivolous and idiotic, and we saw nothing but serious people trying to put the world right. I used to laugh at them, and rather long for my other friends, but now I don't know. Since I was at Perpignan perhaps I have become more serious myself.'

'Everybody is getting more serious, that's the way things are going. But, whatever one may be in politics, right, left, Fascist,

Communist, *les gens du monde* are the only possible ones for friends. You see, they have made a fine art of personal relationships and of all that pertains to them – manners, clothes, beautiful houses, good food, everything that makes life agreeable. It would be silly not to take advantage of that. Friendship is something to be built up carefully, by people with leisure, it is an art, nature does not enter into it. You should never despise social life – *de la haute société* – I mean, it can be a very satisfying one, entirely artificial of course, but absorbing. Apart from the life of the intellect and the contemplative religious life, which few people are qualified to enjoy, what else is there to distinguish man from the animals but his social life? And who understand it so well and who can make it so smooth and so amusing as *les gens du monde*? But one cannot have it at the same time as a love affair, one must be whole-hearted to enjoy it, so I have cancelled all my engagements.'

'What a pity,' said Linda, 'because I'm going back to London to-morrow morning.'

'Ah yes, I had forgotten. What a pity.'

'Allô – allô'

'Hullo.'

'Were you asleep?'

'Yes, of course. What's the time?'

'About two. Shall I come round and see you?'

'Do you mean now?'

'Yes.'

'I must say it would be very nice, but the only thing is, what would the night porter think?'

'*Ma chère*, how English you are. *Eh bien; je vais vous le dire – il ne se fera aucune illusion.*'

'No, I suppose not.'

'But I don't imagine he's under any illusion as it is. After all, I come here for you three times every day – you've seen nobody else, and French people are quite quick at noticing these things, you know.'

'Yes – I see –'
'Alors, c'est entendu – à tout à l'heure.'

The next day Fabrice installed her in a flat, he said it was *plus commode*. He said, 'When I was young I liked to be very romantic and run all kinds of risks. I used to hide in wardrobes, be brought into the house in a trunk, disguise myself as a footman, and climb in at the windows. How I used to climb! I remember once, half-way up a creeper there was a wasps' nest – oh the agony – I wore a Kestos *soutien-gorge* for a week afterwards. But now I prefer to be comfortable, to follow a certain routine, and have my own key.'

Indeed, Linda thought, nobody could be less romantic and more practical than Fabrice, no nonsense about him. A little nonsense, she thought, would have been rather nice.

It was a beautiful flat, large and sunny, and decorated in the most expensive kind of modern taste. It faced south and west over the Bois de Boulogne, and was on a level with the tree-tops. Tree-tops and sky made up the view. The enormous windows worked like the windows of a motor-car, the whole of the glass disappearing into the wall. This was a great joy to Linda, who loved the open air and loved to sunbathe for hours with no clothes on, until she was hot and brown and sleepy and happy. Belonging to the flat, belonging, it was evident, to Fabrice, was a charming elderly *femme de ménage* called Germaine. She was assisted by various other elderly women who came and went in a bewildering succession. She was obviously most efficient, she had all Linda's things out of her suitcase, ironed and folded away, in a moment, and then went off to the kitchen, where she began to prepare dinner. Linda could not help wondering how many other people Fabrice had kept in this flat; however, as she was unlikely to find out, and, indeed, had no wish to know, she put the thought from her. There was no trace of any former occupant, not so much as a scribbled telephone number or the mark of a lipstick anywhere to be seen; the flat might have been done up yesterday.

In her bath, before dinner, Linda thought rather wistfully of Aunt Sadie. She, Linda, was now a kept woman and an adulteress, and Aunt Sadie, she knew, wouldn't like that. She hadn't liked it when Linda had committed adultery with Christian, but he, at least, was English, and Linda had been properly introduced to him and knew his surname. Also, Christian had all along intended to marry her. But how much less would Aunt Sadie like her daughter to pick up an unknown, nameless foreigner and go off to live with him in luxury. It was a long step from lunching in Oxford to this, though Uncle Matthew would, no doubt, have considered it a step down the same road if he knew her situation, and he would disown her for ever, throw her out into the snow, shoot Fabrice, or take any other violent action which might occur to him. Then something would happen to make him laugh, and all would be well again. Aunt Sadie was a different matter. She would not say very much, but she would brood over it and take it to heart, and wonder if there had not been something wrong about her method of bringing up Linda which had led to this; Linda most profoundly hoped that she would never find out.

In the middle of this reverie the telephone bell rang. Germaine answered it, tapped on the bathroom door, and said:

'M. le duc sera légèrement en retard, madame.'

'All right – thank you,' said Linda.

At dinner she said:

'Could one know your name?'

'Oh,' said Fabrice. 'Hadn't you discovered that? What an extraordinary lack of curiosity. My name is Sauveterre. In short, madame, I am happy to tell you that I am a very rich duke, a most agreeable thing to be, even in these days.'

'How lovely for you. And, while we are on the subject of your private life, are you married?'

'No.'

'Why not?'

'My fiancée died.'

'Oh, how sad – what was she like?'

'Very pretty.'

'Prettier than me?'

'Much prettier. Very correct.'

'More correct than me?'

'*Vous – vous êtes une folle, madame, aucune correction. Et elle était gentille – mais d'une gentillesse, la pauvre.*'

For the first time since she knew him, Fabrice had become infinitely sentimental, and Linda was suddenly shaken by the pangs of a terrible jealousy, so terrible that she felt quite faint. If she had not already recognized the fact, she would have known now, for certain and always, that this was to be the great love of her life.

'Five years,' she said, 'is quite a long time when it's all in front of you.'

But Fabrice was still thinking of the fiancée.

'She died much more than five years ago – fifteen years in the autumn. I always go and put late roses on her grave, those little tight roses with very dark green leaves that never open properly – they remind me of her. *Dieu, que c'est triste.*'

'And what was her name?' said Linda.

'Louise. *Enfant unique du dernier Rancé.* I often go and see her mother, who is still alive, a remarkable old woman. She was brought up in England at the court of the Empress Eugénie, and Rancé married her in spite of that, for love. You can imagine how strange everybody found it.'

A deep melancholy settled on them both. Linda saw too clearly that she could not hope to compete with a fiancée who was not only prettier and more correct than she was, but also dead. It seemed most unfair. Had she remained alive her prettiness would surely, after fifteen years of marriage, have faded away, her correctness have become a bore; dead, she was embalmed for ever in her youth, her beauty, and her *gentillesse*.

After dinner, however, Linda was restored to happiness. Being made love to by Fabrice was an intoxication, quite different from anything she had hitherto experienced.

('I was forced to the conclusion,' she said, when telling me about this time, 'that neither Tony nor Christian had an inkling of what we used to call the facts of life. But I suppose all Englishmen are hopeless as lovers.'

'Not all,' I said, 'the trouble with most of them is that their minds are not on it, and it happens to require a very great deal of application. Alfred,' I told her, 'is wonderful.'

'Oh, good,' she said, but she sounded unconvinced I thought.)

They sat until late looking out of the open window. It was a hot evening, and, when the sun had gone, a green light lingered behind the black bunches of the trees until complete darkness fell.

'Do you always laugh when you make love?' said Fabrice.

'I hadn't thought about it, but I suppose I do. I generally laugh when I'm happy and cry when I'm not, I am a simple character, you know. Do you find it odd?'

'Very disconcerting at first, I must say.'

'But why – don't most women laugh?'

'Indeed they do not. More often they cry.'

'How extraordinary – don't they enjoy it?'

'It is nothing to do with enjoyment. If they are young they call on their mothers, if they are religious they call on the Virgin to forgive them. But I have never known one who laughed except you. *Mais qu'est-ce que vous voulez, vous êtes une folle.*'

Linda was fascinated.

'What else do they do?'

'What they all do, except you, is to say: "*Comme vous devez me mépriser.*"'

'But why should you despise them?'

'Oh, really, my dear, one does, that's all.'

'Well, I call that most unfair. First you seduce them, then you despise them, poor things. What a monster you are.'

'They like it. They like grovelling about and saying "*Qu'est-ce que j'ai fait? Mon Dieu, hélas Fabrice, que pouvez-vous bien penser de moi? O, que j'ai honte.*" It's all part of the thing to them. But you,

you seem unaware of your shame, you just roar with laughter. It is very strange. *Pas désagréable, il faut avouer.*'

'Then what about the fiancée,' said Linda, 'didn't you despise her?'

'*Mais non, voyons*, of course not. She was a virtuous woman.'

'Do you mean to say you never went to bed with her?'

'Never. Never would such a thing have crossed my mind in a thousand thousand years.'

'Goodness,' said Linda. 'In England we always do.'

'*Ma chère, c'est bien connu, le côté animal des anglais*. The English are a drunken and an incontinent race, it is well known.'

'They don't know it. They think it's foreigners who are all those things.'

'French women are the most virtuous in the world,' said Fabrice, in the tones of exaggerated pride with which Frenchmen always talk about their women.

'Oh, dear,' said Linda, sadly. 'I was so virtuous once. I wonder what happened to me. I went wrong when I married my first husband, but how was I to know? I thought he was a god and that I should love him for ever. Then I went wrong again when I ran away with Christian, but I thought I loved him, and I did too, much much more than Tony, but he never really loved me, and very soon I bored him, I wasn't serious enough, I suppose. Anyhow, if I hadn't done these things, I shouldn't have ended up on a suitcase at the Gare du Nord and I would never have met you, so, really, I'm glad. And in my next life, wherever I happen to be born, I must remember to fly to the boulevards as soon as I'm of marriageable age, and find a husband there.'

'*Comme c'est gentil*,' said Fabrice, '*et, en effet*, French marriages are generally very very happy you know. My father and mother had a cloudless life together, they loved each other so much that they hardly went out in society at all. My mother still lives in a sort of afterglow of happiness from it. What a good woman she is!'

'I must tell you,' Linda went on, 'that my mother and one of my aunts, one of my sisters and my cousin, are virtuous women, so virtue is not unknown in my family. And anyway, Fabrice, what about your grandmother?'

'Yes,' said Fabrice, with a sigh. 'I admit that she was a great sinner. But she was also *une très grande dame*, and she died fully redeemed by the rites of the Church.'

18

Their life now began to acquire a routine. Fabrice dined with her every night in the flat – he never took her out to a restaurant again – and stayed with her until seven o'clock the following morning. '*J'ai horreur de coucher seul,*' he said. At seven he would get up, dress, and go home, in time to be in his bed at eight o'clock, when his breakfast was brought in. He would have his breakfast, read the newspapers, and, at nine, ring up Linda and talk nonsense for half an hour, as though he had not seen her for days.

'Go on,' he would say, if she showed any signs of flagging. '*Allons, des histoires!*'

During the day she hardly saw him. He always lunched with his mother, who had the first-floor flat in the house where he lived on the ground floor. Sometimes he took Linda sight-seeing in the afternoon, but generally he did not appear until about half-past seven, soon after which they dined.

Linda occupied her days buying clothes, which she paid for with great wads of banknotes given her by Fabrice.

'Might as well be hanged for a sheep as a lamb,' she thought. 'And as he despises me anyway it can't make very much difference.'

Fabrice was delighted. He took an intense interest in her clothes, looked them up and down, made her parade round her drawing-room in them, forced her to take them back to the shops for alterations which seemed to her quite unnecessary, but which proved in the end to have made all the difference. Linda had never before fully realized the superiority of French clothes to English. In London she had been considered exceptionally well dressed, when she was married to Tony; she now realized that never could she have had, by French standards, the smallest pretensions to *chic*. The things she had with her seemed to her so appallingly dowdy, so skimpy and miserable and without line, that she went to the Galeries Lafayette and bought herself a ready-made dress there before she dared to venture into the big houses. When she did finally emerge from them with a few clothes, Fabrice advised her to get a great many more. Her taste, he said, was not at all bad, for an English-woman, though he doubted whether she would really become *élégante* in the true sense of the word.

'Only by trial and error,' he said, 'can you find out your *genre*, can you see where you are going. *Continuez, donc, ma chère, allez-y. Jusqu'à présent, ça ne va pas mal du tout.*'

The weather now became hot and sultry, holiday, seaside weather. But this was 1939, and men's thoughts were not of relaxation but of death, not of bathing-suits but of uniforms, not of dance music but of trumpets, while beaches for the next few years were to be battle and not pleasure grounds. Fabrice said every day how much he longed to take Linda to the Riviera, to Venice and to his beautiful chateau in the Dauphiné. But he was a reservist, and would be called up any day now. Linda did not mind staying in Paris at all. She could sunbathe in her flat as much as she wanted to. She felt no particular apprehensions about the coming war, she was essentially a person who lived in the present.

'I couldn't sunbathe naked like this anywhere else,' she said, 'and it's the only holiday thing I enjoy. I don't like swimming, or tennis, or dancing, or gambling, so you see I'm just as well off here sunbathing and shopping, two perfect occupations for the day, and you, my darling love, at night. I should think I'm the happiest woman in the world.'

One boiling hot afternoon in July she arrived home wearing a new and particularly ravishing straw hat. It was large and simple, with a wreath of flowers and two blue bows. Her right arm was full of roses and carnations, and in her left hand was a striped bandbox, containing another exquisite hat. She let herself in with her latch-key, and stumped, on the high cork soles of her sandals, to the drawing-room.

The green venetian blinds were down, and the room was full of warm shadows, two of which suddenly resolved themselves into a thin man and a not so thin man – Davey and Lord Merlin.

'Good heavens,' said Linda, and she flopped down on to a sofa, scattering the roses at her feet.

'Well,' said Davey, 'you do look pretty.'

Linda felt really frightened, like a child caught out in some misdeed, like a child whose new toy is going to be taken away. She looked from one to the other. Lord Merlin was wearing black spectacles.

'Are you in disguise?' said Linda.

'No, what do you mean? Oh, the spectacles – I have to wear them when I go abroad, I have such kind eyes you see, beggars and things cluster round and annoy me.'

He took them off and blinked.

'What have you come for?'

'You don't seem very pleased to see us,' said Davey. 'We came, actually, to see if you were all right. As it's only too obvious that you are, we may as well go away again.'

'How did you find out? Do Mummy and Fa know?' she added, faintly.

'No, absolutely nothing. They think you're still with Christian. We haven't come in the spirit of two Victorian uncles, my dear Linda, if that's what you're thinking. I happened to see a man I know who had been in Perpignan, and he mentioned that Christian was living with Lavender Davis –'

'Oh good,' said Linda.

'What? And that you had left six weeks ago. I went round to Cheyne Walk and there you obviously weren't, and then Mer and I got faintly worried to think of you wandering about the Continent, so ill suited (we thought, how wrong we were) to look after yourself, and at the same time madly curious to know your whereabouts and present circumstances, so we put in motion a little discreet detective work, which revealed your whereabouts – your circumstances are now as clear as daylight, and I, for one, feel most relieved.'

'You gave us a fright,' said Lord Merlin, crossly. 'Another time, when you are putting on this Cléo de Mérode act, you might send a postcard. For one thing, it is a great pleasure to see you in the part, I wouldn't have missed it for worlds. I hadn't realized, Linda, that you were such a beautiful woman.'

Davey was laughing quietly to himself.

'Oh, goodness, how funny it all is – so wonderfully old-fashioned. The shopping! The parcels! The flowers! So tremendously Victorian. People have been delivering cardboard boxes every five minutes since we arrived. What an interest you are in one's life, Linda dear. Have you told him he must give you up and marry a pure young girl yet?'

Linda said disarmingly: 'Don't tease, Dave. I'm *so* happy you can't think.'

'Yes, you look happy I must say. Oh, this flat is such a joke.'

'I was just thinking,' said Lord Merlin, 'that, however much taste may change, it always follows a stereotyped plan. Frenchmen used to keep their mistresses in *appartements*, each exactly like the other, in which the dominant note, you might say, was lace and velvet. The walls, the bed, the dressing-table, the very bath itself were hung with lace, and everything else was velvet. Nowadays for lace you substitute glass, and everything else is satin. I bet you've got a glass bed, Linda?'

'Yes – but –'

'And a glass dressing-table, and bathroom, and I wouldn't be surprised if your bath were made of glass, with goldfish swimming about in the sides of it. Goldfish are a prevailing motif all down the ages.'

'You've looked,' said Linda sulkily. 'Very clever.'

'Oh, what heaven,' said Davey. 'So it's true! He hasn't looked, I swear, but you see it's not beyond the bounds of human ingenuity to guess.'

'But there are some things here,' said Lord Merlin, 'which do raise the level, all the same. A Gauguin, those two Matisses (chintzy, but accomplished) and this Savonnerie carpet. Your protector must be very rich.'

'He is,' said Linda.

'Then, Linda dear, could one ask for a cup of tea?'

She rang the bell, and soon Davey was falling upon *éclairs* and *mille feuilles* with all the abandon of a schoolboy.

'I shall pay for this,' he said, with a devil-may-care smile, 'but never mind, one's not in Paris every day.'

Lord Merlin wandered round with his tea-cup. He picked up a book which Fabrice had given Linda the day before, of romantic nineteenth-century poetry.

'Is this what you're reading now?' he said. '"*Dieu, que le son du cor est triste au fond des bois.*" I had a friend, when I lived in Paris, who had a boa constrictor as a pet, and this boa constrictor got itself inside a French horn. My friend rang me up in a fearful state, saying: "*Dieu, que le son du boa est triste au fond du cor.*" I've never forgotten it.'

'What time does your lover generally arrive?' said Davey, taking out his watch.

'Not till about seven. Do stay and see him, he's such a terrific Hon.'

'No, thank you, not for the world.'

'Who is he?' said Lord Merlin.

'He's called the Duke of Sauveterre.'

A look of great surprise, mingled with horrified amusement, passed between Davey and Lord Merlin.

'Fabrice de Sauveterre?'

'Yes. Do you know him?'

'Darling Linda, one always forgets, under that look of great sophistication, what a little provincial you really are. Of course we know him, and all about him, and, what's more, so does everyone except you.'

'Well, don't you think he's a terrific Hon?'

'Fabrice,' said Lord Merlin with emphasis, 'is undoubtedly one of the wickedest men in Europe, as far as women are concerned. But I must admit that he's an extremely agreeable companion.'

'Do you remember in Venice,' said Davey, 'one used to see him at work in that gondola, one after another, bowling them over like rabbits, poor dears?'

'Please remember,' said Linda, 'that you are eating his tea at this moment.'

'Yes, indeed, and so delicious. Another *éclair*, please, Linda. That summer,' he went on, 'when he made off with Ciano's girl friend, what a fuss there was, I never shall forget, and then, a week later, he *plaqué*'d her in Cannes and went to Salzburg with Martha Birmingham, and poor old Claud shot at him four times, and always missed him.'

'Fabrice has a charmed life,' said Lord Merlin. 'I suppose he has been shot at more than anybody, and, as far as I know, he's never had a scratch.'

Linda was unmoved by these revelations, which had been forestalled by Fabrice himself. Anyhow, no woman really minds hearing of the past affairs of her lover, it is the future alone that has the power to terrify.

'Come on, Mer,' said Davey. 'Time the *petite femme* got herself into a *négligée*. Goodness, what a scene there'll be when he smells Mer's cigar, there'll be a *crime passionel*, I shouldn't wonder. Goodbye, Linda darling, we're off to dine with our intellectual friends, you know, will you be lunching with us at the Ritz to-morrow? About one, then. Good-bye – give our love to Fabrice.'

When Fabrice came in he sniffed about, and asked whose cigar. Linda explained.

'They say they know you?'

'*Mais bien sûr – Merlin, tellement gentil, et l'autre Warbeck, toujours si malade, le pauvre. Je les connaissais à Venise.* What did they think of all this?'

'Well, they roared at the flat.'

'Yes, I can imagine. It is quite unsuitable for you, this flat, but it's convenient, and with the war coming –'

'Oh, but I love it, I wouldn't like anything else half so much. Wasn't it clever of them, though, to find me?'

'Do you mean to say you never told anybody where you were?'

'I really didn't think of it – the days go by, you know – one simply doesn't remember these things.'

'And it was six weeks before they thought of looking for you? As a family you seem to me strangely *décousu*.'

Linda suddenly threw herself into his arms, and said, with great passion:

'Never, never let me go back to them.'

'My darling – but you love them. Mummy and Fa, Matt and Robin and Victoria and Fanny. What is all this?'

'I never want to leave you again as long as I live.'

'Aha! But you know you will probably have to, soon. The war is going to begin, you know.'

'Why can't I stay here? I could work – I could become a nurse – well, perhaps not a nurse, actually, but something.'

'If you promise to do what I tell you, you may stay here for a time. At the beginning we shall sit and look at the Germans across the Maginot Line, then I shall be a great deal in Paris, between Paris and the front, but mostly here. At that time I shall want you here. Then somebody, we or the Germans, but I am very much afraid the Germans, will pour across the line, and a war of movement will begin. I shall have notice of that *étape*, and what you must promise me is that the very minute I tell you to leave for London you will leave, even if you see no reason for doing so. I should be hampered beyond words in my duties if you were still here. So you will solemnly promise, now?'

'All right,' said Linda. 'Solemnly. I don't believe anything so dreadful could happen to me, but I promise to do as you say. Now will you promise that you will come to London as soon as it's all over and find me again. Promise?'

'Yes,' said Fabrice. 'I will do that.'

Luncheon with Davey and Lord Merlin was a gloomy meal. Preoccupation reigned. The two men had stayed up late and merrily with their literary friends, and showed every sign of having done so. Davey was beginning to be aware of the cruel pangs of dyspepsia,

Lord Merlin was suffering badly from an ordinary straightforward hangover, and, when he removed his spectacles, his eyes were seen to be not kind at all. But Linda was far the most wretched of the three, she was, in fact, perfectly distracted by having overheard two French ladies in the foyer talking about Fabrice. She had arrived, as, from old habits of punctuality drummed into her by Uncle Matthew she always did, rather early. Fabrice had never taken her to the Ritz, she thought it delightful, she knew she was looking quite as pretty, and nearly as well dressed, as anybody there, and settled herself happily to await the others. Suddenly she heard, with that pang which the heart receives when the loved one's name is mentioned by strangers:

'And have you seen Fabrice at all?'

'Well, I have, because I quite often see him at Mme de Sauvet-erre's, but he never goes out anywhere, as you know.'

'Then what about Jacqueline?'

'Still in England. He is utterly lost without her, poor Fabrice, he is like a dog looking for its master. He sits sadly at home, never goes to parties, never goes to the club, sees nobody. His mother is really worried about him.'

'Who would ever have expected Fabrice to be so faithful? How long is it?'

'Five years, I believe. A wonderfully happy *ménage*.'

'Surely Jacqueline will come back soon.'

'Not until the old aunt has died. It seems she changes her will incessantly, and Jacqueline feels she must be there all the time – after all, she has her husband and children to consider.'

'Rather hard on Fabrice?'

'*Qu'est-ce que vous voulez?* His mother says he rings her up every morning and talks for an hour –'

It was at this point that Davey and Lord Merlin, looking tired and cross, arrived, and took Linda off to luncheon with them. She was longing to stay and hear more of this torturing conversation, but, eschewing cocktails with a shudder, they hurried her off to the dining-room, where they were only fairly nice to her, and frankly disagreeable to each other.

She thought the meal would never come to an end, and, when at last it did, she threw herself into a taxi and drove to Fabrice's house. She must find out about Jacqueline, she must know his intentions. When Jacqueline returned would that be the moment for her, Linda, to leave as she had promised? War of movement indeed!

The servant said that M. le Duc had just gone out with Madame la Duchesse, but that he would be back in about an hour. Linda said she would wait, and he showed her into Fabrice's sitting-room. She took off her hat, and wandered restlessly about. She had been here several times before, with Fabrice, and it had seemed, after her brilliantly sunny flat, a little dismal. Now that she was alone in it she began to be aware of the extreme beauty of the room, a grave and solemn beauty which penetrated her. It was very high, rectangular in shape, with grey boiseries and cherry-coloured brocade curtains. It looked into a courtyard and never could get a ray of sunshine, that was not the plan. This was a civilized interior, it had nothing to do with out-of-doors. Every object in it was perfect. The furniture had the severe lines and excellent proportions of 1780, there was a portrait by Lancret of a lady with a parrot on her wrist, a bust of the same lady by Bouchardon, a carpet like the one in Linda's flat, but larger and grander, with a huge coat of arms in the middle. A high carved bookcase contained nothing but French classics bound in contemporary morocco, with the Sauveterre crest, and open on a map table lay a copy of Redouté's roses.

Linda began to feel much more calm, but, at the same time, very sad. She saw that this room indicated a side of Fabrice's character which she had hardly been allowed to apprehend, and which had its roots in old civilized French grandeur. It was the essential Fabrice, something in which she could never have a share – she would always be outside in her sunny modern flat, kept away from all this, kept rigidly away even if their liaison were to go on for ever. The origins of the Radlett family were lost in the mists of antiquity, but the origins of Fabrice's family were not lost at all, there they were, each generation clutching at the next. The English, she thought, throw off their ancestors. It is the great strength of our aristocracy, but Fabrice has his round his neck, and he will never get away from them.

She began to realize that here were her competitors, her enemies, and that Jacqueline was nothing in comparison. Here, and in the grave of Louise. To come here and make a scene about a rival mistress would be utterly meaningless, she would be one unreality complaining about another. Fabrice would be annoyed, as men always are annoyed on these occasions, and she would get no satisfaction. She could hear his voice, dry and sarcastic:

'Ah! Vous me grondez, madame?'

Better go, better ignore the whole affair. Her only hope was to keep things on their present footing, to keep the happiness which she was enjoying day by day, hour by hour, and not to think about the future at all. It held nothing for her, leave it alone. Besides, everybody's future was in jeopardy now the war was coming, this war which she always forgot about.

She was reminded of it, however, when, that evening, Fabrice appeared in uniform.

'Another month I should think,' he said. 'As soon as they have got the harvest in.'

'If it depended on the English,' said Linda, 'they would wait until after the Christmas shopping. Oh, Fabrice, it won't last very long, will it?'

'It will be very disagreeable while it does last,' said Fabrice. 'Did you come to my flat to-day?'

'Yes, after lunching with those two old cross-patches I suddenly felt I wanted to see you very much.'

'Comme c'est gentil,' he looked at her quizzically, as though something had occurred to him, 'but why didn't you wait?'

'Your ancestors frightened me off.'

'Oh, they did? But you have ancestors yourself I believe, madame?'

'Yes, but they don't hang about in the same way as yours do.'

'You should have waited,' said Fabrice, 'it is always a very great pleasure to see you, both for me and for my ancestors. It cheers us all up.'

Germaine now came into the room with huge armfuls of flowers and a note from Lord Merlin, saying:

'Here are some coals for Newcastle. We are tottering home by the ferry-boat. Do you think I shall get Davey back alive? I enclose something which might, one day, be useful.'

It was a note for 20,000 francs.

'I must say,' said Linda, 'considering what cruel eyes he has, he does think of everything.'

She felt sentimental after the occurrences of the day.

'Tell me, Fabrice,' she said, 'what did you think the first moment you ever saw me?'

'If you really want to know, I thought: *"Tiens, elle ressemble à la petite Bosquet."'*

'Who is that?'

'There are two Bosquet sisters, the elder, who is a beauty, and a little one who looks like you.'

'*Merci beaucoup,*' said Linda. '*J'aimerais autant ressembler à l'autre.*'

Fabrice laughed. '*Ensuite, je me suis dit, comme c'est amusant, le côté démodé de tout ça –*'

When the war, which had for so long been pending, did actually break out some six weeks later, Linda was strangely unmoved by the fact. She was enveloped in the present, in her own detached and futureless life, which, anyhow, seemed so precarious, so much from one hour to another: exterior events hardly impinged on her consciousness. When she thought about the war it seemed to her almost a relief that it had actually begun, in so far as a beginning is the first step towards an end. That it had begun only in name and not in fact did not occur to her. Of course, had Fabrice been taken away by it her attitude would have been very different, but his job, an intelligence one, kept him mostly in Paris, and, indeed, she now saw rather more of him than formerly, as he moved into her flat, shutting up his own and sending his mother to the country. He would appear and disappear at all sorts of odd moments of the night and day, and, as the sight of him was a constant joy to Linda, as she could imagine no greater happiness than she always felt when the empty space in front of her eyes became filled by his form, these sudden apparitions kept her in a state of happy suspense and their relationship at fever point.

Since Davey's visit Linda had been getting letters from her family. He had given Aunt Sadie her address and told her that Linda was doing war work in Paris, providing comforts for the French army, he said vaguely, and with some degree of truth. Aunt Sadie was pleased about this, she thought it very good of Linda to work so hard (all night sometimes, Davey said), and was glad to hear that she earned her keep. Voluntary work was often unsatisfactory and expensive. Uncle Matthew thought it a pity to work for foreigners, and deplored the fact that his children were so fond of crossing the oceans, but he also was very much in favour of war work. He was himself utterly disgusted that the War Office were not able to offer him the opportunity of repeating his exploit with the entrenching tool, or, indeed, any job at all, and he went about like a bear with a sore head, full of unsatisfied desire to fight for his King and country.

I wrote to Linda and told her about Christian, who was back in London, had left the Communist party and had joined up. Lavender had also returned; she was now in the A.T.S.

Christian did not show the slightest curiosity about what had happened to Linda, he did not seem to want to divorce her or to marry Lavender, he had thrown himself heart and soul into army life and thought of nothing but the war.

Before leaving Perpignan he had extricated Matt, who, after a good deal of persuasion, had consented to leave his Spanish comrades in order to join the battle against Fascism on another front. He went into Uncle Matthew's old regiment, and was said to bore his brother officers in the mess very much by arguing that they were training the men all wrong, and that, during the battle of Ebro, things had been done thus and thus. In the end his colonel, who was rather brighter in the head than some of the others, hit upon the obvious reply, which was, 'Well anyway, your side lost!' This shut Matt up on tactics, but got him going on statistics – '30,000 Germans and Italians, 500 German planes', and so forth – which were almost equally dull.

Linda heard no more about Jacqueline, and the wretchedness into which she had been thrown by those few chance words overheard at the Ritz were gradually forgotten. She reminded herself that nobody ever really knew the state of a man's heart, not even, perhaps specially not, his mother, and that in love it is actions that count. Fabrice had no time now for two women, he spent every spare moment with her and that in itself reassured her. Besides, just as her marriages with Tony and Christian had been necessary in order to lead up to her meeting with Fabrice, so this affair had led up to his meeting with her: undoubtedly he must have been seeing Jacqueline off at the Gare du Nord when he found Linda crying on her suitcase. Putting herself in Jacqueline's shoes, she realized how much preferable it was to be in her own: in any case it was not Jacqueline who was her dangerous rival, but that dim, virtuous figure from the past, Louise. Whenever Fabrice showed signs of becoming a little less practical, a little more nonsensical, and romantic, it was of his fiancée that he would speak, dwelling with a gentle sadness upon her beauty, her noble birth, her vast estates, and her religious mania. Linda once suggested that, had the fiancée lived to become a wife, she might not have been a very happy one.

'All that climbing,' she said, 'in at other people's bedroom windows, might it not have upset her?'

Fabrice looked intensely shocked and reproachful and said that there never would have been any climbing, that, where marriage was concerned, he had the very highest ideals, and that his whole life would have been devoted to making Louise happy. Linda felt herself rebuked, but was not entirely convinced.

All this time Linda watched the tree-tops from her window. They had changed, since she had been in the flat, from bright green against a bright blue sky, to dark green against a lavender sky, to yellow against a cerulean sky, until now they were black skeletons against a sky of moleskin, and it was Christmas Day. The windows could no longer be opened until they disappeared, but, whenever the sun did come out, it shone into her rooms, and the flat was always as warm as toast. On this Christmas morning Fabrice arrived, quite unexpectedly, before she was up, his arms full of parcels, and soon the floor of her bedroom was covered with waves of tissue paper through which, like wrecks and monsters half submerged beneath a shallow sea, appeared fur coats, hats, real mimosa, artificial flowers, feathers, scent, gloves, stockings, under-clothes, and a bulldog puppy.

Linda had spent Lord Merlin's 20,000 francs on a tiny Renoir for Fabrice: six inches of seascape, a little patch of brilliant blue, which she thought would look just right in his room in the Rue Bonaparte. Fabrice was the most difficult person to buy presents for, he possessed a larger assortment of jewels, knick-knacks, and rare objects of all kinds than anybody she had ever known. He was delighted with the Renoir, nothing, he said, could have pleased him more, and Linda felt that he really meant it.

'Oh, such a cold day,' he said. 'I've just been to church.'

'Fabrice, how can you go to church when there's me?'

'Well, why not.'

'You're a Roman Catholic, aren't you?'

'Of course I am. What do you suppose? Do you think I look like a Calvinist?'

'But then aren't you living in mortal sin? So what about when you confess?'

'*On ne précise pas*,' said Fabrice, carelessly, 'and in any case, these little sins of the body are quite unimportant.'

Linda would have liked to think that she was more in Fabrice's life than a little sin of the body, but she was used to coming up against these closed doors in her relationship with him, and had learnt to be philosophical about it and thankful for the happiness that she did receive.

'In England,' she said, 'people are always renouncing each other on account of being Roman Catholics. It's sometimes very sad for them. A lot of English books are about this, you know.'

'*Les Anglais sont des insensés, je l'ai toujours dit.* You almost sound as if you want to be given up. What has happened since Saturday? Not tired of your war work, I hope?'

'No, no, Fabrice. I just wondered, that's all.'

'But you look so sad, *ma chérie*, what is it?'

'I was thinking of Christmas Day at home. I always feel sentimental at Christmas.'

'If what I said might happen does happen and I have to send you back to England, shall you go home to your father?'

'Oh, no,' said Linda, 'anyway, it won't happen. All the English papers say we are killing Germany with our blockade.'

'*Le blocus,*' said Fabrice, impatiently, '*quelle blague! Je vais vous dire, madame, ils ne se fichent pas mal de votre blocus.* So where would you go?'

'To my own house in Chelsea, and wait for you to come.'

'It might be months, or years.'

'I shall wait,' she said.

The skeleton tree-tops began to fill out, they acquired a pinkish tinge, which gradually changed to golden-green. The sky was often blue, and, on some days, Linda could once more open her windows and lie naked in the sun, whose rays by now had a certain strength. She always loved the spring, she loved the sudden changes of temperature, the dips backward into winter and forward into summer, and, this year, living in beautiful Paris, her perceptions heightened by great emotion, she was profoundly affected by it. There was now a curious feeling in the air, very different from and much more nervous than that which had been current before Christmas, and the town was full of rumours. Linda often thought of the expression '*fin de siècle*'. There was a certain analogy, she thought, between the state of mind which it denoted and that prevailing now, only now it was more like '*fin de vie*'. It was as though everybody around her, and she herself, were living out the last few days of their lives, but this curious feeling did not disturb her, she was possessed by a calm and happy fatalism. She occupied the hours of waiting between Fabrice's visits by lying in the sun, when there was any, and playing with her puppy. On Fabrice's advice she even began to order some new clothes for the summer. He seemed to regard the acquisition of clothes as one of the chief duties of woman, to be pursued through war and revolution, through sickness, and up to death. It was as one who might say, 'Whatever happens the fields must be tilled, the cattle tended, life must go on.' He was so essentially urban that to him the slow roll of the seasons was marked by the spring *tailleurs*, the summer *imprimés*, the autumn *ensembles*, and the winter furs of his mistress.

On a beautiful windy blue and white day in April the blow fell. Fabrice, whom Linda had not seen for nearly a week, arrived from the front looking grave and worried, and told her that she must go back to England at once.

'I've got a place for you in the aeroplane,' he said, 'for this afternoon. You must pack a small suitcase, and the rest of your things must go after you by train. Germaine will see to them. I have to go to the Ministère de la Guerre, I'll be back as soon as possible, and anyhow in time to take you to Le Bourget. Come on,' he added, 'just time for a little war work.' He was in his most practical and least romantic mood.

When he returned he looked more preoccupied than ever. Linda was waiting for him, her box was packed, she was wearing the blue suit in which he had first seen her, and had her old mink coat over her arm.

'*Tiens,*' said Fabrice, who always at once noticed what she had on, 'what is this? A fancy-dress party?'

'Fabrice, you must understand that I can't take away the things you have given me. I loved having them while I was here, and while they gave you pleasure seeing me in them, but, after all, I have some pride. *Je n'étais quand même pas élevée dans un bordel.*'

'*Ma chère*, try not to be so middle-class, it doesn't suit you at all.

165

There's no time for you to change – wait, though –' He went into her bedroom, and came out again with a long sable coat, one of his Christmas presents. He took her mink coat, rolled it up, threw it into the waste-paper basket, and put the other over her arm in its place.

'Germaine will send your things after you,' he said. 'Come now, we must go.'

Linda said good-bye to Germaine, picked up the bulldog puppy, and followed Fabrice into the lift, out into the street. She did not fully understand that she was leaving that happy life behind her for ever.

19

At first, back in Cheyne Walk, she still did not understand. The world was grey and cold certainly, the sun had gone behind a cloud, but only for a time: it would come out again, she would soon once more be enveloped in that heat and light which had left her in so warm a glow, there was still much blue in the sky, this little cloud would pass. Then, as sometimes happens, the cloud, which had seemed at first such a little one, grew and grew, until it became a thick grey blanket smothering the horizon. The bad news began, the terrible days, the unforgettable weeks. A great horror of steel was rolling over France, was rolling towards England, swallowing on its way the puny beings who tried to stop it, swallowing Fabrice, Germaine, the flat, and the past months of Linda's life, swallowing Alfred, Bob, Matt, and little Robin, coming to swallow us all. London people cried openly in the buses, in the streets, for the English army which was lost.

Then, suddenly one day, the English army turned up again. There was a feeling of such intense relief, it was as if the war were over and won. Alfred and Bob and Matt and little Robin all reappeared, and, as a lot of French soldiers also arrived, Linda had a wild hope that Fabrice might be with them. She sat all day by the telephone and when it rang and was not Fabrice she was furious with the unlucky telephoner – I know, because it happened to me. She was so furious that I dropped the receiver and went straight round to Cheyne Walk.

I found her unpacking a huge trunk, which had just arrived from France. I had never seen her looking so beautiful. It made me gasp, and I remembered how Davey had said, when he got back from Paris, that at last Linda was fulfilling the promise of her childhood, and had become a beauty.

'How do you imagine this got here?' she said, between tears and laughter. 'What an extraordinary war. The Southern Railway people brought it just now and I signed for it, all as though nothing peculiar were happening – I don't understand a word of it. What are you doing in London, darling?'

She seemed unaware of the fact that half an hour ago she had spoken to me, and indeed bitten my head off, on the telephone.

'I'm with Alfred. He's got to get a lot of new equipment and see all sorts of people. I believe he's going abroad again very soon.'

'Awfully good of him,' said Linda, 'when he needn't have joined up at all, I imagine. What does he say about Dunkirk?'

'He says it was like something out of the *Boy's Own* – he seems to have had a most fascinating time.'

'They all did, the boys were here yesterday and you never heard anything like their stories. Of course they never quite realized how desperate it all was until they got to the coast. Oh, isn't it wonderful to have them back. If only – if only one knew what had happened to one's French buddies –' She looked at me under her eyelashes, and I thought she was going to tell me about her life, but, if so, she changed her mind and went on unpacking.

'I shall have to put these winter things back in their boxes really,' she said. 'I simply haven't any cupboards that will hold them all, but it's something to do, and I like to see them again.'

'You should shake them,' I said, 'and put them in the sun. They may be damp.'

'Darling, you are wonderful, you always know.'

'Where did you get that puppy?' I said enviously. I had wanted a bulldog for years, but Alfred never would let me have one because of the snoring.

'Brought him back with me. He's the nicest puppy I ever had, so anxious to oblige, you can't think.'

'What about quarantine, then?'

'Under my coat,' said Linda, laconically. 'You should have heard him grunting and snuffling, it shook the whole place, I was terrified, but he was so good. He never budged. And talking of puppies, those ghastly Kroesigs are sending Moira to America, isn't it typical of them? I've made a great thing with Tony about seeing her before she goes, after all I am her mother.'

'That's what I can't ever understand about you, Linda.'

'What?'

'How you could have been so dreadful to Moira.'

'Dull,' said Linda. 'Uninteresting.'

'I know, but the point is that children are like puppies, and if you never see puppies, if you give them to the groom or the gamekeeper to bring up, look how dull and uninteresting they always are. Children are just the same – you must give them much more than their life if they are to be any good. Poor little Moira – all you gave her was that awful name.'

'Oh, Fanny, I do know. To tell you the truth I believe it was always in the back of my mind that, sooner or later, I should have to run away from Tony, and I didn't want to get too fond of Moira, or to make her too fond of me. She might have become an anchor, and I simply didn't dare let myself be anchored to the Kroesigs.'

'Poor Linda.'

'Oh, don't pity me. I've had eleven months of perfect and unalloyed happiness, very few people can say that, in the course of long long lives, I imagine.'

I imagined so too. Alfred and I are happy, as happy as married people can be. We are in love, we are intellectually and physically suited in every possible way, we rejoice in each other's company, we have no money troubles and three delightful children. And yet, when I consider my life, day by day, hour by hour, it seems to be composed of a series of pin-pricks. Nannies, cooks, the endless drudgery of housekeeping, the nerve-racking noise and boring repetitive conversation of small children (boring in the sense that it bores into one's very brain), their absolute incapacity to amuse themselves, their sudden and terrifying illnesses, Alfred's not infrequent bouts of moodiness, his invariable complaints at meals about the pudding, the way he will always use my tooth-paste and will always squeeze the tube in the middle. These are the components of marriage, the wholemeal bread of life, rough, ordinary, but sustaining; Linda had been feeding upon honey-dew, and that is an incomparable diet.

The old woman who had opened the door to me came in and said was that everything, because, if so, she would be going home.

'Everything,' said Linda. 'Mrs Hunt,' she said to me, when she had gone. 'A terrific Hon – she comes daily.'

'Why don't you go to Alconleigh,' I said, 'or to Shenley? Aunt Emily and Davey would love to have you, and I'm going there with the children as soon as Alfred is off again.'

'I'd like to come for a visit some time, when I know a little more what is happening, but at the moment I must stop here. Give them my love though. I've got such masses to tell you, Fanny, what we really need is hours and hours in the Hons' cupboard.'

After a great deal of hesitation Tony Kroesig and his wife, Pixie, allowed Moira to go and see her mother before leaving England. She arrived at Cheyne Walk in Tony's car, still driven by a chauffeur in uniform not the King's. She was a plain, stodgy, shy little girl, with no echo of the Radletts about her; not to put too fine a point on it she was a real little Gretchen.

'What a sweet puppy,' she said, awkwardly, when Linda had kissed her. She was clearly very much embarrassed.

'What's his name?'

'Plon-plon.'

'Oh. Is that a French name?'

'Yes it is. He's a French dog, you see.'

'Daddy says the French are terrible.'

'I expect he does.'

'He says they have let us down, and what can we expect if we have anything to do with such people.'

'Yes, he would.'

'Daddy thinks we ought to fight with the Germans and not against them.'

'M'm. But Daddy doesn't seem to be fighting very much with anybody, or against anybody, or at all, as far as I can see. Now, Moira, before you go I have got two things for you, one is a present and the other is a little talk. The talk is very dull, so we'll get that over first, shall we?'

'Yes,' said Moira, apathetically. She lugged the puppy on to the sofa beside her.

'I want you to know,' said Linda, 'and to remember, please, Moira (stop playing with the puppy a minute and listen carefully to what I am saying) that I don't at all approve of you running away like this, I think it most dreadfully wrong. When you have a country which has given you as much as England has given all of us, you ought to stick to it, and not go wandering off as soon as it looks like being in trouble.'

'But it's not my fault,' said Moira, her forehead puckering. 'I'm only a child and Pixie is taking me. I have to do what I'm told, don't I?'

'Yes, of course, I know that's true. But you'd much rather stay, wouldn't you?' said Linda, hopefully.

'Oh no, I don't think so. There might be air-raids.'

At this Linda gave up. Children might or might not enjoy air-raids actually in progress, but a child who was not thrilled by the idea of them was incomprehensible to her, and she could not imagine having conceived such a being. Useless to waste any more time and breath on this unnatural little girl. She sighed and said:

'Now wait a moment and I'll get your present.'

She had in her pocket, in a velvet box, a coral hand holding a diamond arrow, which Fabrice had given her, but she could not bear to waste anything so pretty on this besotted little coward. She went to her bedroom and found a sports wristwatch, one of her wedding presents when she had married Tony and which she had never worn, and gave this to Moira, who seemed quite pleased by it, and left the house as politely and unenthusiastically as she had arrived.

Linda rang me up at Shenley and told me about this interview.

'I'm in such a temper,' she said, 'I must talk to somebody. To think I ruined nine months of my life in order to have that. What do your children think about air-raids, Fanny?'

'I must say they simply long for them, and I am sorry to say they also long for the Germans to arrive. They spend the whole day making booby-traps for them in the orchard.'

'Well that's a relief anyhow – I thought perhaps it was the generation. Actually of course, it's not Moira's fault, it's all that bloody Pixie – I can see the form only too clearly, can't you? Pixie is frightened to death and she has found out that going to America is like the children's concert, you can only make it if you have a child in tow. So she's using Moira – well, it does serve one right for doing wrong.' Linda was evidently very much put out. 'And I hear Tony is going too, some Parliamentary mission or something. All I can say is what a set.'

All through those terrible months of May, June, and July, Linda waited for a sign from Fabrice, but no sign came. She did not doubt that he was still alive, it was not in Linda's nature to imagine that anyone might be dead. She knew that thousands of Frenchmen were in German hands, but felt certain that, had Fabrice been taken prisoner (a thing which she did not at all approve of, incidentally, taking the old-fashioned view that, unless in exceptional circumstances, it is a disgrace), he would undoubtedly manage to escape. She would hear from him before long, and, meanwhile, there was nothing to be done, she must simply wait. All the same, as the days went by with no news, and as all the news there was from France was bad, she did become exceedingly restless. She was really more concerned with his attitude than with his safety – his attitude towards events and his attitude towards her. She felt sure that he would never be associated with the armistice, she felt sure that he would want to communicate with her, but she had no proof, and, in moments of great loneliness and depression, she allowed herself to lose faith. She realized how little she really knew of Fabrice, he had seldom talked seriously to her, their relationship having been primarily physical while their conversations and chat had all been based on jokes.

They had laughed and made love and laughed again, and the months had slipped by with no time for anything but laughter and love. Enough to satisfy her, but what about him? Now that life had become so serious, and, for a Frenchman, so tragic, would he not have forgotten that meal of whipped cream as something so utterly unimportant that it might never have existed? She began to think, more and more, to tell herself over and over again, to force herself to realize, that it was probably all finished, that Fabrice might never be anything for her now but a memory.

At the same time the few people she saw never failed when talking, as everybody talked then, about France, to emphasize that the French 'one knew', the families who were *'bien'*, were all behaving very badly, convinced Pétainists. Fabrice was not one of them, she thought, she felt, but she wished she knew, she longed for evidence.

In fact, she alternated between hope and despair, but as the months went by without a word, a word that she was sure he could have sent if he had really wanted to, despair began to prevail.

Then, on a sunny Sunday morning in August, very early, her telephone bell rang. She woke up with a start, aware that it had been ringing already for several moments, and she knew with absolute certainty that this was Fabrice.

'Are you Flaxman 2815?'

'Yes.'

'I've got a call for you. You're through.'

'Allô – allô?'

'Fabrice?'

'Oui.'

'Oh! Fabrice – *on vous attend depuis si longtemps.'*

'Comme c'est gentil. Alors, on peut venir tout de suite chez vous?'

'Oh, wait – yes, you can come at once, but don't go for a minute, go on talking, I want to hear the sound of your voice.'

'No, no, I have a taxi outside, I shall be with you in five minutes. There's too much one can't do on the telephone, *ma chère, voyons –*' Click.

She lay back, and all was light and warmth. Life, she thought, is sometimes sad and often dull, but there are currants in the cake and here is one of them. The early morning sun shone past her window on to the river, her ceiling danced with water-reflections. The Sunday silence was broken by two swans winging slowly upstream, and then by the chugging of a little barge, while she waited for that other sound, a sound more intimately connected with the urban love affair than any except the telephone bell, that of a stopping taxicab. Sun, silence, and happiness. Presently she heard it in the street, slowly, slower, it stopped, the flag went up with a ring, the door slammed, voices, clinking coins, footsteps. She rushed downstairs.

Hours later Linda made some coffee.

'So lucky,' she said, 'that it happens to be Sunday, and Mrs Hunt isn't here. What would she have thought?'

'Just about the same as the night porter at the Hotel Montalembert, I expect,' said Fabrice.

'Why did you come, Fabrice? To join General de Gaulle?'

'No, that was not necessary, because I have joined him already. I was with him in Bordeaux. My work has to be in France, but we have ways of communicating when we want to. I shall go and see him, of course, he expects me at midday, but actually I came on a private mission.'

He looked at her for a long time.

'I came to tell you that I love you,' he said, at last.

Linda felt giddy.

'You never said that to me in Paris.'

'No.'

'You always seemed so practical.'

'Yes, I suppose so. I had said it so often and often before in my life, I had been so romantic with so many women, that when I felt this to be different I really could not bring out all those stale old phrases again, I couldn't utter them. I never said I loved you, I never *tutoyé*'d you, on purpose. Because from the first moment I knew that this was as real as all the others were false, it was like recognizing somebody – there, I can't explain.'

'But that is exactly how I felt too,' said Linda, 'don't try to explain, you needn't, I know.'

'Then, when you had gone, I felt I had to tell you, and it became an obsession with me to tell you. All those dreadful weeks were made more dreadful because I was being prevented from telling you.'

'How ever did you get here?'

'*On circule*,' said Fabrice, vaguely. 'I must leave again tomorrow morning, very early, and I shan't come back until the war is over, but you'll wait for me, Linda, and nothing matters so much now that you know. I was tormented, I couldn't concentrate on anything, I was becoming useless in my work. In future I may have much to bear, but I shan't have to bear you going away without knowing what a great love I have for you.'

'Oh, Fabrice, I feel – well, I suppose religious people sometimes feel like this.'

She put her head on his shoulder, and they sat for a long time in silence.

When he had paid his visit to Carlton Gardens they lunched at the Ritz. It was full of people Linda knew, all very smart, very gay, and talking with the greatest flippancy about the imminent arrival of the Germans. Had it not been for the fact that all the young men there had fought bravely in Flanders, and would, no doubt, soon be fighting bravely again, and this time with more experience, on other fields of battle, the general tone might have been considered shocking. Even Fabrice looked grave, and said they did not seem to realize –

Davey and Lord Merlin appeared. Their eyebrows went up when they saw Fabrice.

'Poor Merlin has the wrong kind,' Davey said to Linda.

'The wrong kind of what?'

'Pill to take when the Germans come. He's just got the sort you give to dogs.'

Davey brought out a jewelled box containing two pills, one white and one black.

'You take the white one first and then the black one – he really must go to my doctor.'

'I think one should let the Germans do the killing,' said Linda. 'Make them add to their own crimes and use up a bullet. Why should one smooth their path in any way? Besides, I back myself to do in at least two before they get me.'

'Oh, you're so tough, Linda, but I'm afraid it wouldn't be a bullet for me, they would torture me, look at the things I've said about them in the *Gazette*.'

'No worse than you've said about all of us,' Lord Merlin remarked.

Davey was known to be a most savage reviewer, a perfect butcher, never sparing even his dearest friends. He wrote under several pseudonyms, which in no way disguised his unmistakable style, his cruellest essays appearing over the name Little Nell.

'Are you here for long, Sauveterre?'

'No, not for long.'

Linda and Fabrice went in to luncheon. They talked of this and that, mostly jokes. Fabrice told her scandalous stories about some of the other lunchers known to him of old, with a wealth of unlikely detail. He spoke only once about France, only to say that the struggle must be carried on, everything would be all right in the end. Linda thought how different it would have been with Tony or Christian. Tony would have held forth about his experiences and made boring arrangements for his own future, Christian would have launched a monologue on world conditions subsequent to the recent fall of France, its probable repercussions in Araby and far Cashmere, the inadequacy of Pétain to deal with such a wealth of displaced persons, the steps that he, Christian, would have taken had he found himself in his, the Marshal's, shoes. Both would have spoken to her exactly, in every respect, as if she had been some chap in their club. Fabrice talked to her, at her, and for only her, it was absolutely personal talk, scattered with jokes and allusions private to them both. She had a feeling that he would not allow himself to be serious, that if he did he would have to embark on tragedy, and that he wanted her to carry away a happy memory of his visit. But he also gave an impression of boundless optimism and faith, very cheering at that dark time.

Early the next morning, another beautiful, hot, sunny morning, Linda lay back on her pillows and watched Fabrice while he dressed, as she had so often watched him in Paris. He made a certain kind of face when he was pulling his tie into a knot, she had quite forgotten it in the months between, and it brought back their Paris life to her suddenly and vividly.

'Fabrice,' she said, 'Do you think we shall ever live together again?'

'But of course we shall, for years and years and years, until I am ninety. I have a very faithful nature.'

'You weren't very faithful to Jacqueline.'

'Aha – so you know about Jacqueline, do you? *La pauvre, elle était si gentille – gentille, élégante, mais assommante, mon Dieu! Enfin*, I was immensely faithful to her and it lasted five years, it always does with me (either five days or five years). But as I love you ten times more than the others that brings it to when I am ninety, and, by then, *j'en aurai tellement l'habitude –*'

'And how soon shall I see you again?'

'*On fera la navette*.' He went to the window. 'I thought I heard a car – oh yes, it is turning round. There, I must go. *Au revoir*, Linda.'

He kissed her hand politely, almost absentmindedly, it was as if he had already gone, and walked quickly from the room. Linda went to the open window and leaned out. He was getting into a large motor-car with two French soldiers on the box and a Free

French flag waving from the bonnet. As it moved away he looked up.

'*Navette – navette –*' cried Linda with a brilliant smile. Then she got back into bed and cried very much. She felt utterly in despair at this second parting.

20

The air-raids on London now began. Early in September, just as I had moved there with my family, a bomb fell in the garden of Aunt Emily's house in Kent. It was a small bomb compared with what one saw later, and none of us were hurt, but the house was more or less wrecked. Aunt Emily, Davey, my children, and I, then took refuge at Alconleigh, where Aunt Sadie welcomed us with open arms, begging us to make it our home for the war. Louisa had already arrived there with her children, John Fort William had gone back to his regiment and their Scottish home had been taken over by the Navy.

'The more the merrier,' said Aunt Sadie. 'I should like to fill the house, and, besides, it's better for rations. Nice, too, for your children to be brought up all together, just like old times. With the boys away and Victoria in the Wrens, Matthew and I would be a very dreary old couple here all alone.'

The big rooms at Alconleigh were filled with the contents of some science museum and no evacuees had been billeted there, I think it was felt that nobody who had not been brought up to such rigours could stand the cold of that house.

Soon the party received a very unexpected addition. I was upstairs in the nursery bathroom doing some washing for Nanny, measuring out the soap-flakes with wartime parsimony and wishing that the water at Alconleigh were not so dreadfully hard, when Louisa burst in.

'You'll never guess,' she said, 'in a thousand thousand years who has arrived.'

'Hitler,' I said, stupidly.

'Your mother, Auntie Bolter. She just walked up the drive and walked in.'

'Alone?'

'No, with a man.'

'The Major?'

'He doesn't look like a major. He's got a musical instrument with him and he's very dirty. Come on, Fanny, leave those to soak –'

And so it was. My mother sat in the hall drinking a whisky-and-soda and recounting in her birdlike voice with what incredible adventures she had escaped from the Riviera. The major with whom she had been living for some years, always having greatly preferred the Germans to the French, had remained behind to collaborate, and the man who now accompanied my mother was a ruffianly-looking Spaniard called Juan, whom she had picked up during her travels, and without whom, she said, she could never have got away from a ghastly prison camp in Spain. She spoke of him exactly as though he were not there at all, which produced rather a curious effect, and indeed seemed most embar-rassing until we realized that Juan understood no word of any language except Spanish. He sat staring blankly into space, clutch-ing a guitar and gulping down great draughts of whisky. Their relationship was only too obvious, Juan was undoubtedly (nobody doubted for a moment, not even Aunt Sadie), the Bolter's lover, but they were quite incapable of verbal exchange, my mother being no linguist.

Presently Uncle Matthew appeared, and the Bolter told her adventures all over again to him. He said he was delighted to see her, and hoped she would stay as long as she liked, he then turned his blue eyes upon Juan in a most terrifying and uncompromising stare. Aunt Sadie led him off to the business-room, whispering, and we heard him say:

'All right then, but only for a few days.'

One person who was off his head with joy at the sight of her was dear old Josh.

'We must get her ladyship up on to a horse,' he said, hissing with pleasure.

My mother had not been her ladyship since three husbands

(four if one were to include the Major), but Josh took no account of this, she would always be her ladyship to him. He found a horse, not worthy of her, in his eyes, but not an absolute dud either, and had her out cub-hunting within a week of her arrival.

As for me it was the first time in my life that I had found myself really face to face with my mother. When a small child I had been obsessed by her and the few appearances she had made had absolutely dazzled me, though, as I have said, I never had any wish to emulate her career. Davey and Aunt Emily had been very clever in their approach to her, they, and especially Davey, had gradually and gently and without in any way hurting my feelings, turned her into a sort of joke. Since I was grown up I had seen her a few times, and had taken Alfred to visit her on our honeymoon, but the fact that, in spite of our intimate relationship, we had no past life in common put a great strain upon us and these meetings were not a success. At Alconleigh, in contact with her morning, noon, and night, I studied her with the greatest curiosity, apart from anything else she was, after all, the grandmother of my children. I couldn't help rather liking her. Though she was silliness personified there was something engaging about her frankness and high spirits and endless good nature. The children adored her, Louisa's as well as mine, and she soon became an extra unofficial nursery-maid, and was very useful to us in that capacity.

She was curiously dated in her manner, and seemed still to be living in the 1920s. It was as though, at the age of thirty-five, having refused to grow any older, she had pickled herself, both mentally and physically, ignoring the fact that the world was changing and that she was withering fast. She had a short canary-coloured shingle (windswept) and wore trousers with the air of one still flouting the conventions, ignorant that every suburban shopgirl was doing the same. Her conversation, her point of view, the very slang she used, all belonged to the late twenties, that period now deader than the dodo. She was intensely unpractical, foolish, and apparently fragile, and yet she must have been quite a tough little person really, to have walked over the Pyrenees, to have escaped from a

Spanish camp, and to have arrived at Alconleigh looking as if she had stepped out of the chorus of *No, No, Nanette*.

Some confusion was caused in the household at first by the fact that none of us could remember whether she had, in the end, actually married the Major (a married man himself and father of six) or not, and, in consequence, nobody knew whether her name was now Mrs Rawl or Mrs Plugge. Rawl had been a white hunter, the only husband she had ever lost respectably through death, having shot him by accident in the head during a safari. The question of names was soon solved, however, by her ration book, which proclaimed her to be Mrs Plugge.

'This Gewan,' said Uncle Matthew, when they had been at Alconleigh a week or so, 'what's going to be done about him?'

'Well, Matthew dulling,' she larded her phrases with the word darling, and that is how she pronounced it. 'Hoo-arn saved my life, you know, over and over again, and I can't very well tear him up and throw him away, now can I, my sweet?'

'I can't keep a lot of dagoes here, you know.' Uncle Matthew said this in the same voice with which he used to tell Linda that she couldn't have any more pets, or if she did they must be kept in the stables. 'You'll have to make some other arrangements for him, Bolter, I'm afraid.'

'Oh, dulling, keep him a little longer, please, just a few more days, Matthew dulling,' she sounded just like Linda, pleading for some smelly old dog, 'and then I promise I'll find some place for him and tiny me to go to. You can't think what a lousy time we had together, I must stick to him now, I really must.'

'Well, another week if you like, but it's not to be the thin end of the wedge, Bolter, and after that he must go. You can stay as long as you want to, of course, but I do draw the line at Gewan.'

Louisa said to me, her eyes as big as saucers: 'He rushes into her room before tea and lives with her.' Louisa always describes the act of love as living with. 'Before tea, Fanny, can you imagine it?'

*

'Sadie, dear,' said Davey. 'I am going to do an unpardonable thing. It is for the general good, for your own good too, but it is unpardonable. If you feel you can't forgive me when I've said my say, Emily and I will have to leave, that's all.'

'Davey,' said Aunt Sadie in astonishment, 'what can be coming?'

'The food, Sadie, it's the food. I know how difficult it is for you in wartime, but we are all, in turns, being poisoned. I was sick for hours last night, the day before Emily had diarrhoea, Fanny has that great spot on her nose, and I'm sure the children aren't putting on the weight they should. The fact is, dear, that if Mrs Beecher were a Borgia she could hardly be more successful – all that sausage mince is poison, Sadie. I wouldn't complain if it were merely nasty, or insufficient, or too starchy, one expects that in the war, but actual poison does, I feel, call for comment. Look at the menus this week – Monday, poison pie; Tuesday, poison burger steak; Wednesday, Cornish poison –'

Aunt Sadie looked intensely worried.

'Oh, dear, yes, she is an awful cook, I know, but Davey, what can one do? The meat ration only lasts about two meals, and there are fourteen meals in a week, you must remember. If she minces it up with a little sausage meat – poison meat (I do so agree with you really) – it goes much further, you see.'

'But in the country surely one can supplement the ration with game and farm produce? Yes, I know the home farm is let, but surely you could keep a pig and some hens? And what about game? There always used to be such a lot here.'

'The trouble is Matthew thinks they'll be needing all their ammunition for the Germans, and he refuses to waste a single shot on hares or partridges. Then you see Mrs Beecher (oh, what a dreadful woman she is, though of course, we are lucky to have her) is the kind of cook who is quite good at a cut off the joint and two veg., but she simply hasn't an idea of how to make up delicious foreign oddments out of little bits of nothing at all. But you are quite, absolutely right, Davey, it's not wholesome. I really will make an effort to see what can be done.'

'You always used to be such a wonderful housekeeper, Sadie dear, it used to do me so much good, coming here. I remember one Christmas I put on four and a half ounces. But now I am losing steadily, my wretched frame is hardly more than a skeleton and I fear that, if I were to catch anything, I might peter out altogether. I take every precaution against that, everything is drenched in T.C.P., I gargle at least six times a day, but I can't disguise from you that my resistance is very low, very.'

Aunt Sadie said: 'It's quite easy to be a wonderful housekeeper when there are a first-rate cook, two kitchenmaids, a scullerymaid, and when you can get all the food you want. I'm afraid I am dreadfully stupid at managing on rations, but I really will try and take a pull. I'm very glad indeed that you mentioned it, Davey, it was absolutely right of you, and of course, I don't mind at all.'

But no real improvement resulted. Mrs Beecher said 'yes, yes' to all suggestions, and continued to send up Hamburger steaks, Cornish pasty, and shepherd pie, which continued to be full of poison sausage. It was very nasty and very unwholesome, and, for once, we all felt that Davey had not gone a bit too far. Meals were no pleasure to anybody and a positive ordeal to Davey, who sat, a pinched expression on his face, refusing food and resorting more and more often to the vitamin pills with which his place at the table was surrounded – too many by far even for his collection of jewelled boxes – a little forest of bottles, Vitamin A, vitamin B, vitamins A and C, vitamins B_3 and D, one tablet equals two pounds of summer butter – ten times the strength of a gallon of cod-liver oil – for the blood – for the brain – for muscle – for energy – anti this and protection against that – all but one bore a pretty legend.

'And what's in this, Davey?'

'Oh, that's what the panzer troops have before going into action.'

Davey gave a series of little sniffs. This usually denoted that his nose was about to bleed, pints of valuable red and white corpuscles so assiduously filled with vitamins would be wasted, his resistance still further lowered.

Aunt Emily and I looked up in some anxiety from the rissoles we were sadly pushing round our plates.

'Bolter,' he said, severely, 'you've been at my Mary Chess again.'

'Oh, Davey dulling, such a tiny droppie.'

'A tiny drop doesn't stink out the whole room. I'm sure you have been pouring it into the bath with the stopper out. It is a shame. That bottle is my quota for a month, it is too bad of you, Bolter.'

'Dulling, I swear I'll get you some more – I've got to go to London next week, to have my wiggie washed, and I'll bring back a bottle, I swear.'

'And I very much hope you'll take Gewan with you and leave him there,' growled Uncle Matthew. 'Because I won't have him in this house much longer, you know. I've warned you, Bolter.'

Uncle Matthew was busy from morning to night with his Home Guard. He was happy and interested and in a particularly mellow mood, for it looked as if his favourite hobby, that of clocking Germans, might be available again at any moment. So he only hunted Juan from time to time, and, whereas in the old days he would have had him out of the house in the twinkling of an eye, Juan had now been an inmate of Alconleigh for nearly a month. However, it was beginning to be obvious that my uncle had no intention of putting up with his presence for ever and things were clearly coming to a head where Juan was concerned. As for the Spaniard himself, I never saw a man so wretched. He wandered about miserably, with nothing whatever to do all day, unable to talk to anybody, while at mealtimes the disgust on his face fully equalled that of Davey. He hadn't even the spirit to play his guitar.

'Davey, you must talk to him,' said Aunt Sadie.

My mother had gone to London to have her hair dyed, and a family council was gathered in her absence to decide upon the fate of Juan.

'We obviously can't turn him out to starve, as the Bolter says he saved her life, and, anyhow, one has human feelings.'

'Not towards Dagoes,' said Uncle Matthew, grinding his dentures.

'But what we can do is to get him a job, only first we must find out what his profession is. Now, Davey, you're good at languages, and you're so clever, I'm sure if you had a look at the Spanish dictionary in the library you could just manage to ask him what he used to do before the war. Do try, Davey.'

'Yes, darling, do,' said Aunt Emily. 'The poor fellow looks too miserable for words at present, I expect he'd love to have some work.'

Uncle Matthew snorted.

'Just give me the Spanish dictionary,' he muttered. 'I'll soon find the word for "get out".'

'I'll try,' said Davey, 'but I can guess what it will be I'm afraid. G for gigolo.'

'Or something equally useless, like M for matador or H for hidalgo,' said Louisa.

'Yes. Then what?'

'Then B for be off,' said Uncle Matthew, 'and the Bolter will have to support him, but not anywhere near me, I beg. It must be made perfectly clear to both of them that I can't stand the sight of the sewer lounging about here any longer.'

When Davey takes on a job he does it thoroughly. He shut himself up for several hours with the Spanish dictionary, and wrote down a great many words and phrases on a piece of paper. Then he beckoned Juan into Uncle Matthew's business-room and shut the door.

They were there a short time, and, when they emerged, both were wreathed in happy smiles.

'You've sacked him, I hope?' Uncle Matthew said, suspiciously.

'No, indeed, I've not sacked him,' said Davey, 'on the contrary, I've engaged him. My dears, you'll never guess, it's too absolutely glamorous for words, Juan is a cook, he was the cook, I gather, of some cardinal before the Civil War. You don't mind I hope, Sadie. I look upon this as an absolute lifeline – Spanish food, so delicious, so unconstipating, so digestible, so full of glorious garlic. Oh, the joy, no more poison-burger – how soon can we get rid of Mrs Beecher?'

Davey's enthusiasm was fully justified, and Juan in the kitchen was the very greatest possible success. He was more than a first-class cook, he had an extraordinary talent for organization, and soon, I suspect, became king of the local black market. There was no nonsense about foreign dishes made out of little bits of nothing at all; succulent birds, beasts, and crustaceans appeared at every meal, the vegetables ran with extravagant sauces, the puddings were obviously based upon real ice-cream.

'Juan is wonderful,' Aunt Sadie would remark in her vague manner, 'at making the rations go round. When I think of Mrs Beecher – really, Davey, you were so clever.'

One day she said: 'I hope the food isn't too rich for you now, Davey?'

'Oh no,' said Davey. 'I never mind rich food, it's poor food that does one such an infinity of harm.'

Juan also pickled and bottled and preserved from morning till night, until the store cupboard, which he had found bare except for a few tins of soup, began to look like a pre-war grocer's shop. Davey called it Aladdin's Cave, or Aladdin for short, and spent a lot of his time there, gloating. Months of tasty vitamins stood there in neat rows, a barrier between him and that starvation which had seemed, under Mrs Beecher's régime, only just round the corner.

Juan himself was now a very different fellow from the dirty and disgruntled refugee who had sat about so miserably. He was clean, he wore a white coat and hat, he seemed to have grown in stature, and he soon acquired a manner of great authority in his kitchen. Even Uncle Matthew acknowledged the change.

'If I were the Bolter,' he said, 'I should marry him.'

'Knowing the Bolter,' said Davey, 'I've no doubt at all that she will.'

Early in November I had to go to London for the day, on business for Alfred, who was now in the Middle East, and to see my doctor. I went by the eight o'clock train, and, having heard nothing of Linda for some weeks, I took a taxi and drove straight to Cheyne

Walk. There had been a heavy raid the night before, and I passed through streets which glistened with broken glass. Many fires still smouldered, and fire engines, ambulances, and rescue men hurried to and fro, streets were blocked, and several times we had to drive quite a long way round. There seemed to be a great deal of excitement in the air. Little groups of people were gathered outside shops and houses, as if to compare notes; my taxi-driver talked incessantly to me over his shoulder. He had been up all night, he said, helping the rescue workers. He described what he had found.

'It was a spongy mass of red,' he said, ghoulishly, 'covered with feathers.'

'Feathers?' I said, horrified.

'Yes. A feather bed, you see. It was still breathing, so I takes it to the hospital, but they say that's no good to us, take it to the mortuary. So I sews it in a sack and takes it to the mortuary.'

'Goodness,' I said.

'Oh, that's nothing to what I have seen.'

Linda's nice daily woman, Mrs Hunt, opened the door to me at Cheyne Walk.

'She's very poorly, ma'am, can't you take her back to the country with you? It's not right for her to be here, in her condition. I hate to see her like this.'

Linda was in her bathroom, being sick. When she came out she said:

'Don't think it's the raid that's upset me. I like them. I'm in the family way, that's what it is.'

'Darling, I thought you weren't supposed to have another baby.'

'Oh, doctors! They don't know anything, they are such fearful idiots. Of course I can, and I'm simply longing for it, this baby won't be the least like Moira, you'll see.'

'I'm going to have one too.'

'No – how lovely – when?'

'About the end of May.'

'Oh, just the same as me.'

'And Louisa, in March.'

'Haven't we been busy? I do call that nice, they can all be Hons together.'

'Now, Linda, why don't you come back with me to Alconleigh? Whatever is the sense of stopping here in all this? It can't be good for you or the baby.'

'I like it,' said Linda. 'It's my home, and I like to be in it. And besides, somebody might turn up, just for a few hours you know, and want to see me, and he knows where to find me here.'

'You'll be killed,' I said, 'and then he won't know where to find you.'

'Darling Fanny, don't be so silly. There are seven million people living in London, do you really imagine they are all killed every night? Nobody is killed in air-raids, there is a great deal of noise and a great deal of mess, but people really don't seem to get killed much.'

'Don't – don't –' I said. 'Touch wood. Apart from being killed or not it doesn't suit you. You look awful, Linda.'

'Not so bad when I'm made up. I'm so fearfully sick, that's the trouble, but it's nothing to do with the raids, and that part will soon be over now and I shall be quite all right again.'

'Well, think about it,' I said, 'it's very nice at Alconleigh, wonderful food –'

'Yes, so I hear. Merlin came to see me, and his stories of caramelized carrots swimming in cream made my mouth water. He said he was preparing to throw morality to the winds and bribe this Juan to go to Merlinford, but he found out it would mean having the Bolter too and he couldn't quite face that.'

'I must go,' I said uncertainly. 'I don't like to leave you, darling, I do wish you'd come back with me.'

'Perhaps I will later on, we'll see.'

I went down to the kitchen and found Mrs Hunt. I gave her some money in case of emergency, and the Alconleigh telephone number, and begged her to ring me up if she thought there was anything I could do.

'She won't budge,' I said. 'I've done all I can to make her, but it doesn't seem to be any good, she's as obstinate as a donkey.'

'I know, ma'am. She won't even leave the house for a breath of air, sits by that telephone day in day out playing cards with herself. It ain't hardly right she should sleep here all alone in my opinion, either, but you can't get her to listen to sense. Last night, ma'am, whew! it was terrible, walloping down all night, and those wretched guns never got a single one, what ever they may tell you in the papers. It's my opinion they must have got women on those guns, and, if so, no wonder. Women!'

A week later Mrs Hunt rang me up at Alconleigh. Linda's house had received a direct hit and they were still digging for her.

Aunt Sadie had gone on an early bus to Cheltenham to do some shopping, Uncle Matthew was nowhere to be found, so Davey and I simply took his car, full of Home Guard petrol, and drove to London, hell for leather. The little house was an absolute ruin, but Linda and her bulldog were unhurt, they had just been got out and put to bed in the house of a neighbour. Linda was flushed and excited, and couldn't stop talking.

'You see,' she said. 'What did I tell you, Fanny, about air-raids not killing people. Here we are, right as rain. My bed simply went through the floor, Plon-plon and I went on it, most comfortable.'

Presently a doctor arrived and gave her a sedative. He told us she would probably go to sleep and that when she woke up we could drive her down to Alconleigh. I telephoned to Aunt Sadie and told her to have a room ready.

The rest of the day was spent by Davey in salvaging what he could of Linda's things. Her house and furniture, her beautiful Renoir, and everything in her bedroom was completely wrecked, but he was able to rescue a few oddments from the splintered, twisted remains of her cupboards, and in the basement he found, untouched, the two trunks full of clothes which Fabrice had sent after her from Paris. He came out looking like a miller, covered with white dust from head to foot, and Mrs Hunt took us round to her own little house and gave us some food.

'I suppose Linda may miscarry,' I said to Davey, 'and I'm sure it's to be hoped she will. It's most dangerous for her to have this child – my doctor is horrified.'

However, she did not, in fact she said that the experience had done her a great deal of good, and had quite stopped her from feeling sick. She demurred again at leaving London, but without much conviction. I pointed out that if anybody was looking for her and found the Cheyne Walk house a total wreck they would be certain at once to get into touch with Alconleigh. She saw that this was so, and agreed to come with us.

21

Winter now set in with its usual severity on those Cotswold uplands. The air was sharp and bracing, like cold water; most agreeable if one only goes out for short brisk walks or rides, and if there is a warm house to go back to. But the central-heating apparatus at Alconleigh had never been really satisfactory and I suppose that by now the pipes, through old age, had become thoroughly furred up – in any case they were hardly more than tepid. On coming into the hall from the bitter outside air one did feel a momentary glow of warmth; this soon lessened, and gradually, as circulation died down, one's body became pervaded by a cruel numbness. The men on the estate, the old ones that is, who were not in the army, had no time to chop up logs for the fires; they were occupied from morning till night, under the leadership of Uncle Matthew, in drilling, constructing barricades and blockhouses, and otherwise preparing to make themselves a nuisance to the German army before ending up as cannon-fodder.

'I reckon,' Uncle Matthew would say proudly, 'that we shall be able to stop them for two hours – possibly three – before we are all killed. Not bad for such a little place.'

We made our children go out and collect wood, Davey became an assiduous and surprisingly efficient woodman (he had refused to join the Home Guard, he said he always fought better out of uniform), but, somehow, they produced only enough to keep the nursery fire going, and the one in the brown sitting-room, if it was lit after tea, and, as the wood was pretty wet, this really got warm only just when it was time to tear oneself away and go up the freezing stairs to bed. After dinner the two armchairs on each side of the fire were always occupied by Davey and my mother. Davey pointed out that it would be more trouble for everybody in the end if he got one of his chills; the Bolter just dumped herself down. The rest of us sat in a semicircle well beyond the limits of any real warmth, and looked longingly at the little flickering yellow flames, which often subsided into sulky smoke. Linda had an evening coat, a sort of robe from head to foot, of white fox lined with white ermine. She wrapped herself in this for dinner, and suffered less than we others did. In the daytime she either wore her sable coat and a pair of black velvet boots lined with sable to match, or lay on the sofa tucked up in an enormous mink bedspread lined with white velvet quilting.

'It used to make me so laugh when Fabrice said he was getting me all these things because they would be useful in the war, the war would be fearfully cold he always said, but I see now how right he was.'

Linda's possessions filled the other females in the house with a sort of furious admiration.

'It does seem rather unfair,' Louisa said to me one afternoon when we were pushing our two youngest children out in their prams together. We were both dressed in stiff Scotch tweeds, so different from supple flattering French ones, in woollen stockings, brogues, and jerseys, knitted by ourselves, of shades carefully chosen to 'go with' though not 'to match' our coats and skirts. 'Linda goes off and has this glorious time in Paris, and comes back covered with rich furs, while you and I – what do we get for sticking all our lives to the same dreary old husbands? Three-quarter-length shorn lamb.'

'Alfred isn't a dreary old husband,' I said loyally. But of course I knew exactly what she meant.

Aunt Sadie thought Linda's clothes too pretty.

'What lovely taste, darling,' she would say when another ravishing garment was brought out. 'Did that come from Paris too? It's really wonderful what you can get there, on no money, if you're clever.'

At this my mother would give tremendous winks in the direction of anybody whose eye she might happen to catch, including Linda herself. Linda's face would then become absolutely stony.

She could not bear my mother; she felt that, before she met Fabrice, she had been heading down the same road herself, and she was appalled to see what lay at the end of it. My mother started off by trying a 'let's face it, dear, we are nothing but two fallen women' method of approach to Linda, which was most unsuccessful. Linda became not only stiff and cold, but positively rude to the poor Bolter, who, unable to see what she could have done to offend, was at first very much hurt. Then she began to be on her dignity, and said it was great nonsense for Linda to go on like this; in fact, considering she was nothing but a high-class tart, it was most pretentious and hypocritical of her. I tried to explain Linda's intensely romantic attitude towards Fabrice and the months she had spent with him, but the Bolter's own feelings had been dulled by time, and she either could not or would not understand.

'It was Sauveterre she was living with, wasn't it?' my mother said to me, soon after Linda arrived at Alconleigh.

'How do you know?'

'Everybody knew on the Riviera. One always knew about Sauveterre somehow. And it was rather a thing, because he seemed to have settled down for life with that boring Lamballe woman; then she had to go to England on business and clever little Linda nabbed him. A very good cop for her, dulling, but I don't see why she has to be so high-hat about it. Sadie doesn't know, I quite realize that, and of course wild horses wouldn't make me tell her, I'm not that kind of a girl, but I do think, when we're all together, Linda might be a tiny bit more jolly.'

The Alconleighs still believed that Linda was the devoted wife of Christian, who was now in Cairo, and, of course, it had never occurred to them for a moment that the child might not be his. They had quite forgiven her for leaving Tony, though they thought themselves distinctly broadminded for having done so. They would ask her from time to time what Christian was doing, not because they were interested, but so that Linda shouldn't feel out of it when Louisa and I talked about our husbands. She would then be obliged to invent bits of news out of imaginary letters from Christian.

'He doesn't like his Brigadier very much,' or,

'He says Cairo is great fun, but one can have enough of it.'

In point of fact Linda never got any letters at all. She had not seen her English friends now for so long, they were scattered in the war to the ends of the earth, and, though they might not have forgotten about Linda, she was no longer in their lives. But, of course, there was only one thing she wanted, a letter, a line even, from Fabrice. Just after Christmas it came. It was forwarded in a typewritten envelope from Carlton Gardens with General de Gaulle's stamp on it. Linda, when she saw it lying on the hall table, became perfectly white. She seized it and rushed up to her bedroom.

About an hour later she came to find me.

'Oh, darling,' she said, her eyes full of tears. 'I've been all this time and I can't read one word. Isn't it torture? Could you have a look?'

She gave me a sheet of the thinnest paper I ever saw, on which were scratched, apparently with a rusty pin, a series of perfectly incomprehensible hieroglyphics. I could not make out one single word either, it seemed to bear no relation to handwriting, the marks in no way resembled letters.

'What can I do?' said poor Linda. 'Oh, Fanny.'

'Let's ask Davey,' I said.

She hesitated a little over this, but feeling that it would be better, however intimate the message, to share it with Davey than not to have it all, she finally agreed.

Davey said she was quite right to ask him.

'I am very good at French handwriting.'

'Only you wouldn't laugh at it?' Linda said, in a breathless voice like a child.

'No, Linda, I don't regard it as a laughing matter any longer,' Davey replied, looking with love and anxiety at her face, which had become very drawn of late. But when he had studied the paper for some time, he too was obliged to confess himself absolutely stumped by it.

'I've seen a lot of difficult French writing in my life,' he said, 'and this beats them all.'

In the end Linda had to give up. She went about with the piece of paper, like a talisman, in her pocket, but never knew what Fabrice had written to her on it. It was cruelly tantalizing. She wrote to him at Carlton Gardens, but this letter came back with a note regretting that it could not be forwarded.

'Never mind,' she said. 'One day the telephone bell will ring again and he'll be there.'

Louisa and I were busy from morning to night. We now had one Nanny (mine) between eight children. Fortunately they were not at home all the time. Louisa's two eldest were at a private school, and two of hers and two of mine went for lessons to a convent Lord Merlin had most providentially found for us at Merlinford. Louisa got a little petrol for this, and she and I or Davey drove them there in Aunt Sadie's car every day. It can be imagined what Uncle Matthew thought of their arrangement. He ground his teeth, flashed his eyes, and always referred to the poor good nuns as 'those damned parachutists'. He was absolutely convinced that whatever time they could spare from making machine-gun nests for other nuns, who would presently descend from the skies, like birds, to occupy the nests, was given to the seduction of the souls of his grandchildren and great nieces.

'They get a prize you know for anybody they can catch – of course you can see they are men, you've only got to look at their boots.'

Every Sunday he watched the children like a lynx for genuflections, making the sign of the Cross, and other Papist antics, or even for undue interest in the service, and when none of these symptoms was to be observed he was hardly reassured.

'These Romans are so damned artful.'

He thought it most subversive of Lord Merlin to harbour such an establishment on his property, but only really what one might expect of a man who brought Germans to one's ball and was known to admire foreign music. Uncle Matthew had most conveniently forgotten all about 'Una voce poco fa', and now played, from morning to night, a record called 'The Turkish Patrol', which started piano, became forte, and ended up pianissimo.

'You see,' he would say, 'they come out of a wood, and then you can hear them go back into the wood. Don't know why it's called Turkish, you can't imagine Turks playing a tune like that, and of course there aren't any woods in Turkey. It's just the name, that's all.'

I think it reminded him of his Home Guard, who were always going into woods and coming out of them again, poor dears, often covering themselves with branches as when Birnam Wood came to Dunsinane.

So we worked hard, mending and making and washing, doing any chores for Nanny rather than actually look after the children ourselves. I have seen too many children brought up without Nannies to think this at all desirable. In Oxford, the wives of progressive dons did it often as a matter of principle; they would gradually become morons themselves, while the children looked like slum children and behaved like barbarians.

As well as looking after the clothes of our existing families we also had to make for the babies we were expecting, though they did inherit a good deal from brothers and sisters. Linda, who naturally had no store of baby clothes, did nothing of all this. She arranged one of the slatted shelves in the Hons' cupboard as a sort of bunk, with pillows and quilts from spare bedrooms, and here, wrapped in her mink bedspread, she would lie all day with Plonplon beside her, reading fairy stories. The Hons' cupboard, as of old, was the warmest, the one really warm place in the house. Whenever I could I brought my sewing and sat with her there, and then she would put down the blue or the green fairy book, Anderson or Grimm, and tell me at length about Fabrice and her happy life with him in Paris. Louisa sometimes joined us there, and then Linda would break off and we would talk about John Fort William and the children. But Louisa was a restless busy creature, not much of a chatter, and, besides, she was irritated to see how Linda did absolutely nothing, day after day.

'Whatever is the baby going to wear, poor thing,' she would say crossly to me, 'and who is going to look after it, Fanny? It's quite plain already that you and I will have to, and really, you know, we've got enough to do as it is. And another thing, Linda lies there covered in sables or whatever they are, but she's got no money at all, she's a pauper – I don't believe she realizes that in the least. And what is Christian going to say when he hears about the baby, after all, legally his, he'll have to bring a suit to illegitimize it, and then there'll be such a scandal. None of these things seem to have occurred to Linda. She ought to be beside herself with worry, instead of which she is behaving like the wife of a millionaire in peacetime. I've no patience with her.'

All the same, Louisa was a good soul. In the end it was she who went to London and bought a layette for the baby. Linda sold Tony's engagement ring at a horribly low price, to pay for it.

'Do you never think about your husbands?' I asked her one day, after she had been talking for hours about Fabrice.

'Well, funnily enough, I do quite often think of Tony. Christian, you see, was such an interlude, he hardly counts in my life at all, because, for one thing, our marriage lasted a very short time, and then it was quite overshadowed by what came after. I don't know, I find these things hard to remember, but I think that my feelings for him were only really intense for a few weeks, just at the very beginning. He's a noble character, a man you can respect, I don't blame myself for marrying him, but he has no talent for love.

'But Tony was my husband for so long, more than a quarter of my life, if you come to think of it. He certainly made an impression. And I see now that the thing going wrong was hardly his fault, poor Tony, I don't believe it would have gone right with anybody (unless I happened to meet Fabrice) because in those days I was so extremely nasty. The really important thing, if a marriage is to go well, without much love, is very very great niceness – *gentillesse* – and wonderful good manners. I was never *gentille* with Tony, and often I was hardly polite to him, and, very soon after our honeymoon, I became exceedingly disagreeable. I'm ashamed now to think what I was like. And poor old Tony was so good-natured, he never snapped back, he put up with it all for years and then just ambled off to Pixie. I can't blame him. It was my fault from beginning to end.'

'Well, he wasn't very nice really, darling. I shouldn't worry yourself about it too much, and look how he's behaving now.'

'Oh, he's the weakest character in the world, it's Pixie and his parents who made him do that. If he'd still been married to me he would have been a Guards officer by now, I bet you.'

One thing Linda never thought about, I'm quite sure, was the future. Some day the telephone bell would ring and it would be Fabrice, and that was as far as she got. Whether he would marry her, and what would happen about the child, were questions which not only did not preoccupy her, but which never seemed to enter her head. Her mind was entirely on the past.

'It's rather sad,' she said one day, 'to belong, as we do, to a lost generation. I'm sure in history the two wars will count as one war and that we shall be squashed out of it altogether, and people will forget that we ever existed. We might just as well never have lived at all, I do think it's a shame.'

'It may become a sort of literary curiosity,' Davey said. He sometimes crept, shivering, into the Hons' cupboard to get up a little circulation before he went back to his writing. 'People will be interested in it for all the wrong reasons, and collect Lalique dressing-table sets and shagreen boxes and cocktail cabinets lined with looking-glass and find them very amusing. Oh good,' he said, peering out of the window, 'that wonderful Juan is bringing in another pheasant.'

(Juan had an invaluable talent, he was expert with a catapult. He spent all his odd moments – how he had odd moments was a mystery, but he had – creeping about the woods or down by the river armed with this weapon. As he was an infallible shot, and moreover, held back by no sporting inhibitions, that a pheasant or a hare should be sitting or a swan the property of the King being immaterial to Juan, the results of these sallies were excellent from the point of view of larder and stock-pot. When Davey really wanted to relish his food to the full he would recite, half to himself, a sort of little grace, which began: 'Remember Mrs Beecher's tinned tomato soup.'

The unfortunate Craven was, of course, tortured by these goings on, which he regarded as little better than poaching. But his nose, poor man, was kept well to the grindstone by Uncle Matthew, and, when he was not on sentry-go, or fastening the trunks of trees to bicycle-wheels across the lanes to make barricades against tanks, he was on parade. Uncle Matthew was a byword in the county for the smartness of his parades. Juan, as an alien, was luckily excluded from these activities, and was able to devote all his time to making us comfortable and happy, in which he very notably succeeded.)

'I don't want to be a literary curiosity,' said Linda. 'I should like to have been a living part of a really great generation. I think it's too dismal to have been born in 1911.'

'Never mind, Linda, you will be a wonderful old lady.'

'You will be a wonderful old gentleman, Davey,' said Linda.

'Oh, me? I fear I shall never make old bones,' replied Davey, in accents of the greatest satisfaction.

And, indeed, there was a quality of agelessness about him. Although he was quite twenty years older than we and only about five years younger than Aunt Emily, he had always seemed much nearer to our generation than to hers, nor had he altered in any respect since the day when he had stood by the hall fire looking unlike a captain and unlike a husband.

'Come on, dears, tea, and I happen to know that Juan has made a layer-cake, so let's go down before the Bolter gets it all.'

Davey carried on a great meal-time feud with the Bolter. Her table manners had always been casual, but certain of her habits, such as eating jam with a spoon which she put back into the jam-pot, and stubbing out her cigarette in the sugarbasin, drove poor Davey, who was very ration-conscious, to a frenzy of irritation, and he would speak sharply to her, like a governess to a maddening child.

He might have spared himself the trouble. The Bolter took

absolutely no notice whatever, and went on spoiling food with insouciance.

'Dulling,' she would say, 'whatever does it matter, my perfectly divine Hoo-arn has got plenty more up his tiny sleeve, I promise you.'

At this time there was a particularly alarming invasion scare. The arrival of the Germans, with full paraphernalia of airborne troops dressed as priests, ballet dancers, or what you will, was expected from one day to the next. Some unkind person put it about that they would be the doubles of Mrs Davis, in W.V.S. uniform. She had such a knack of being in several places at once that it already seemed as if there were a dozen Mrs Davises parachuting about the countryside. Uncle Matthew took the invasion very seriously indeed, and one day he gathered us all together, in the business-room and told us in detail the part that we were expected to play.

'You women, with the children, must go to the cellar while the battle is on,' he said, 'there is an excellent tap, and I have provisioned you with bully-beef for a week. Yes, you may be there several days, I warn you.'

'Nanny won't like that,' Louisa began, but was quelled by a furious look.

'While we are on the subject of Nanny,' Uncle Matthew said, 'I warn you, there's to be no question of cluttering up the roads with your prams, mind, no evacuation under any circumstances at all. Now, there is one very important job to be done, and that I am entrusting to you, Davey. You won't mind it I know, old boy, if I say that you are a very poor shot – as you know, we are short of ammunition, and what there is must, under no circumstances, be wasted – every bullet must tell. So I don't intend to give you a gun, at first, anyhow. But I've got a fuse and a charge of dynamite (I will show you, in a moment), and I shall want you to blow up the store-cupboard for me.'

'Blow up Aladdin,' said Davey. He turned quite pale. 'Matthew, you must be mad.'

'I would let Gewan do it, but the fact is, though I rather like old

Gewan now, I don't altogether trust the fella. Once a foreigner always a foreigner in my opinion. Now I must explain to you why I regard this as a most vital part of the operations. When Josh and Craven and I and all the rest of us have been killed there is only one way in which you civilians can help, and that is by becoming a charge on the German army. You must make it their business to feed you – never fear, they'll do so, they don't want any typhus along their lines of communication – but you must see that it's as difficult as possible for them. Now that store cupboard would keep you going for weeks, I've just had a look at it; why, it would feed the entire village. All wrong. Make them bring in the food and muck up their transport, that's what we want, to be a perfect nuisance to them. It's all you'll be able to do, by then, just be a nuisance, so the store cupboard will have to go, and Davey must blow it up.'

Davey opened his mouth to make another observation, but Uncle Matthew was in a very frightening mood and he thought better of it.

'Very well, dear Matthew,' he said, sadly, 'you must show me what to do.'

But as soon as Uncle Matthew's back was turned he gave utterance to loud complaints.

'No, really, it is too bad of Matthew to insist on blowing up Aladdin,' he said. 'It's all right for him, he'll be dead, but he really should consider us a little more.'

'But I thought you were going to take those black and white pills,' said Linda.

'Emily doesn't like the idea, and I had decided only to take them if I were arrested, but now I don't know. Matthew says the German army will have to feed us, but he must know as well as I do that if they feed us at all, which is extremely problematical, it will be on nothing but starch – it will be Mrs Beecher again, only worse, and I can't digest starch especially in the winter months. It is such a shame. Horrid old Matthew, he's so thoughtless.'

'Well, but, Davey,' said Linda, 'how about us? We're all in the same boat, but we don't grumble.'

'Nanny will,' said Louisa with a sniff, which plainly said, 'and I wish to associate myself with Nanny.'

'Nanny! She lives in a world of her own,' said Linda. 'But we're all supposed to know why we're fighting, and, speaking for myself, I think Fa is absolutely right. And if I think that, in my condition –'

'Oh, you'll be looked after,' said Davy, bitterly, 'pregnant women always are. They'll send you vitamins and things from America, you'll see. But nobody will bother about me, and I am so delicate, it simply won't do for me to be fed by the German army, and I shall never be able to make them understand about my inside. I know Germans.'

'You always said nobody understood as much about your inside as Dr Meyerstein.'

'Use your common sense, Linda. Are they likely to drop Dr Meyerstein over Alconleigh? You know perfectly well he's been in a camp for years. No, I must make up my mind to a lingering death – not a very pleasant prospect, I must say.'

Linda took Uncle Matthew aside after that, and made him show her how to blow up Aladdin.

'Davey's spirit is not so frightfully willing,' she said, 'and his flesh is definitely weak.'

There was a certain coldness between Linda and Davey for a little while after this, each thought the other had been quite unreasonable. It did not last, however. They were much too fond of each other (in fact, I am sure that Davey really loved Linda most in the world) and, as Aunt Sadie said, 'Who knows, perhaps the necessity for these dreadful decisions will not arise.'

So the winter slowly passed. The spring came with extraordinary beauty, as always at Alconleigh, with a brilliance of colouring, a richness of life, that one had forgotten to expect during the cold grey winter months. All the animals were giving birth, there were young creatures everywhere, and we now waited with longing and impatience for our babies to be born. The days, the very hours, dragged slowly by, and Linda began to say 'better than that' when asked the time.

'What's the time, darling?'

'Guess.'

'Half-past twelve?'

'Better than that, a quarter to one.'

We three pregnant women had all become enormous, we dragged ourselves about the house like great figures of fertility, heaving tremendous sighs, and feeling the heat of the first warm days with exaggerated discomfort.

Useless to her now were Linda's beautiful Paris clothes, she was down to the level of Louisa and me in a cotton smock, maternity skirt, and sandals. She abandoned the Hons' cupboard, and spent her days, when it was fine weather, sitting by the edge of the wood, while Plon-plon, who had become an enthusiastic, though unsuccessful, rabbiter, plunged panting to and fro in the green mists of the undergrowth.

'If anything happens to me, darling, you will look after Plon-plon,' she said. 'He has been such a comfort to me all this time.'

But she spoke idly, as one who knows, in fact, that she will live for ever, and she mentioned neither Fabrice nor the child, as surely she would have done had she been touched by any premonition.

Louisa's baby, Angus, was born at the beginning of April. It was her sixth child and third boy, and we envied her from the bottom of our hearts for having got it over.

On the 28th May both our babies were born – both boys. The doctors who said that Linda ought never to have another child were not such idiots after all. It killed her. She died, I think, completely happy, and without having suffered very much, but for us at Alconleigh, for her father and mother, brothers and sisters, for Davey and for Lord Merlin a light went out, a great deal of joy that never could be replaced.

At about the same time as Linda's death Fabrice was caught by the Gestapo and subsequently shot. He was a hero of the Resistance, and his name has become a legend in France.

I have adopted the little Fabrice, with the consent of Christian, his legal father. He has black eyes, the same shape as Linda's blue ones, and is a most beautiful and enchanting child. I love him quite as much as, and perhaps more than, I do my own

The Bolter came to see me while I was still in the Oxford nursing home where my baby had been born and where Linda had died.

'Poor Linda,' she said, with feeling, 'poor little thing. But, Fanny, don't you think perhaps it's just as well? The lives of women like Linda and me are not so much fun when one begins to grow older.'

I didn't want to hurt my mother's feelings by protesting that Linda was not that sort of woman.

'But I think she would have been happy with Fabrice,' I said. 'He was the great love of her life, you know.'

'Oh, dulling,' said my mother, sadly. 'One always thinks that. Every, every time.'

PENGUIN ESSENTIALS

BROOKLYN/COLM TÓIBÍN

'In the United States there would be plenty of work for someone like you and with good pay.'

It is Ireland in the early 1950s and for Eilis Lacey, as for so many young Irish girls, opportunities are scarce. So when Father Flood speaks of a job in New York, Eilis knows she must go.
Living in a crowded lodging house in Brooklyn, Eilis is far from home – and homesick. Yet after taking her first tentative steps towards friendship, and perhaps something more, Eilis thinks she might find happiness. Until bad news sends her back to Ireland, where a terrible dilemma awaits her – a devastating choice between duty and love.

'Unforgettable' *Spectator*

PENGUIN ESSENTIALS

EXTREMELY LOUD AND INCREDIBLY CLOSE/JONATHAN SAFRAN FOER

'In the end, everyone loses everyone. There was no invention to get around that, and so I felt, that night, like the turtle that everything else in the universe was on top of . . .'

A couple of years after his father dies in 9/11, nine-year-old Oskar discovers a key. Convinced it belonged to his father, he sets out to find which of New York's 162 million locks it opens. It's a quest that throws Oskar into the paths of friends, relatives and complete strangers, into their tumbled, jumbled lives. With each lock tries, he dreams he's getting a little step closer to his lost father. In fact, he is approaching ever nearer to the heart of a family mystery that stretches back more than fifty years . . .

'Utterly engaging' *Spectator*

PENGUIN ESSENTIALS

AGE OF IRON/J. M. COETZEE

'Care: the true root of charity. I look for him to care, and he does not. Because he is beyond caring. Beyond caring and beyond care . . .'

Capetown, South Africa. Mrs Curren, a dying classics professor, is writing to her daughter in America. Having quietly opposed apartheid all her life, she is suddenly confronted by its true horrors: the burning of a township, the persecution of her servant's son, the murder of an activist who seeks sanctuary in her home. When a homeless man appears on her doorstep, Mrs Curren gradually awakens to her own complicity in a regime of iron in which no soul can survive unblemished . . .

'Remarkable' *Wall Street Journal*

PENGUIN ESSENTIALS

AUSTERLITZ/W. G. SEBALD

**'The longer I think about it the more it seems to me that we
who are still alive are unreal in the eyes of the dead, that only
occasionally, in certain lights and atmospheric conditions, do we
appear in their field of vision.'**

In 1939, five-year-old Jacques Austerlitz is sent to England on a
Kindertransport and placed with foster parents. This childless couple
promptly erase from the boy all knowledge of his identity and he grows
up ignorant of his past. Later in life, after a career as an architectural
historian, Austerlitz – having avoided all clues that might point to his
origin – finds the past returning to haunt him and is forced to explore
what happened to him fifty years before . . .

'An extraordinary, mesmeric story' *Observer*

PENGUIN ESSENTIALS

THE HOUND OF THE BASKERVILLES/ARTHUR CONAN DOYLE

'**A hound it was, an enormous coal-black hound, but not such a hound as mortal eyes have ever seen. Fire burst from its open mouth, its eyes glowed with a smouldering glare, its muzzle and hackles and dewlap were outlined in flickering flame.**'

Sir Charles Baskerville has died suddenly, and mysteriously. As rumours of the terrible beast said to haunt the family spread, consulting detective Sherlock Holmes and his faithful companion Dr Watson are asked to ensure the protection of the new heir to Baskerville Hall in Devon.

But it is there, in an isolated mansion, surrounded by wild, barren moors, that the pair must confront a terrifying evil which has lain dormant for centuries . . .

'Sherlock Holmes's best. It remains a classic' *The Times*

PENGUIN ESSENTIALS

THREE NOVELS/CÉSAR AIRA

Three novels by the cult Argentinian writer

In *Ghosts* a new apartment block is haunted by a collection of spectres, beguiling and threatening the life of the daughter of one family. *An Episode in the Life of a Landscape Painter* follows nineteenth-century German artist Johann Moritz Rugendas on an expedition in Argentina at the behest of his friend, explorer Alexander von Humboldt. Finally, in The Literary Conference, one Cesar Aira is attempting to take over the world using an army of Carlos Fuentes clones.

'Once you've started to read Aira, you don't want to stop'
Roberto Bolaño

PENGUIN ESSENTIALS

THE CHRYSALIDS/JOHN WYNDHAM

'WATCH THOU FOR THE MUTANT!'

It is many years since God sent the Tribulation to punish the forebears for their sins, and in the rural settlement of Waknuk David Strorm's father decries any and all blasphemies against nature. Little does he realise that David and his cousin Rosalind, have their own secret aberration which would label them as mutants. But as they grow older it becomes more difficult to conceal their differences from the village elders. Soon they face a choice: wait for eventual discovery, or flee to the terrifying and mutable Badlands. . .

'An outstanding success' *New York Times*

Penguin Essentials

VILLAGES/JOHN UPDIKE

'Some days, half-aroused, he finds the way back to sleep only by remembering one of the women, Alissa or Vanessa or Karen or Faye, who shared with him the town of Middle Falls, Connecticut, in the sixties and seventies.'

The life of Owen Mackenzie – a son, father, husband and serial adulterer – abounds with sin and seduction, domesticity and debauchery. As he looks back on his youthful indiscretions from the craggy hills of old age – marriage to his college sweetheart, his first betrayal leading to a succession of affairs, desperately pursuing fleeting happiness in small towns across New England – he finally catches a glimpse of the man, the authentic man, he has been running from his whole life.

'Wonderful stuff' *Daily Mail*

PENGUIN ESSENTIALS

LIBRA/DON DELILLO

**'Think of two parallel lines. One is the life of Lee H. Oswald. One
is the conspiracy to kill the President. What bridges the space
between them? What makes a connection inevitable? There is a
third line. It comes out of dreams, visions, intuitions, prayers, out
of the deepest levels of the self.'**

A troubled adolescent endlessly riding New York's subway cars,
Lee Harvey Oswald enters adulthood believing himself to be an
agent of history. This makes him fair game to a pair of discontented
CIA operatives convinced that a failed attempt on the life of the US
president will force the nation to tackle the threat of communism head
on.

Libra is a gripping, masterful blend of fact and fiction, laying bare the
wounded American psyche and the dark events that still torment it.

'An audacious blend of fiction and fact' *The Times*

PENGUIN ESSENTIALS

The Penguin Essentials are some of our most important books.
When they were first published they changed the way we thought about
literature and life. And they have remained vital reading ever since.
These new, stylish editions remind readers that once upon a time each
book in the Essentials series was the only book worth being seen with.

The Hound of the Baskervilles by Arthur Conan Doyle

Extremely Loud and Incredibly Close by Jonathan Safran Foer

The Pursuit of Love by Nancy Mitford

The Chrysalids by John Wyndham

Three Novels by César Aira

Age of Iron by J. M. Coetzee

Brooklyn by Colm Tóibín

Villages by John Updike

Austerlitz by W. G. Sebald

Libra by Don DeLillo